Detective Francis "Sheik" Yoshikawa is back! Scott Kikkawa's hard-living, Chaucer-quoting knight in a Cadillac Eldorado peels back the veneer of respectability over 1950s Honolulu to reveal the violence—and hope—buried just below. His latest homicide case hits close to home when a guest is murdered inside the residence of his high-school buddy and fellow veteran, Wally Yoshida. As the bodies pile up and the masks fall away, The Sheik fights doggedly to shelter his friend and bring the killers to justice, even as those goals seem to become ever-less compatible.

—Zakariah Johnson, crime writer and *Mystery Tribun*e reviewer

Only Scott Kikkawa can blend Chaucer with noir, throw Middle English in with Japanese and Hawaiian pidgin in a rare look at postwar Honolulu through the eyes of a local. Complex, diverse, compelling characters and gripping story showcase both the beauty and underbelly of Hawai'i in Kikkawa's wonderful novel.

—Jennifer K. Morita, award-winning author of *Ghosts of Waikīkī*

Kikkawa shows a real talent for the kind of character-driven comedy that makes watching or reading the great noirs of the 1930s, such as *The Maltese Falcon* and *The Big Sleep*, so enjoyable.

—*HONOLULU Magazine*

# Sporting Girl

**Sporting Girl**

ISBN 978-1-943756-15-5

This is issue #129 of *Bamboo Ridge, Journal of Hawai'i Literature and Arts* (ISSN # 0733-0308).



Published by Bamboo Ridge Press

Printed in the United States of America

Bamboo Ridge Press is a member of the Community of Literary Magazines and Presses (CLMP).

Typesetting and design: Jui-Lien Sanderson

Cover art: Tommy Hite, *Sporting Girl Cover*, 2025, oil on wood panel, 19″ × 24″. Collection of Scott Kikkawa, Honolulu.

Bamboo Ridge Press is a nonprofit, tax-exempt corporation formed in 1978 to foster the appreciation, understanding, and creation of literary, visual, and performing arts by, for, or about Hawai'i's people. The organization is funded by book sales, subscriptions, and individual donors. This project was made possible in part by funding from the National Endowment for the Arts.

*Bamboo Ridge* is published twice a year. For orders, subscription information, and back issues, contact:

Bamboo Ridge Press
P.O. Box 61781
Honolulu, Hawai'i 96839-1781
808.626.1481
read@bambooridge.org
www.bambooridge.org

5 4 3 2 1 26 27 28 29 30

# Sporting Girl

Scott Kikkawa

BAMBOO RIDGE PRESS

*For Juliet*

*Because your lessons have stayed with me,*
*you will always be my editor.*

# Prologue

The love of money is the root of all evil. How many times have you heard that one? I think I got that line growing up, in sermons at Makiki Christian Church, or in passing from one of my sanctimonious older sisters, or even from a matinee cartoon feature. Maybe it was Bugs Bunny. It was like a Bing Crosby lyric, something that sounded right but most folks couldn't care less about, an adage designed to enter one ear and exit the other. It wasn't until I got to college that I learned that it was first popularized by Geoffrey Chaucer:

*Radix malorum est Cupiditas.*

"The Pardoner's Tale" is where the famous statement makes its appearance. *My theme is alwey oon, and evere was, Radix Malorum est Cupiditas.* Of course, the Pardoner turns out to be a hypocrite by his own admission, but isn't anyone who has uttered those words? Especially today in 1954, here in Honolulu, T.H.

It probably came from the Bible at first, like all quoted nuggets of wisdom. An admonishment thrown about among priests and scholars, when all the important haoles in the world spoke Latin to each other in their private clubs under gothic arches.

Only the deluded would say that the love of money is the root of all evil in a world where everyone is trying to grab as much of it as they can. In our time and place, the pursuit of money is not only not evil, it's admirable. Anyone who isn't chasing money is a hermit, a lunatic, or just plain lazy.

Money will buy almost anything you want, contrary to the Bible and Chaucer. Money buys happiness: ask anyone who works in an air-conditioned office who put a down payment on a once-covenant-restricted house in Manoa. Money buys love: ask any lucky "guest" of a Hotel Street "hotel" who purchased a half-hour honeymoon without the prison sentence of marriage. Money even buys a World Series championship.

What it doesn't buy is the truth. In fact, money is often used to bury it.

The whole world is trying to hire an assassin who will kill the truth. Beauty parlor treatments to hide the crow's feet of long, hard living. Greased palms in kid gloves to treat an average schmoe like the king he feels he should be. Hush money to silence the critics, squash testimony, or make witnesses vanish.

Everybody wants to buy a lie.

Everybody, except us cops.

It's not that we're more honest or better people. It's just that when others throw the truth out of their lives, we're stuck holding the bag of it.

# 1

My knuckles were beginning to hurt from knocking on the splintery wooden frames of all those screen doors. My knees were beginning to hurt from climbing all those short steps to creaky lanais. My pride was already hurt because I was too slow to get the drop on him.

Happy Tokuda had vanished into thin air. Again. On an island. Who the hell does that? Maybe it shouldn't surprise me. Happy had a hundred friends and just as many people who weren't friends but who owed him favors. Often, he used what many a Hongwanji-volunteer matron referred to as his "natural charm"; they all swooned over his "rugged" good looks. I thought he just looked like the mechanics at my folks' shop, only with a little extra pomade in his hair and better teeth. And then there were those he could dupe. There were lots of those. More than I could count.

Happy was Chaucer's miller, the perpetual vagabond who dared to match his betters and somehow managed to upstage them. It's true that many found Happy and his ways offensive at a distance, but they had to look his way with rapt attention despite their disgust and contempt, and that is where he managed to fleece them.

Not me. I never fell for it.

I first met Harry "Happy" Tokuda when I was in my junior year at McKinley High School. McKinley was a big block just Diamond Head of downtown Honolulu; it was bordered by King

Street on its mauka side and Kapiolani Boulevard on its makai side. It was hemmed in by lands belonging to the Victoria Ward Estate and Pensacola Street. McKinley's location made it convenient to both Kakaako and Sheridan Tract, neighborhoods crammed with Japanese families and businesses, which earned it the moniker of "Tokyo High." My four older sisters preceded me in attendance there.

I had earned a starting spot on the varsity baseball team as a first baseman, probably owing to my size. At just a fraction of an inch shy of six feet, I was big for a Japanese boy. Even the Hawaiian kids on Kamehameha's team who played outfield backed up when I approached the plate. I always got a kick out of that.

Happy Tokuda was in his late twenties at the time, a man with enough time on his hands to drop in on a high school baseball practice when most grown men had things in their lives that robbed them of time, like jobs. Happy wasn't burdened that way. He was what the obasans called "chanbara handsome," like the one samurai movie protagonist that had a wild mane of long, tousled hair instead of a shaved pate. He walked with B-movie swagger, like a poor man's John Wayne in chaps. He dressed like the foppish, low-rent confidence man that he was, a silly little black wool beret tilted at a rakish angle on his pomade-slicked head, the kind I had seen painters and schoolgirls wear when I was in France during the war. His lean frame was dressed up with a checkered sports coat and a bright shirt with no tie, baggy trousers, and saddle shoes.

And Happy smiled. A lot. I think it was probably his normal expression. The idiotic grin was a natural feature. Almost everyone who met Happy thought his smile was what gave him his name, but it was really his poor penmanship that was responsible. When he signed his name, Harry, his *r*'s looked like *p*'s thanks to the fact that he mixed uppercase and lowercase letters in his printed signature, like a slow child.

Happy dropped by our practice to sell bubble gum and chewing tobacco and occasionally much more wicked contraband like cigarettes and girlie magazines, and all at dirt cheap prices. He carried his wares in a worn leather briefcase, like he was some kind of businessman headed to the boardroom. We all gave Happy many of our nickels for something to stick in our mouths during batting practice. Guys without fathers who kept liquor in the house or without the guts to pilfer it often put clandestine orders for hooch in with Happy, who would obtain a pint of bourbon or bottles of beer and deliver the goods at the gate behind centerfield on Queen Kapiolani Boulevard after practice.

I went on patronizing Happy's portable store like everyone else for a couple of weeks until I learned that his goods were shoplifted from a few nearby mom-and-pop stores. Wally Yoshida and Sam Nomura were talking about it during batting practice. They muttered under their breath about overhearing the owners of the Wong Market talking to the police about the Japanese man with the funny hat and how a lot of their merchandise had gone missing. Wally was so goody-goody and gullible he even mused aloud that the shop owners had to be mistaken. I knew better: the smarmy son-of-a-bitch couldn't have obtained his cheap goods any other way.

When I found out that my hard-earned nickels were being spent on stolen goods, I was livid. I told Happy so. If there was one thing I could never tolerate, it was people who thought they could leapfrog others by breaking the rules. Kids who cut in line to get the last of the penny candy. Adults who called in favors to get a better seat, better view, better deal than the masses who had no such favors to call in. They thought they were better. They weren't. They were just cheaters. Few things gave me more satisfaction than putting them where they belonged, whether it was at the back of the line, behind bars, or under my self-righteous foot.

"What's eating you?" Happy asked. "No big deal, First Base." First Base. That's what Happy called me. He called us all by our positions, like a one-man Abbott and Costello.

"No big deal? You sold me something you stole," I said. "That makes me a recipient of stolen goods. I could go to jail same as you."

"Who's going to call the cops and tell them? You? How about you, Shortstop?" He looked at Wally, who shook his head.

"No way," said Wally. "I like my cheap chew."

"You're no help," I said. I cuffed Wally on the side of the head with my glove.

"You see, First Base? No big deal," said Happy. He smiled wide so I could see the gap between his front teeth. The neighborhood housewives thought it gave his face "character." It just made me think of a rodent.

Disgusted, I spit my barely chewed bubble gum into the infield dirt.

"Don't ever sell me stolen shit again," I said. "I gave you nickels for something that didn't cost you a goddamn thing."

"Sure, it costs me," said Happy. "I take all the risks. You could, too, and get all this stuff for free, but you don't. I do. What you pay me isn't just for the stuff, it's for me sticking my neck out. For you. You know what would happen if that crazy Pake or his old lady caught you? They'd beat the shit out of you with that big broom handle that they keep by the cash register, that's what they'd do. And they'd catch you, First Base. They would. But not me. I'm too fast, too slick."

"They wouldn't catch me," I said.

"Yeah, they would."

"No, they wouldn't. That's because I wouldn't steal their shit in the first place." Stealing was just another form of bullying. Taking something you weren't entitled to. If everyone did that shit, nobody would have anything. I figured this out early on with four older sisters who were, at one point, bigger and stronger, then later claimed seniority privilege or "reasoned" their way into things that were rightfully mine. Then there were kids in grammar school, overgrown and patently stupid who demanded lunch money. I detested people who flouted rules.

Happy smiled at me. His grin was a little lopsided, something all the old ladies in Kakaako thought was charming. I thought it was goofy; it made me think of the slow kid on our block who followed the manapua man around and mimicked his cries. But his stupid smile was admittedly endearing and disarming, and that I had to acknowledge that, even to myself, irritated me. I had a point to prove, though, so I stood my ground and didn't smile back.

Happy snapped open his briefcase and withdrew a fistful of bubble gum. He thrust the pink pieces of gum twisted in wax paper into my glove.

"Suit yourself, First Base," he said. "For free." He nodded at the gum in my glove. "We're even now, so no hard feelings, okay?"

I turned my glove upside down and let the little bits of pink happiness fall into the dirt at my feet.

"Crook," I said.

Happy just smiled and snapped his briefcase shut.

"So serious," he said. He turned and walked away to the fence at the back of centerfield.

Wally dropped to his knees to scoop up my discarded bribe.

"You don't want it?" he asked.

"Be my guest," I said.

I watched Happy strut confidently across centerfield to the fence on Kapiolani where he let himself out through the gate. He turned and waved. My shameless teammates, his satisfied customers, waved back and cheered him on his way. The cheerleaders who had been going over their routines had drifted near right field in their little satin dresses and white gloves to catch a glimpse of the con man and titter shamelessly. Happy blew them kisses as he turned to them and elicited squeals. Cattle. It made me want to wretch.

"Smile, First Base," he shouted. "It won't break your face."

"Go to hell, criminal," I yelled back.

Happy waved one more time, then he disappeared behind the fence, leaving the gate swinging.

When I was sure he was gone and when nobody was looking, I allowed myself a smile.

That was in the spring of 1941. A few months after that, the world would change. That was a long time ago. It's now 1954 and I'm knocking on doors in a Waialua plantation village because a tip had come in that Happy Tokuda had been sighted there the day before. I'd been showing all the obasans and young mothers his photograph and asking if they had seen him.

No, they said. All of them. It was going to be a long day.

A lot had happened since I first met Happy Tokuda, our bubble gum and tobacco fence. In the intervening years, I had grown up, if you want to call it that. I had graduated from McKinley and gone overseas to fight in the Great War for a country that treated me and mine like traitors and spies. I had gone to a big deal college with the government's thank-you money and obtained a degree in an obscure subject. I had come home and had become a cop. I got married, got a house with a mortgage and even got a kid. Grown up. A man. A citizen and a taxpayer, like all the rest of the folks who, somewhere along the way, quit being children and sold their souls for a paycheck.

The name on the pebble glass window on the door to my office read, "Francis H. Yoshikawa, Detective Lieutenant, Homicide Detail." My mother called me Hide-kun. My sisters, my wife and my friends called me Frankie. To other cops, I was the Sheik. The last time anyone called me Francis was when I was still at McKinley falling asleep in algebra. And nobody called me First Base except for Happy Tokuda.

That day back in 1941, when I confronted Happy about the stolen shit he sold me, was my first real encounter with the loveable, charismatic grifter. It wouldn't be my last. When I was first promoted to detective and assigned to the central detective bureau, I was detailed for a time to the bunco squad to work some of their overflow cases. About half of them involved Happy Tokuda as the primary suspect. I arrested Happy in every single one of those cases, and in every single one of those cases he walked.

"Tough luck, First Base," he'd say with that ever-present lopsided grin gracing his tanned face. He'd do his best Gene Kelly shuffle down the Spanish tiled stairs of the station foyer and out the door onto Bethel Street.

It irritated me to get beat by Happy, particularly because all my collars of him were clean and they all took so much work. In the end, I managed to nab him because even creatures as slippery as Happy Tokuda were creatures of habit, and I got to know Happy's habits over the years. Which wasn't to say that catching Happy was easy. It was one thing to be able to anticipate his moves, but quite another to keep up with them. Keep up with him I did, though, and my perseverance was always rewarded by the inevitable arrest.

"What can I say? You got me, First Base," he'd say, and hold out his wrists for cuffing, all the while smiling and offering me one of his pilfered cigarettes. More often than not, I'd accept the smoke and we'd talk on the way over to the station about old times. When we got there, I'd get him out of my car and we'd walk up the stairs together, then I'd turn him over to the Receiving Desk for booking.

Predictably, before I could finish my paperwork, I'd get word that Happy was being released. Some witness always recanted, saying that they were mistaken. Sometimes, it was the complainant who recanted.

Tough luck, First Base.

This time, in line with my hunch, the tip that had come in said that there was an hours-long cockfight in the Filipino village and that there had been a Japanese man in attendance who had made sales of "virility feed" to a couple of bird trainers that turned out to be nothing more than seed corn dyed red. One of the birds that ate the miracle corn won all its bouts. That bird's trainer regaled the Japanese salesman with okolehao and adobo made from the losers' carcasses and had him dancing and flirting with his pretty cousins to the music of a plantation guitar-and-ukulele ensemble. The ecstatic and appreciative winning trainer even placed a standing order for more of the magical "virility feed." The salesman stayed until very late in the evening, dancing, drinking, and eating. Then he said he'd be back with more of the feed for his host in a couple of days and turned down an invitation to stay the night, saying that he had a cousin in the Japanese village who had a bed prepared and was expecting him.

The other trainer he had sold his fraudulent chicken drug to was not so successful. His bird was torn apart by a sickly-looking opponent. Needless to say, this was the tipster.

After a long morning of interviewing all of the post-fight revelers and receiving credible descriptions of the man I knew as Happy Tokuda, along with positive photograph confirmation, I made the short drive to the Japanese village and started the tedious process of knocking on each and every door and questioning whoever opened them. I said the same shit over and over in both Japanese and English. I asked the same damn question and got the same damn answer: no. Nope. Nai. Never seen him. Most of the time, I didn't even get that, just a silent frown and a shake of the head, or the wave of a wrinkled, leathery hand, signifying a negative response.

My whole morning had been full of the ghost of Happy Tokuda. With us, it had been cat and mouse. I was always playing Tom to his Jerry.

Happy Tokuda was something of a Kakaako Robin Hood. He'd liberally hand out bubble gum, chocolate, and senbei to the children, for free. I had put a stop to his black market sales at McKinley for the time I was there, much to the chagrin of my morally ambiguous teammates. Over the years, my moral compass would also shift, admittedly more so as the result of police work than the result of combat, but I always reserved a healthy dose of righteous indignation for Happy, as hypocritical as it was. That Happy could always rally every kenjinkai picnic-goer or bartender or bus driver to see him as misunderstood or wrongly accused only increased my irritation. It seemed that whenever he wasn't taking people's money from right under their noses, Happy Tokuda was promoting himself as a helpful, loveable ne'er-do-well. He was able to live on free musubis, manapua, and bottles of Primo, gifts from his benefactors of the moment, and those folks were all too willing to support him that way, especially the neighborhood women, young and old, who giggled and made sloppy eyes at him when they invited him to stay for dinner.

This is what rankled me so. Every time I'd arrest Happy, Kakaako and its expatriates knew immediately through the coconut wireless of every bowling league, Hongwanji, and grammar school. I was always the villain, the Sheriff of Nottingham to Happy's Robin Hood, the knight whose tale was usurped in Chaucer by that of the crude miller. *Alwey the nye slye maketh the ferre leve to be looth.* Happy was in the right place at the right time, and I was playing catch-up.

Absalom and Nicholas.

Tom and Jerry.

"Don't you have real criminals to chase?" asked my sister, Iris.

"Let it go, Frankie. It's all in good fun," said Wally Yoshida, now an attorney seeking Territorial office. "You always let Happy get under your skin." Wally was one of those guys who saw Happy as harmless because the folks he fleeced never seemed to have a problem with being fleeced. "You see, Frankie? Everybody's fine with him." *Except you.*

"What's your issue with this guy? Whatever it is, it doesn't seem healthy," said my boss, Captain Gideon Hanohano. "High blood pressure, Sheik. It can kill you. This guy's not worth it."

"I think you're just upset because you've never beaten him," said Ellen. "You're so competitive." Jesus. Ellen, too. My own wife. The whole world was telling me to stop picking on poor, good-natured handsome Happy Tokuda.

This was always the narrative. Happy breaks the law, I find out about it. I chase Happy. Happy evades me. I grit my teeth, take a deep dive into the pool of obsession, and finally catch him. I book him. They let him go.

Tough luck, First Base.

The more I thought about it, the more determined I became to nail him. I had talked to every post-cockfight partygoer from the previous night, and had knocked on twenty rickety screen doors in the Japanese plantation village and had more than twenty to go. I knew that all that lay ahead of me were more "no" and "nai" and polite head shaking. And I knew that at least half of them, usually honest to a fault, would be liars on his behalf.

Sometimes it seemed that I was the only human being in the whole, big world who didn't think that Happy Tokuda's fleecing was adorable or entertaining. In his almost lifelong career as a con artist,

I was the only cop who managed to bring him in. In my career as a detective, Happy was the only arrestee of mine who never received justice. While I was not the sole nuisance to his success and he was not the sole focus of my daily crusades, we somehow managed to bump up against each other from time to time, and when we did, it was off to the races.

Maybe Ellen was right. She almost always was. Maybe I had a sore spot for Happy the way that almost everyone else had a soft spot for him and maybe it was because I had never beaten him. When I examined my life and anyone I ever considered to be an opponent—opposing pitchers, Hitler's Wehrmacht, rival suitors—I could say that on the final scorecard I had bested each one of them, at least by decision if not by knockout. All of them. Except Happy Tokuda.

The funny, ironic thing was that on a personal level, I really didn't hate him or harbor any real animosity toward him. In a sense, I inwardly found him as amusing as the rest of the world did, and in most cases the cat and mouse game we played was a refreshing diversion from the gravitas of looking at corpses and hunting down their makers. Sometimes the game was almost fun. But it was always frustrating as hell. I was the kid who never mastered the kendama, who always got the wooden ball close to the cup only to have it jump out immediately. Happy was the wooden ball on the string, taunting me with his nearness.

More screen doors knocked on. More toothless old ladies, more moms with their hair in kerchiefs and brats at their feet, more drunks interrupted from their hangover naps. All of them shook their heads when they were shown Happy's photograph. None of them had ever seen his grinning face in their lives, though more than half of their eyes flickered with unmistakable recognition. He had legions of sympathizers. Enough to delay me for an entire morning.

Happy probably thought he had beaten me.

Again.

Tough luck, First Base.

Not this time.

This time it's not about some widow's life savings or some lovestruck idiot's paycheck or some high school first baseman's hard-earned nickels. It wasn't even really about his fake miracle chicken feed.

This time Happy Tokuda was wanted for murder.

# 2

I was there when it started. Two days before I found myself out in Waialua chasing down the loveable grifter, I was at Wally Yoshida's house.

Wally Yoshida and I had known each other since McKinley, since we both made the varsity as sophomores. We were best friends, though we were as opposite as two best friends could be. Wally stood about five feet four inches tall and weighed just over 120 pounds; I was almost six feet and about 180 in high school. Wally was our class valedictorian; I turned in half of my assignments late. Wally listened to his mother; I begged forgiveness instead of asking for permission. Wally was quick, nimble, and had good hands. He played shortstop. I was big, strong and could smash the ball over the fence. I played first base.

Pearl Harbor was bombed near the end of the first semester of our senior year. Wally and I both saw our fathers taken away to Sand Island. His old man was a fisherman with his own sampan and radio and therefore a potential spy; mine taught calligraphy at a Japanese language school in Moiliili and was therefore a potential propagandist. Wally's dad was shipped off to the mainland and spent some months at the "relocation camp" at Jerome, Arkansas. Mine caught pneumonia waiting for the boat and died in a wet tent.

Wally and I both enlisted as soon as we got the chance and ended up together in the 442nd. Wally enlisted to serve his country; I enlisted so my country would leave my family the hell alone.

When we were in Europe, a German grenade took Wally's leg off. I made a tourniquet and saved his life. Wally was shipped back stateside and never had to experience the carnage in the Vosges Woods where we rescued some boxed-in haoles from Texas. I took a bullet to the shoulder—a graze, really—and got shipped back, too. We both used the G.I. Bill to go to Ivy League schools. Wally went to Harvard, I went to Columbia. Wally studied history and stuck around at Harvard for law school. I got my degree in Medieval and Renaissance Literature and came home and became a cop.

I was at Wally's to celebrate his new house and his new wife. He went away to New York City for a meeting with National Democratic Party leadership as one of the party's up-and-coming young candidates out in the T.H. and came home with campaign funds for the coming elections and a bride.

Her name was Lydia French. She was an actress who had seen a couple of minor roles on Broadway and had something of a claim to fame as a one-time understudy to Joan Roberts in the role of Laurey in *Oklahoma!*—though she never took the stage in that capacity. Lydia was an active supporter of the Democratic Party and an "ardent admirer of FDR" in her own words. She met Wally at a cocktail party given by the National Committee at the Waldorf Astoria. After striking up a conversation with him about his wooden leg, they fell for each other and married before a Manhattan justice of the peace after a forty-eight-hour whirlwind courtship. I was extremely jealous: she took him to a game at Yankee Stadium.

Wally had not bothered contacting anyone in his family or any of his friends. If he had talked to me, I would've advised him against it. But in a way, I could understand his impulse to take the plunge into sudden matrimony. Up to that point, Wally's love life had been fraught with bad luck. His steady from McKinley, Polly Yamanaka, had not waited for him while he was overseas getting shot at with me. Polly started seeing Ted Kawamoto secretly, got pregnant, and married him. Wally found out the day he got home with his brand-new fake leg. Ever the saint, he congratulated them and even made a wedding gift of the gold ring he had picked up in Italy, which he was going to present to Polly when he proposed to her. Jesus, what a sap. I would've punched Ted in the mouth for a wedding gift and hocked the ring and got drunk. Wally always was too nice for his own good.

Then came his hard luck at Harvard. He dated a Radcliffe co-ed from a family of Massachusetts fishermen named Marie Gouveia and wrote to me often about her. On the day he was accepted to the law school, he was going to propose to her at dinner, but the cab she was in got broadsided by a bus in a busy Boston intersection. Both Marie and the driver were killed.

So, when Wally came home from his political vacation as a married man, I was not surprised. He told me over lunch in town that Lydia had received a polite but cool reception from his folks, who were none too pleased that he had brought home some mystery haole girl after marrying her without telling anyone, but he was convinced that they would warm to her in time because she was such a wonderful person. I told Wally that the world was full of wonderful people and that his folks didn't care for most of them. Lydia was different, he told me. Special. I would find out for myself just how much, he said. That's when he invited me over for dinner.

Wally and Lydia had just moved into a nice, new home up on Maunalani Heights. I was only a few minutes away down in Palolo Valley, and the irony was not lost on me that I lived at Kaimuki's lowest elevation and Wally lived at its highest. He had finally gotten taller than me.

When I told my wife, Ellen, she became excited at the prospect of visiting the new Yoshida home and meeting the new Mrs. Yoshida.

"It looks like good things come to those who wait," she said.

"How's that?" I asked. "It didn't look to me like he waited at all."

"Poor Wally," she said. "After all that's happened to him. And he was such a good sport about everything. Someone like that deserves all the happiness in the world. And she's a Broadway actress!"

"I've never heard of her."

"Frankie Yoshikawa! The sun doesn't rise and set based on your personal knowledge. There are plenty of important things that happen every day with or without your knowing about them. Just because you've never heard about Lydia doesn't mean that millions of others don't know and adore her."

The former Miss Ellen Aeran Park became Mrs. Ellen Yoshikawa about a year before. When I met her a few months before that, she had been a part-time reporter for the *Honolulu Record*, Koji Ariyoshi's progressive—some would say "revolutionary," and not in a nice way—weekly newspaper. She had been covering a case of mine. We fell for each other and started dating. When the House Un-American Activities Committee, or HUAC, had sent an investigator to snoop after all of the so-called Hawaii Seven's associates, I feared that Ellen would be a target of the witch-hunt. So, I asked her to quit working at the *Record* and marry me to throw the HUAC off her scent. Well, that, and we found out that she was pregnant, too.

It all worked out for us in the end. I was planning to ask her to marry me anyway, and she was planning to say yes. I bought a house in Palolo Valley with a mango tree in the front and big, heavy note payments. For a time, I took stand-in bagman work to make up some of the shortfall, but that heinous arrangement fortunately came to an end when all of that scheme's Department perpetrators came to an end. In the aftermath, Gideon Hanohano, my lieutenant, was promoted to captain, I was promoted to take his place and the bump in salary gave me enough breathing room on my note payments so that I no longer had to resort to strong-arming Chinatown vice lords to raise additional cash.

A couple of months after I was promoted, our daughter was born. Everyone in the family, including Ellen, thought that she was going to be a boy. So much for old wives' tales about how Ellen carried low or how active the baby was. We named her Elizabeth Hideko Mi Ok Yoshikawa. Ellen felt that Elizabeth had a regal sound to it, as if anyone with that name was destined to appear on television in white gloves and a hat with a veil, waving daintily from the back seat of a Rolls-Royce at a sea of stiff haoles holding little Union Jacks.

My sisters called her Lizzie and the nickname stuck. She was a plump and beautiful baby with a mostly sweet temperament, except when she got hungry or wet in the dead of night and her wailing would set off all the dogs in the valley barking. Thanks to Lizzie, my evenings were suddenly filled with something besides scotch and KGMB-TV.

Though Ellen very much enjoyed motherhood, I got the sense that without reporting, a significant void was left in her life, and that manifested itself in her use of me as her outlet for opinion. Her hobby these days was putting me in my place, which she had always been good at, but now the act seemed somehow essential to her. When I got home from work, a litany of personal editorial awaited me along with dinner.

Still, I can't complain. From the moment I met her, I knew that Ellen was a verbal fencer who never backed down when the gauntlet was thrown. And I pursued her anyway. It was really my fault, too, for always throwing the gauntlet. I have yet to learn that I'll never win.

Just before we went to Wally's, Ellen slipped into the role of the drill sergeant she had recently become since Lizzie was born.

"Frankie Yoshikawa," she said. "What are you wearing?"

"It's called a shirt." I had just come out of the shower and was pulling on a short-sleeved madras plaid shirt.

"Don't you think that's a little casual?" she asked.

"It isn't Buckingham Palace we're going to. It's Wally's house."

"We're meeting his wife for the first time," she said. "We couldn't attend their wedding, so this is like we're attending it belatedly."

"Attending belatedly? Where do you come up with stuff like that?"

"Change your shirt. I picked out a tie for you. It's on the bed. I need you to make a good first impression. Besides, she's not from here. She's from Broadway."

"Nobody's really from Broadway. They're from a bus or a train that brought them to Broadway. But she's here now. She'll have to learn to relax a little."

"But not tonight. I already told you. We're belatedly . . ."

". . . attending their wedding. Yeah, you said."

I looked up at Ellen. She was holding out a white, long-sleeved shirt that had been pressed and starched. She was wearing a black cocktail dress and looking up at me, even in heels. Her hair had been done professionally, up in a shiny black regal coif like Audrey Hepburn. She was wearing her big glasses but I knew that she'd remove them once we were in the car. She was stunning and she made me feel like a stock boy in my plaid shirt. I blew out a sigh and changed.

When I was dressed, I helped Ellen with her pearls and she went to check on the baby while I poured myself a quick drink from the crystal decanter next to the television.

Ellen emerged as I finished my drink. She was carrying Lizzie who had been dressed in a little pink dress with a matching bonnet. The baby was probably adorable as hell but I couldn't tell because Ellen had also wrapped her in what looked like five blankets.

"Would you put the top up on the car?" Ellen asked. "We'll wait here in the living room until you're done."

"Put the top up? We're just going up the hill. This is a visit to Wally's house, not a polar expedition." I looked pointedly at my poor daughter bundled up beyond recognition.

"I don't want her to catch a cold," said Ellen. "This is why I told you that the Cadillac has to go. We have a family now, Frankie. Your Eldorado with the top down is not a family car."

I'd heard this tune from Ellen before. Chevrolet was coming out soon with something they called the Nomad, which looked like a candy-colored hearse. It was just terrible. Ellen had cut the advertisement out of a *Life* magazine and stuck it up on the ice-box door with a magnet.

"Soon," I said, "I'll trade it in for one of those." I pointed at the ad. I didn't mean it.

I relented and acquiesced to my wife's wishes and put the top up on the Eldorado. We had originally planned to call my sister Daisy to come over and watch the baby while we went over to Wally's, but Wally insisted that we bring her, even if it meant having to leave early. He said that Lydia loved babies and really wanted to meet Lizzie.

We arrived at Wally's to find a number of cars parked around the new house. The house itself was modern in design, with a lanai that wrapped all the way around the structure to take advantage of the breathtaking view of Honolulu and the deep blue Pacific, with Diamond Head as the centerpiece. All of the house's wood parts were redwood stained with a red-brown varnish, and there was precious little of it because most of it was glass. Out front there were hibiscus bushes, a Japanese-style rock garden complete with a genuine koi pond filled with genuine koi, and a single tall coconut palm whose fronds moved languidly in the breeze.

It was a nice place.

As it turned out, Wally's new wife was just as nice as his new house.

I knocked on the door and it opened a few seconds later. Standing in the doorway was a stunning little blonde with clear blue eyes. Her golden hair was coiffed in a fashionable short cut. She wore a knee-length silk dress printed with large pink roses. She had the erect carriage of a ballerina and the dazzling smile of a toothpaste ad. She looked like Broadway.

"You must be Frankie!" she exclaimed. Before I could so much as nod, she threw her arms around me and tiptoed to plant a kiss on my cheek. I simply leaned in to her, unable to return the hug as my arms were filled with the two gifts that Ellen insisted we bring: one for the wedding and one for the house. I didn't really see much of a difference as both gifts were really for the house, but I always deferred to my wife on matters of social protocol as most of the house visits I made at work had nothing to do with celebrations.

Lydia was short—about the same height as Wally—and she wasn't wearing any shoes. She had already taken to our custom of removing footwear while indoors.

"You must be Ellen! You're so beautiful! I love your dress and your pearls! And this must be little Miss Lizzie! How adorable!" Lydia embraced Ellen and fawned over Lizzie, stroking her multiple blankets gently. Then she took the gifts off my hands after thanking us profusely. I thought I even caught her bowing, like my mother did when expressing gratitude. Lydia was a quick study.

"E komo mai," she said. "I've been practicing that all day."

"It's perfect," said Ellen. "It's like you've been here for a long time!"

"Come in and have a drink!"

Lydia left us momentarily to put the gifts down near the kitchen. I looked across the living room to the lanai on the opposite side, where I saw Wally waving at us. He was having a highball with a couple of guys I recognized from our high school baseball team. They looked up and waved, too. We moved into the entryway, where we removed our shoes. The living room was full of people, eating, drinking, laughing. Most looked familiar or vaguely familiar.

"She's really nice," said Ellen.

"Looks like Wally found someone his own size," I said. That earned me an elbow in the ribs.

I took a quick glance around. Everything in sight looked modern or futuristic, or at least like it had come from a place some designer envisioned the future would be. And that place wasn't Maunalani Heights. Stepping into Wally's living room was like stepping into *Buck Rogers*, except for the view. The lampshades were in shapes I had only seen under a microscope and even the koa furniture looked like it had been made on Mars. On the boomerang-shaped coffee table was a large floral arrangement of red torch ginger, bird of paradise, lobster claw heliconia, fern, and ti leaves. The walls were hung with paintings that looked like they were done by blindfolded monkeys given paint to sling instead of their turds.

Overall, the living room had the feeling of a high-priced law firm's waiting room. I'd say that Wally hired the same guy who did his office if his office didn't look like a dentist's office.

I took notice of the fact that none of Wally's family was there. All I saw were old friends from McKinley, a couple of 442nd guys, and a slew of people I didn't know who probably knew Wally through work or his campaign, and their families.

Lydia monopolized Ellen and Lizzie while I made myself a drink at Wally's well-stocked bar cart. I took a couple of ice cubes out of a bucket that would be more at home as the component of a jet engine, with tongs that were probably the talons of Picasso's pet parrot, and dropped them into a tumbler with little gold triangles all over it. I covered them with scotch and headed for the lanai.

I was greeted enthusiastically by my old high school teammates and we spent some time catching up and reminiscing before they moved off to join their wives in getting food, leaving me alone with Wally.

"Well, what do you think?" Wally asked.

"Nice, if you like living in a modern art gallery but without the free white wine," I said, knowing that Wally probably could have had all the free white wine he wanted.

"I mean about Lydia. What do you think?"

"I think she's swell," I said. "So does Ellen." Relief crossed over Wally's face like a cool wave. He swirled the melting ice in his drink and took a sip.

"That's good," he said. "The folks are still a little bit guarded about her, but I know they'll come around. She's just the most genuine person. When I told her about my leg, she said she didn't care. Didn't hesitate at all."

"You're a lucky guy."

"I know it. Almost everything is perfect."

"Almost?"

"See that lady in the corner next to the bookcase? The tall haole lady with the dark hair?"

I looked at the woman Wally referred to. She was about forty with unremarkable features. She was what I'd call plain but had a patrician air about her that commanded some attention, with alabaster skin and large, dark eyes. Her nose was perpetually up in the air and she held her drink with a natural, sophisticated ease. She wore a deep green dress and a couple of large gold bangles that didn't look cheap on her right wrist. She was about five feet and six inches of cold, hard class, new money that could pass as old.

"What about her?" I asked.

"That's Aunt Meg. She's one of Lydia's aunts from the mainland. She turned up a couple of days ago out of the blue, and Lydia asked if it would be okay if she stayed with us for a week or so. I told her of course she's welcome; she's family and we have plenty of room. She could stay as long as she likes."

"So, what's the problem?"

Wally took a sip of his highball and looked out at Diamond Head and the ocean beyond. The sun was beginning to sink and tinted the sky and sea with fire. "I can't put my finger on exactly why, Frankie," he said, "but Lydia's been a wreck ever since Aunt Meg turned up."

"She seems fine to me."

"That's how she usually is, and she's putting up a pretty good front for all the guests tonight. But when it's just me and her, it's tense and quiet. I caught her sobbing earlier today when she thought I wasn't paying attention. I asked her what was wrong, and she just smiled and said it was nothing I'd understand. New bride nerves, or something like that. But I heard her and Aunt Meg arguing in the guest room last night and, though I couldn't make out what they were saying, I did catch all the nasty names Aunt Meg called her. I asked Lydia about it this morning, and she told me not to worry about it, that Aunt Meg is just 'a little old-fashioned,' which I took to mean that Aunt Meg doesn't approve of Lydia's marriage to a Japanese man. But do you know what's strange? Aunt Meg has been nothing but nice to me."

"Strange," I said, agreeing absently. Admittedly, I had only partially been paying attention to Wally, watching instead his bubbly

Broadway wife dote on my baby girl. Ellen seemed to be completely captivated by Lydia. I found her interesting. She had suddenly shown up in Wally's life and, almost as suddenly, this Aunt Meg had also shown up.

"Look, Wally," I said, "maybe you're overthinking this. After all, you're still getting to know each other, you and Lydia. Maybe this is normal for her."

"Well, maybe," he said.

It was a strange little exchange, but largely unmemorable outside the context of what was to follow. The new Mrs. Lydia Yoshida seemed for all the world to be full of charisma and verve and even I could believe that she could've been an understudy to Joan Roberts. I'd never even seen *Oklahoma!* but I thought she might be able to pull off the lead even in a production that big with flying colors.

I made my rounds with all the folks there I knew and Wally introduced me to a few people I didn't know, including the enigmatic Aunt Meg. I found her charming, cultured, and sincere and she held my attention despite her plain appearance. I didn't get the impression at all that she was revolted by my being Japanese or from Hawaii. I asked her how she was enjoying her visit, and she told me that she loved it here.

We ate meatballs with teriyaki sauce and pineapple. Wally told me that Lydia made all the food herself. It was good, and I was beginning to believe all of the good press he had given her.

After being there for a couple of hours, Ellen told me that it was time to go; she needed to feed Lizzie and put her down for the night. We said our goodbyes to everyone and were getting into our shoes near the front door when there was a knock. Wally ran up, drink in hand, and opened the door.

The voice outside the door said, "How's things, Shortstop? Long time no see."

# 3

Happy Tokuda. Chaucer's miller. *Heere folwen the wordes betwene the Hoost and the Millere.* Shit, here we go. The voice was jarring the same way the odor of something rotten in the back of the ice-box is when it finally hits your nose after weeks of resting undiscovered behind the fresh stuff. It was too damn late for me to run away and hide. I was trapped in Wally's fancy entryway in a pair of wingtips with untied laces.

I tried my best to disappear right where I was, kneeling on one knee and bowing my head with my hat on, concentrating intensely on tying my shoes. I heard Wally greet him enthusiastically, saying something to the effect of what a pleasant surprise it was to see him and come inside, come inside, come inside.

Shit. I bit the bullet after finishing with my shoes and looked up to find that familiar tanned face and its idiot smile a few inches away from mine. He was wearing a bright orange shirt under his sports coat with a matching orange pocket handkerchief. The little black beret was perched precariously sideways on his slick hair.

"Eh! First Base! You're looking good!"

"And you're looking guilty of something."

Happy laughed like a demented chimp. "Same old First Base," he said.

"Who the hell invited you?" I asked.

"Right Field told me about it," he said. "He didn't think

Shortstop would mind if I stopped by. I told him not to say I was coming. I wanted to surprise everybody."

"Caught me off guard," I said.

"Yeah, just like old times," said Happy.

Ellen was suddenly behind us, holding Lizzie in one arm and using the other to brace herself against my back while she stepped into her pumps.

"Who's this pretty girl?" Happy asked. "Don't tell me you married this one, First Base!"

"Yeah, he did," said Ellen. "He knocked me over the head with his club and dragged me by the hair into his cave. I'm Ellen."

"They call me Happy, but my real name is Harry. Harry Tokuda. But you can call me Happy. Everybody else does."

"Happy Tokuda? I've heard a lot about you," said Ellen.

"Really? I'm touched. I didn't think you liked me, First Base."

"I don't," I said.

"Who's this?" asked Happy, ignoring me and leaning over the bundled up Lizzie.

"This is Elizabeth, our baby girl," said Ellen. She did so with the same joyful, shiny pride she always did when introducing our baby to anyone, including, it seemed, to perpetrators of every misdemeanor on the books with an occasional grand theft thrown in.

"She can't be yours, First Base! She's too cute." Happy reached into his hip pocket and pulled out a crisp twenty-dollar bill. He held it out between two fingers toward Ellen.

"Here," he said. "For the baby's college."

I snatched the bill from between them and held it up in front of Happy's face.

"Which old coot's pension did you steal this from?" I asked. I flipped the bill at his face. It hit him squarely between the eyes and fluttered to the floor.

"Frankie!" Ellen scolded. "Be nice!"

Unfazed, Happy squatted down, picked up the bill, straightened back up and tucked it into Lizzie's blankets then gave her a gentle pat. He grinned broadly at Ellen. He was working the same smarmy charm he reserved for his female marks, but this time he was directing it at my wife. I balled up my hand in a fist and got ready to launch, but Ellen got between us.

"Just like before," he said. "Same old First Base."

Wally ambled over in an attempt to smooth things between me and Happy. I noticed how well he moved; one would be hard-pressed to guess that one of his legs was artificial.

"Hey, come on, Frankie," he said. "You and Happy go way back together. We all do. He just dropped in to wish us all well, didn't you, Happy?"

"Of course," said Happy. "Shortstop with his new house and new wife, and First Base, too. What a cute little baby!"

Happy beamed. Ellen beamed back at the compliment to Lizzie. I suddenly felt like a heel. Happy stood in the entryway holding his black beret in front of his chest, reminding me of a dog begging for table scraps.

"Thanks, Happy," I said. I said it through clenched teeth, but I said it. I even stuck my hand out in a gesture of conciliation, to make up for the uptight jerk I was being. Happy grasped my hand and shook it heartily.

"You're a lucky guy, First Base," he said, fairly oozing goodwill and ease of character. I managed a grin and nodded.

"How about we go inside and have a drink together?" Happy suggested. "We can catch up."

"Thank you, he'd love to, but we have to get going," said Ellen. "It's our little girl's bedtime."

"Yeah," I said. "It's my bedtime, too."

"Okay, then," said Happy. "Stay in a good mood, First Base. I'll see you next time."

"Stay out of trouble, Happy," I said. "Or next time I'll arrest you. Again."

Happy laughed. "Same old First Base," he said.

The purring engine of my Cadillac Eldorado lulled the baby into a quiet doze. The car was almost two years old and still sounded as good as it did the day I drove it off the Schuman Carriage lot. Ellen sang quietly to Lizzie about doggies in the window with waggly tails, swaying slightly in the back seat. I stole a furtive glance at them through the rearview mirror as I drove down Waialae Avenue. This was my contentment. I had taken my time winding downhill along Sierra Drive to give Lizzie time to enjoy the soft hum of the car. She was the picture of peace.

We were home in just under ten minutes. Ellen put Lizzie down in her crib while I took my jacket and tie off. I let my eyes roam over the living room and dining room that was my domain, my great hall. The hard-won castle had come at a price. A lot of note payments had been made in blood money, my take as a part-time bagman until I found a way out of the arrangement and received a fortuitous promotion. In that sense, I was no better than Happy Tokuda. What the hell gave me the right to judge him?

I told myself that what I did, I did for my family. For Ellen. For Lizzie. Our koa-framed sofa in the living room, once a symbol of our transcendence above our plantation origins, was now a resting place for folded pink blankets, fresh diapers, and a brown teddy bear damp with drool. Happy never pulled any of his scams to fund anything like it.

Who the hell was I kidding? None of it made me better than him. I became annoyed at the fact that I had left Happy behind on Maunalani Heights and yet I had carried him all the way back into Palolo Valley into the sanctity of my castle in my head.

As was becoming nearly always the case, Ellen had read my mind. I met her in our bedroom after she put the baby down to help her remove her pearls and unzip her dress.

"So that was Happy Tokuda," she said. "What is it about him that bothers you so much? He seems jolly and harmless. I didn't expect him to be so handsome, too."

Jesus, not my wife, too. Like all the old ladies in the Kakaako neighborhood, she was willing to let him off the hook for all his shit just because he looked nice.

"He's a criminal," I said. "Happy has separated not just stupid bad people from their money, but stupid good people, too. He does it with a smile, but he still does it."

"Frankie, you've put plenty of worse ones away, and some of them more than once. But they never got under your skin the way this one does. I've told you this before: I think Happy bothers you because you've never beaten him."

"So?"

"So, you're something of a sore loser, Frankie Yoshikawa. Why can't you just let it go? Wally doesn't seem to have a problem with him, and neither do the rest of your friends, for that matter. You're a homicide detective now, not just a bunco squad dick. You caught the ones who mattered. This Happy is a small fish. Let it go. Nobody thinks any less of you just because he's never been convicted."

Ellen slipped out of her black dress and opened a drawer to select a nightgown. I stood and admired her from behind. One of my great pleasures was watching her get dressed and undressed. It was comforting as well as arousing; that she would perform these simple but private tasks in my presence told me that to her, I was home. It made me feel content and ashamed that I had let someone as insignificant as Happy Tokuda annoy me with all I had going for me.

Ellen was right. I was slowly but surely learning to just shut up and listen to her. Life was easier that way.

Ellen slipped into something pink chiffon that she had pulled from her fragrant drawer of sheer things. She sat down at the vanity to brush her shiny black hair. I threw my shirt into the wicker hamper in the bathroom and brushed my teeth.

When we were both ready for bed, I turned off the light and lay down next to Ellen. Her bedtimes had lately been coinciding with Lizzie's because she'd have to wake up when Lizzie did in the middle of the night, screaming about the discomfort of an empty stomach or a full diaper.

I reached over and touched one of Ellen's warm, soft breasts through the sheer fabric shrouding it. Too late. It rose and fell in my grasp to the languid rhythm of sleep. Defeated, I flopped over on my back, closed my eyes, then opened them again, staring at the ceiling in darkness.

I had been lasciviously thinking of Ellen ever since watching her slip out of her cocktail dress, but was now once again thinking of Happy Tokuda. Nothing in the world could be more different.

My mind wandered back to the spring of 1942, when I was a senior at McKinley. After the Japanese had bombed Pearl Harbor, school had been shut down for a few weeks and had just re-opened. We were all playing catch-up with reading assignments so we could graduate on time. All interscholastic sports had been cancelled, so I had played my last inning of high school baseball months before and had a spring of no baseball ahead of me. Plenty of time to study. I needed Wally's help with some math and he told me no problem, but I'd have to take a walk with him to downtown, where he could keep an eye on his little brother, Clarence, who must have been twelve or thirteen at the time. Clarence had put together a shinebox and was one of the first of hundreds of enterprising kids his age who would be intent on making a fortune in nickels on Hotel Street where all the haole G.I.s would be lined up for the brothels.

Clarence, like Wally, though athletic, was diminutive in stature. He looked more like a nine year old than a kid who would be starting high school in a couple of years.

Wally felt it was necessary to keep an eye on Clarence while he was out raking in the silver with his homemade shinebox. He had heard that haole servicemen, especially those from the South, could be cruel and sometimes violent when dealing with the Japanese kids. He was happy to have me along for added intimidation, though in truth I would have been of little use in a brawl with ten or twenty drunken sailors.

"It's nice to have a big guy with us," said Wally. "Thanks for coming along."

"Sure," I said. "All you need now is fifty more of me."

We got to Hotel Street right after school let out, thanks to no baseball practice. At a little after two o'clock, the lines for the brothels were still a block long, though the buses had already taken most of the G.I.s back to base. Thanks to curfew and command restrictions the de facto "evening" for the servicemen ran from a little before nine in the morning until just after two in the afternoon. There was drinking in the filthy little bars at a time when the bakeries still had fresh goods for sale. The whole uniformed world was lined up for three-dollar sex in the middle of the morning. Nightlife in broad daylight.

At that stage of the game, Hotel Street had not yet become the out-of-control sea of uniformed white bodies reeking of cheap cologne, cheap liquor, and cheap steaks it was to be a year down the road, but it was still a grotesque version of Pinocchio's Pleasure Island, and all it took was a few drinks to turn a disciplined fighting man into a braying donkey.

Just like ants to a picnic, the haole whores with their brassy hair and crimson-painted mouths came by the boatload to the Hotel Street goldmine. Japanese and Pake vendors and kids like Clarence Yoshida could smell the money above the dead fish and wino piss stink, too. Many dropped everything and got their asses down to Hotel Street to sell whatever the hell they could. In the time after the bombing of Pearl Harbor when the schools were closed, the shine boys spent their mornings working the lines to the brothels and made a killing.

Even after the schools had reopened, many of the shine boys continued to show up faithfully with their boxes as soon as the brothels opened up for business. As long as there were queues to get into the whorehouses, there were shoes to be shined. Most of the kanaka and Portuguese boys could skip school to make money with the tacit approval of their folks, but the Oriental boys had a harder time, and Clarence Yoshida was no exception. His folks insisted on his being in school, but gave him permission to earn his nickels after school as long as his marks remained sufficiently high.

"Nothing but scraps," he complained to me and Wally. "I can make a nickel a shine just like the other guys, but I have to work fast—I only get an hour or so, if I'm lucky, before they all get on the bus."

"You're lucky Mom and Pop allow you at all," said Wally. "Quit your complaining."

I laughed. "You're making a hell of a lot more than I am," I said. "I can't even afford to take Millie out for a soda. That's why I'm here getting help with my math from your brother." Millie Miyasaki, my erstwhile high school girlfriend who'd later end up in one of my case files. At the time, though, my concern about her was keeping her sufficiently buttered up with gifts and outings.

"Well, let me know when you do get enough to take her out," said Clarence. "I'll shine your shoes for three cents. Special friend's discount."

We all laughed. Clarence got going, working a line of desperate navy whites queued up to get into something called the Statesman Hotel. All the brothels had names like that, and in a technical sense they were hotels where the guests stayed for a staggering rate of a dollar a minute. Three bucks was the going rate for a roll in the hay, and those girls had them out in literally three minutes. Like Clarence and his shinebox, they understood that time was money.

Wally and I stood not far away at the corner of Hotel and Nuuanu, going over a few equations I had scrawled on a piece of notebook paper and torn out and folded pocket-sized for convenience. Every now and then, we'd glance up to make sure Clarence was doing fine. He was. My presence there was more or less superfluous as there were cops on every corner and a couple of M.P.s tooling around in a jeep, looking for any crooked nails needing a good pounding down. Most of the G.I.s in line were antsy with hopes that they could make it up the stairs before the madam shut the door for the day. I had my face buried in my crumpled page of equations, making corrections in pencil as I held it fast against the plate glass window of some liquor store, when I heard his voice.

"Hey, Shortstop! First Base! What you guys selling?"

"Nothing," Wally replied. "Just keeping an eye on my kid brother. How's it going, Happy?"

I turned away from my equations to see Happy Tokuda standing next to Wally holding a large, hand-painted sign: TWO PICTURES WITH A GENUWINE HULA GIRL. 75 CENTS. Happy was sporting his black felt beret, checked sport coat with his open shirt collar spread out over the lapels, and baggy trousers with his trademark black-and-white saddle shoes. Devil-may-care, or maybe just the devil. He carried the sign under one arm and had the other draped over a dark, slender girl in a grass skirt and coconut shell brassiere and a lot of pink plumerias. She had a dazzling, permanent toothpaste advertisement smile and a giant yellow hibiscus that may or may not have been artificial in her shiny, dark hair.

"This is Esmerelda," Happy said. "I'm good friends with her brother from Big Island plantation time."

"Hi," said Esmerelda, waving a hand graced with long, slender fingers capped with candy-red nails.

"I know these boys long time," Happy said to her. "Ball players. Good ones, from McKinley. Isn't that right, First Base?"

"You spelled 'genuine' wrong, stupid," I said.

Happy put the sign down and spun it so it faced him. He screwed his face up like he was thinking hard. I knew it was an act; he was too goddamn stupid to know what I was really talking about. He unloaded a wooden tripod and a camera bag from his shoulder and put them down on the sidewalk. He used both of his hands to hold the sign up at eye level, as if bringing it closer to his face would make him see his error more clearly.

"I don't know," he said. "What you think, Esme? Looks okay to me. Nobody said nothing all day."

"Looks okay," said the fake hula girl.

"Where the hell are you going to develop those pictures, Happy?" I asked. "You don't have a dark room." I knew Happy rented a single bedroom and shared a furo in a Kakaako "camp."

"I don't need one," he said. "I tell these G.I.s that I'll meet them in front of the chop suey house near River Street tomorrow and then I don't. I collect the money in full up front, then tomorrow I'll work the mauka side of the street and tell them the same thing."

"I should take you to the cops on the corner," I said.

Happy laughed. Wally and Esmerelda laughed with him.

"Same old First Base," he said.

Same old First Base.

Some things never change. I leaned over and kissed Ellen's sleeping face on the cheek and slept until the telephone woke me.

# 4

I was in that state between dreaming and thinking when the telephone on my nightstand jarred me into a fuzzy consciousness. I could feel Ellen stir next to me and sit up, faster than I could. When I found the receiver and lifted it to stop the ringing, I could hear Lizzie crying in her crib. Ellen had heard Lizzie above the cacophonous telephone bells and was already on her feet, moving swiftly toward the baby.

I brought the receiver to my head, miraculously putting the right end to my ear.

"Hello," I said, though it sounded more like I was clearing my throat.

"How now, Lieutenant?" said the voice in my ear.

"Tired," I said. It was Detective Sergeant Paris Lau, dropping his Shakespearean affectations on me at four o'clock in the morning. "But at your service," I said. I returned the affectation at him out of habit. Paris had been an English major at Stanford and I studied Medieval and Renaissance Literature at Columbia. Our strange, flowery cracks to one another were an in-joke and a mystery to most of our colleagues.

"Thanks, and thanks, and ever thanks," said Paris. "Look, Sheik, I know we usually don't pull you out of bed much for this kind of stuff these days, but under the circumstances we don't have much of a choice. Besides, I think you probably don't want to sleep in on this one."

"What circumstances?"

"You were here at the scene a few hours ago, we just found out."

My mind raced. Wally.

"What?" was all I could get out of my mouth.

"Haole female. Looks like asphyxiation. Smothered with a pillow, probably. Maunalani Heights."

"What?"

"The residence of one Wallace Yoshida, Esquire. He said you're a friend and were here around dinner."

"Shit," I said. "His wife?"

"No," said Paris. "The victim was a houseguest. Mrs. Yoshida's aunt from the mainland."

"Shit. I'll be there in a few minutes."

I hung up, jumped out of bed and threw the lights on. The white-yellow glow was blinding. I stumbled into the bathroom. I threw cold water on my face, put toothpaste on my toothbrush and stuck it in my mouth.

"Shit," I said.

In what felt like only two minutes, I was dressed, shoulder holster and all. I found Ellen sitting on the sofa in the living room, nursing Lizzie. She was bleary-eyed but as content and serene as I had ever seen her.

"Nice to see you awake at this hour, too, for a change," she said. She let out one of her dainty yawns. "Is everything all right?"

"No," I said. "I don't think so."

I glanced down at my daughter, little eyes closed in feeding bliss. I made a snap decision not to tell Ellen at the moment. I usually gave her a synopsis of my strange hour calls, but this one was sure to upset her. I'd tell her about it later.

"Something happened not too far from here," I said. "They need me on this one. Short drive, at least. I'll tell you about it when

I get back." I leaned down and kissed Ellen and stroked Lizzie's downy little head.

I felt bad about leaving my perfect little home with my two perfect little ladies for Wally's nightmare up on Maunalani Heights. Not too long ago, he had a perfect little home, too. Now it was hell. Any residual jealousy I felt a few hours earlier over his shiny new house and shiny new bride was burned away by gnawing fear of, and anxiety over, what I'd find—and find out—up there.

I hadn't had time to put on coffee. I didn't need it. I was tortured into alertness by a sickening jolt of adrenaline. I didn't bother taking the top back down on the Eldorado, either, which was probably a good thing because I shouted profanity all the way up Waialae Avenue. It was that, or vomit.

A decade before, I had seen Wally lose a leg to a German grenade in a dirty bunker. I had stopped the bleeding with a tourniquet and probably saved his life. I could still smell the ferrous tang of his blood and feel its nauseating warmth all over my hands. Now I was on my way to his not so dirty house at the loss of his in-law, less sure if I could save him this time. The tourniquet was easy by comparison. Thanks to my job, I had seen houses instantly transformed several times from places of refuge to places of horror. Though I always felt bad for the survivors, their homes-turned-crime-scenes in a sick way had come to have a familiar feel of an office. My office. A place where I put my nose to the grindstone. This time, it was different. This time, I was going to share the horror. This shit is different when it's your friend's house—and his life.

I made a beeline up Wilhelmina Rise, blowing through the intersections where Sierra Drive crisscrossed over the steep thoroughfare, committing a dozen moving violations as I pushed the Cadillac uphill. The streets were fortunately empty thanks to the ungodly hour, so nothing was damaged except my common sense.

I couldn't get within a block of Wally's castle in the air. The street was choked with prowlers and there were old women with their blue hair in curlers and their shriveled bodies in fuzzy bathrobes, craning their necks for a glimpse of something other than a uniform. I slipped through their ranks with my badge out and headed for the front door.

The flatfoot at the door greeted me. "Morning, Loot," he said. "Sergeant Lau is inside the guest bedroom. He told me to look out for you."

"Thanks," I said. I reflexively stooped to remove my shoes, then my heart dropped when I realized that I needed to keep them on. This wasn't the social call that my earlier visit was. I was no longer setting foot as a welcome guest into a friend's house. I was entering a slaughterhouse, and homicide dicks never remove their shoes when stepping onto a killing floor.

The first thing I saw when I moved from the entryway into the living room was Lydia's blonde head drooping down, her hair a hanging golden curtain obscuring her face. She was huddled on the long sofa with a heavy quilted futon draped over her shoulders. Wally was sitting next to her, arms around his blanket-encased wife. Both were in sleep clothes but neither looked like they had done much sleeping.

I cautiously stepped toward them, willing my feet to keep moving. Wally looked up at me with bloodshot eyes.

"Hi, Frankie," he said. His voice was a dry croak, like a martini drunk's but steadier and without the gin mill reek. I laid a hand on his shoulder and squeezed lightly.

"I'll be back," I said.

I turned to the hallway and walked to the guest room, where the noise and movement of men with badges at work filled that tiny corner of the early morning.

I shielded my eyes from the flashbulbs exploding in angry, lightning-white bursts of sudden, fleeting illumination. A couple of bespectacled technicians in white gloves dusted the headboard of the bed for prints. The photographer momentarily ceased his assault on my eyesight to change a roll of film. A big Pake in a dark suit with clean fingernails and a mom-pressed handkerchief sticking out of his pocket scrawled away in a hand-sized notepad with a yellow Ticonderoga pencil, the kind schoolgirls chewed to quell their amorous frustrations.

"Paris," I said.

"How now, Sheik?"

"I was about to ask you."

"Have a look for yourself."

The woman I had been told was Aunt Meg a few hours earlier lay on the bed. Naked. Blindfolded. Wrists tied to the posts with white silk cord. After getting a nod from one of the lab technicians, I moved the blindfold. Her eyes, once a sharp and thoughtful-looking soft brown, were now dull and muddy and pointed vacantly at the ceiling fan.

"I saw her earlier," I said. "I only knew her as Lydia's Aunt Meg. Who was she?"

Paris flipped a couple of pages back in his notepad. He used the eraser on his pencil to scan the page, stopping and tapping when he reached the relevant entries.

"The missus told me her name was Margaret Albert, an aunt on her mother's side," said Paris. He stuck the pencil behind his ear. The pencil gave him a strange, unfamiliar look. Paris Lau rarely did anything so pedestrian or sloppy as tucking a pencil behind his ear. That was the kind of shit cub reporters and regular dicks did. I guess he was picking up all kinds of bad habits in Homicide. There was hope for him. We'd turn him into a real detective yet.

"Was she mom's older sister or younger? Her form looks well-tended," I said. I gave her naked body a clinical glance. "I'm going to guess younger."

"Actually, neither," said Paris. "According to Mrs. Yoshida, she was some kind of cousin of her mother's."

"Distant?"

"Something like that."

I took another look at Aunt Meg. She was fit, but not tennis pro fit. She was bedroom fit: slim in the right places, full in the right places. It made me think that maybe there was some hidden appeal to her beyond her plain face. That led me to my next question.

"Any idea who tied her up and blindfolded her? I don't see any signs of a struggle, so Aunt Meg must have been a willing participant in her own restraining."

"Well," said Paris, "according to our host and hostess, the party broke up just before midnight. Mr. Yoshida told me you were gone by eight o'clock. Only a handful of guests remained to finish up their drinking, old friends of Mr. Yoshida. He stayed up to chat with them in the living room until almost one in the morning, when he saw the last of the small group out. At that point, there was only one remaining guest who had been drinking with Aunt Meg and retreated with her to the guest room."

Paris pointed to a couple of heavy old-fashioned glasses, one smeared with lipstick matching the corpse's, the other clean. I took my handkerchief out of my pocket and lifted the clean glass to my nose.

"Scotch," I said. "Good stuff."

I picked up the other glass and sniffed the same residue.

"Haig and Haig," said Paris. He jerked his chin toward the floor by the nightstand where the empty dimpled bottle lay on one of its beveled sides.

"Wally's got good taste," I said. "Seems like it was quite the private little party. Who the hell was this last, lucky guest?"

"Another old friend of Mr. Yoshida's," said Paris. He opened his notebook again, took the pencil from behind his ear and used the little pink eraser as his pointer. "A guy named Harry Tokuda."

Jesus, Happy. What the hell have you done?

"Who found her?" I asked.

"Mr. Yoshida did. He came out of his bedroom at a little after two o'clock for an aspirin and noticed the open door. He went over, knocked, called out Aunt Meg's name. When he got no answer, he turned on the lights and saw this. He called the station right away."

I didn't need any special ability to predict the future to know that when the lab results were in, traces of Happy would be all over the room and on and in the late Aunt Meg. The two scotch glasses had already been dusted for prints, and no doubt they'd be Happy's, just like the prints they lifted from the bedposts and headboard. Happy's blood type would be in the semen in the corpse.

My head was starting to hurt from not enough sleep and no coffee.

"When did Hap—uh—Mr. Tokuda leave?" I asked. As soon as the question left my mouth, I knew I wasn't going to get a good answer.

"Nobody saw him go," said Paris. "He left some time before Mr. Yoshida came out and found this. That would put it between one and two o'clock."

An hour. Stick a pillow on her face then walk the hell out. Plenty of time.

I got a brief on the cold, hard physical facts from the guy in the white lab coat. Caucasian female. Age somewhere between thirty-five and forty-five. Prints were taken and she had all her teeth, so positive ID would not be an issue, though it may take time as all her records are somewhere on the mainland. She had engaged in coitus prior to expiring as evidenced by the presence of semen in the vaginal canal, samples of which had been taken. As I guessed, she had been tied to the bedposts and blindfolded willingly as there were no signs of a struggle nor any damage to the skin under the silk cord bonds. It was some kind of twisted sex game and she had signed up to play.

And she was drunk. Very drunk. Toxicology reports would bear that out, but all the physical signs were there. I was willing to bet that when the results were in, they'd show she was marinated.

It was after the games were over that something had happened. She was unconscious when she asphyxiated, probably due to the large amount of alcohol in her system. Chances were she never even knew it was happening when it was happening.

"How do we know it was the pillow?" I asked.

"It was still on her face when we got here," said Paris. "The linen case is full of her scotchy saliva and lipstick. Someone pressed down hard."

At that point, the only thing left to do was the most unpleasant task of all: talking to Wally and Lydia. This was ten times worse than looking at the corpse. You didn't need to be sensitive with the corpse, didn't need to tiptoe around its fragile feelings. I could have deferred the whole thing to Paris, and maybe I should have, but a nagging sense of obligation and responsibility, an unwanted heirloom from my Japanese parents, caused me to take the proverbial bullet after biting it.

"Are you sure, Sheik? I can do this," said Paris. "He's your friend."

"I know. It's why I have to do this. Thanks, anyway."

I made my way back into the living room and swallowed hard before I approached Wally and Lydia, still huddled together on the sofa. Wally looked up at me and gave me a smile diluted with shock.

"Hey, Frankie," he said.

"Hey," I said. "Long time no see." Wally cracked a weak little smile at my joke. "How're you folks holding up? Can you talk?"

"I told your partner in there, Sergeant Lau, just about everything I know. Are you going to ask me the same questions?"

"No," I said. "Not quite." I took a knee on the floor next to the sofa and propped myself up with an elbow on an armrest. "I'm sorry, Wally. I'm sorry this happened and I'm sorry you folks are going through this. Sergeant Lau already talked to you. He's a good detective, and I know he's covered all the bases. I'm not going to go over any of the stuff he went over again, except one: where the hell is Happy?"

"I don't know," said Wally. "Do you really think he'd . . . do something like this?"

"Oh my God not again!" wailed Lydia. "You're still defending him. That . . . that . . . drunk!" She started sobbing loudly, stood up and ran off to the master bedroom with the futon still draped over her. We heard the door slam. Inside, I cringed for Wally. He didn't go after her. He stayed on the sofa in a limp, deflated pose and stared at the floor.

"Sorry, Frankie," he said. "She's not taking this well at all."

"No need to apologize to me," I said. "Can you blame her? The facts as they stand don't look good for Happy."

"Come on, Frankie," he said. He had found his litigator's voice again, spurred, it seemed, by desperation and disbelief. The sudden confidence was more to convince himself than it was for me. "You know Happy as well as I do."

"Better."

"Okay, better. Then you should know this isn't really Happy. You should know he's never hurt anybody." Wally looked at the floor and back at me. "Wouldn't he? I mean, I don't think so . . ."

"It depends on how you define 'hurt.' He's ruined more than a few lives. He has a rap sheet as long as your koa dining table."

"But it's all for minor stuff. You told me yourself. Misdemeanors, Frankie. He's never been convicted."

"A five-dollar bribe to a witness will buy you that. He's bought several."

"Look, I know you and Happy have never seen eye to eye. But I don't think he'd do this awful, awful thing. At least, I hope he didn't. But if you think about this, it doesn't sound like the Happy we know." Then he added, "Does it?"

"I *am* thinking about it. And do you know what I'm thinking? I'm thinking that I don't know he didn't do this."

"Frankie . . ."

"But I don't know that he did, either," I said. It was time to change my angle on this. Wally and I had gone a few rounds with each other over the years about Happy Tokuda's merits or lack of them. Wally had a soft spot for lost causes. Maybe that's why he was my best friend: I, too, was a lost cause in some ways. So, I smoothed it out. The last thing I wanted to do was get into an argument with Wally while a corpse was in his guest room.

"Shoot, Frankie, it was kind of a surprise when Happy showed up. I guess one of the guys from our team saw him and told him. It was nice to see him, at first. I didn't know he drank so much, though."

"You need to tell me all you can, Wally. I need to know just what the hell he did here, so I know what he didn't do. And I've got to find him and talk to him myself. You're right. I never saw eye to eye with Happy and I never will. But if he didn't do this thing, I'm the best chance he's got."

Wally looked down at his feet. They were covered in a pair of fuzzy plaid slippers, the kind you see dads wearing in front of the fireplace and Christmas tree in pipe tobacco ads aimed at middle management haole schmoes in every big and small town from Cape Cod to San Diego. They looked ridiculously warm on his feet—or foot. I wondered why he even bothered covering up the artificial one. That foot never got cold. Then again, neither did the real foot. Not in Kaimuki. It was all an affectation, one that afflicted island folks looking to elevate themselves into the ranks of haole good taste, which compelled all kinds of illogical behavior. Like wearing fall clothes in the fall, or marrying a bleach blonde Broadway understudy and sneaking bites of your mother's "stinky" tsukemono while the blonde was out shopping so as not to offend her with "foreign" fare.

"After you left, Happy started hitting the punchbowl really hard," said Wally. "He was talking to all the McKinley guys at first, telling a few of them that he was going into automobile sales."

"I hope nobody bought a car from him last night," I said. "They'd just find themselves a couple of grand poorer this morning."

"It's not what you might think. It's something different. Cars made in Japan. They're small and cute, kind of like the girls there. Something called a Toyopet." Wally managed to crack a weak smile.

"Sounds like a wind-up poodle. I hope you didn't buy one."

"No," said Wally. "I'm happy with the Oldsmobile I bought at Schuman Carriage." He let out a sigh and scratched his fake knee out of nervous habit. I couldn't imagine the thing actually itched. "While Happy was drinking and talking up the baseball guys I think he saw Aunt Meg on the other side of the living room. He broke off the sales pitch and went over to her. It was like he was drawn to her. They talked a little and he got them some punch, then they talked some more. I'd seen Happy on the make with girls before, but this time was different."

"How so?"

"There wasn't any laughing and joking like there was before with the other girls, especially the haole girls. This time he was quiet, more subdued. They talked quietly, but pleasantly, I guess. They smiled a lot. But there was something unusual about it."

"What?"

"It's strange, but it seemed like they already knew each other. They just seemed really familiar with each other. Though I think it's impossible. Happy's never left Hawaii."

"Did you discuss any of this with Lydia?"

"No. She's too upset. If I even mention Aunt Meg, she starts crying."

I took a pack of Lucky Strikes out of my coat pocket and offered one to Wally. He declined by shaking his head, but he pushed a table lighter the size of a jet engine my way along with an ashtray you could toss a salad in. I lit a stick up and thought, without producing any flashes of brilliance.

"What happened after their little talk?" I asked. "Did they spend the rest of the evening together?"

"No," said Wally. "Eventually, Happy went back to trying to take orders for his little Japanese cars and Aunt Meg went outside to talk to Lydia on the lanai. Everybody started leaving after a while until it was just Happy and Aunt Meg sitting at the kitchen table with the new bottle of Haig and Haig. We told them goodnight. I told Happy when he was ready to go, he could help himself to the food we put away in the icebox and he could see himself out. Then Lydia and I went to bed. Lydia was exhausted, but happy. She talked about you and Ellen and Lizzie and how much she liked you guys before she went to sleep. I didn't sleep as well. I drifted in and out. Headache. Too much punch, I guess. I got up to take an aspirin. I saw the guest room door was open, so I went to check on Aunt Meg. I thought maybe she left with Happy. I knocked and called out but there wasn't any answer, so I pushed the door all the way open and turned on the lights. That's when I found her. Like that."

Wally shut his eyes and rubbed his forehead. The front door opened and a young guy in thick glasses made a godawful noise when wheeling a gurney through the front door, clattering and rattling like a swordfight on a Hollywood pirate ship.

"Sorry," he said. He eyed us sitting on the sofa and flashed an embarrassed look our way before pushing the gurney through the living room and down the hall.

"This is very important," I said. "Do you have any idea where Happy may have gone? Any idea where he may be staying?"

Wally shook his head and sat in silence. We listened for a moment to the commotion down the hall in the guest room where the body was being moved at last from the bed.

"Come on, Wally," I said. "I told you, it's important and I mean it. Better I find him than a trigger-happy flatfoot trying to make a name for himself on the APB."

"I don't know where he's living these days. Nobody really does. You know that, Frankie. But he said he had a partner in the auto import thing."

# 5

The only human being stupider than the one who gave Happy Tokuda business was the one who went into business with him. I was about to meet that person. Wally coughed the name up when he was convinced that I wasn't going to shoot Happy on sight. The genius was a Schuman Carriage salesman named Joe Matsukawa who suffered from delusions of grandeur. Matsukawa felt that he, too, could have a Carriage like Schuman. A Japanese automobile baron with enough green to send his kids to private school, keep his wife in a house with a koi pond in Manoa Valley on the edge of the covenant homes, and maintain a pale, fragrant mistress at Club Ginza.

Sorry, Joe. Not if you're dumb enough to entrust Happy Tokuda with *any* of your money.

I thanked Wally for the information and told him I'd be in touch with him soon, and that I would need to talk to Lydia when she was ready. He nodded and thanked me for showing up. I told him it was my job.

"And Frankie?"

"Yeah?"

"Please don't shoot him. I know you said you wouldn't, but please."

"I'll try like hell not to."

I motioned for Wally to stay seated while I made my exit, reminding myself once again that this time he was no host and I was no guest. Once outside, I put my hat on and started toward my Cadillac down the street, but nearly ran into a human wall before I got off the Yoshida property. Captain Gideon Hanohano was a solid three hundred pounds of former left tackle in a smart brown suit. He was a beloved teacher and mentor and my boss since the day I came into Homicide.

"Got a lead, Gid," I said. I hadn't broken my stride after nearly running him over. He was agile enough to dodge me, a ballerina the size of a pachyderm.

"Good morning, Sheik," he said.

His simple, quiet greeting made me stop in my tracks. Gid had a way of restoring my humanity by example. The big man was always civil, no matter the circumstances. He once told me that bad manners never got anyone anything except a closed door. I told him that probably explained why I ended up drinking on the lanai so often.

"Good morning, Gid," I said.

"What's the hurry?" he asked, as if to emphasize the point that he himself was rarely ever in a hurry. He leisurely reached in his inside coat pocket and produced a pack of cigarettes and offered me one. I took it and pulled out the Zippo lighter Gid had given me for Christmas when I first came under his command then lit us up. His trick had worked. I relaxed.

"I just got a lead on the suspect from the homeowner," I said. I took a couple of drags and relaxed some more.

"He's a friend of yours, isn't he?"

"Yeah. Wally Yoshida and I go way back."

"I meant the suspect."

"Happy Tokuda's no friend," I said. I couldn't help how coldly that came out.

"Sorry," said Gid. "He always seemed so friendly with you back in your bunco case days whenever you brought him in for booking."

"*He* was friendly. I wasn't always. He irritated me. He always knew he'd get off. Even if I always caught him. And I always did."

"The bunco guys told me you knew him for a long time. Since school."

"Yeah. When we were at McKinley, he used to come around and sell us bubble gum and chewing tobacco for cheap when we had baseball practice. It was stolen shit. He lifted it from Wong Market and some other Pake stores. I told him not to come back with stolen goods or I'd beat his ass."

"Did you?"

"No. He stopped coming around practice after that. My teammates were sore at me for a while, but they got over it."

"You see, Sheik?" said Gid. He shook with some of his dry, silent chuckles. "You *did* stop him. He didn't get off *that* time."

"I didn't really," I said. "I heard he just moved on to Roosevelt and sold his stuff to all the Portuguese and haoles when *they* had batting practice."

Amused, Gid shook some more with his silent laughter then took a slow drag off his cigarette. He smiled his small, crooked half-smile at me and looked at me thoughtfully.

"You sure you want to do this?" he asked. I knew this was coming. "It would be an easy thing for me to relieve you on this case. You're too close by the standards of some."

"I didn't know the victim," I said. "And though I know the suspect, I don't have any love for him. Just look at my reports. I brought him in six times."

"Take it easy, Sheik," said Gid. He held his hands up in a surrender gesture. "I'm not saying you've got a conflict or that you wouldn't do an outstanding job on this investigation. I know how close you and Wallace Yoshida are. All I'm saying is that if you don't feel like doing this because of that, then I don't have a problem with it. Paris can take it with someone else."

I stood on Wally's front lawn smoking my cigarette and pondering my captain's offer. He stood with me while I thought. That was Gid. Always supporting, never encroaching. He nonchalantly looked off at Diamond Head and the stunning azure of the ocean behind it in the morning sun while he smoked, one huge hand in his pocket, the other holding his cigarette.

His offer was not without its charms. Elizabeth, our little bundle of joy and wake-up calls, had blown into our lives a few months before, right on the heels of my promotion to lieutenant. Ellen had become the conductor of our little three-piece orchestra in Palolo Valley and her daily demands made paperwork at the station seem like a vacation. I could take Gid up on his offer, wash my hands of Happy Tokuda and what would certainly be a shitstorm of a case, and look forward to a cup of bad coffee, a stale malasada, and a stack of reports on my desk. It would be dull and monotonous and absolute heaven after a night of no sleep thanks to my little human air raid siren.

It also brought to mind another offer Gid had made to me, just after Ellen had given birth. He proposed that he would assign me Homicide's administrative oversight for a year, proofreading and signing off on case reports and files and sitting in on meetings with the brass. I declined. I didn't know why. Maybe it was an addiction to casework. Maybe it was fear of becoming a housepet. Whatever the reason, I took a pass on the opportunity to ride my desk for a year. I never told Ellen about it.

But here it was again and this time, it smelled beautiful. This time I was tired. This time I was a mere husk of the man who had declined the initial offer. I had worked a half-dozen cases with Paris since Lizzie was born. Riding elevators and climbing stairs where there were no elevators to squeeze information out of liars, idiots, and false leads had all taken its toll on me.

I almost bit. I almost took the prize and made a sprint to the promised land with it. Almost.

Then I thought about Wally.

My best friend lost a leg overseas. I still had both legs because I got up to fetch a candy bar out of my pack. Now Wally was on the verge of losing a lot more—maybe his wife, maybe an election—thanks to an ugly thing that happened under his roof that wasn't his fault. I couldn't save his leg, but maybe I could save his marriage and his career. Maybe, if I could bring Happy Tokuda in one more time.

Gid would tell me to leave it; someone else would bring Happy in. Better that I take it easy until my little girl got a little less little.

But the problem was that nobody else could bring Happy in. All those dicks in bunco couldn't make the collar, and most of them were pretty damn good at what they did. When it came to Happy Tokuda, there was only one cop on the island who was capable of finding him. Me. First Base. The kid who kicked him and his stolen goods out of McKinley. The only dick who knew him well enough to ferret him out of his hiding places and intractable enough to ignore his begging and his bribes and book his ass.

In the end, I was not only Happy's best chance at a fair shake as I told Wally, I was also Wally's at bringing a resolution to the chaos in his life.

"No need," I told Gid at last. This time the words burned my throat like a steak dinner vomited up after a night of heavy drinking, and they tasted just as bad.

What the hell. It was a dream. Peace and quiet never had a chance. I fished my car keys from my pocket and dangled the ring from my forefinger. They jingled without luster and cheer. Funeral bells for my year of relaxation.

"You sure?" asked Gid.

"Yeah," I said. "I'm sure. I'm not thrilled about it, but I'm sure."

Gid laid one of his giant hands on my shoulder, gave a gentle squeeze, then lumbered toward the front door.

"You can always change your mind," he said. He didn't even turn around when he said it. "You just let me know, Sheik."

"Thanks, Captain, but this is something I need to see through. Maybe I'll take you up on your offer next case."

"Okay, but try not to wait until your daughter's wedding to redeem your rain check."

Gid disappeared into the entryway to find Paris and get a briefing from him. I continued down the street until I reached my car and got into it. I started the engine, turned the corner, and started my descent down Wilhelmina Rise and into investigative hell.

Schuman Carriage was a familiar place to me. I purchased my Cadillac Eldorado there almost two years before when the Eldorado was the new, coveted automobile to own. I stopped by on occasion when my sister Violet asked me to pick up parts she needed. She ran an automobile repair shop in Kakaako with her husband, Masa. Masa was the mechanic in charge of the other mechanics and ran the shop. Violet ran the office and the books, which really meant she ran the business. My brother-in-law detested paperwork and was more than happy to let my sister do it. I took my Cadillac to my sister's shop where they serviced it for free, so I was only too happy to return the favor and act as their shop's intermediary with Schuman Carriage when they needed parts in a hurry. Especially if those parts were for my car.

Schuman Carriage was located at the corner of Richards and Beretania across from Washington Place where the governor of the Territory lived. It was housed in a building that looked wrong.

A theatre-like marquee above the showroom door proclaimed all the new models over the big, modern plate glass windows meant to entice the passerby like a filmy negligee. Sprouting out of the top of this new car showcase was an old stone church. It had been Central Union Church before that church moved to a nice green spacious lot several blocks Diamond Head, to the corner of Beretania and Punahou Streets. The old stone edifice at Richards still stood, with Schuman Carriage eventually fitting its showroom around it. The steepled roof above stared down at all those who humbly entered the showroom as a reminder that in exchange for heaven on asphalt, one would have to tithe his life away in monthly payments. It was something right out of "The Knight's Tale" in Chaucer:

*And al above, depeynted in a tour*
*Saw I conquest sittinge in greet honour*
*With the sharpe swerde over his heed*
*Hanginge by a sotil twynes threed*

I knew the feeling all too well as the owner of a not yet two-year-old Cadillac Eldorado. Talk about conquest: my bank account was overrun. It was probably more accurate to say the car owned me than the other way around.

I pulled up to the curb fronting the showroom and got out. A couple of haole salesmen abandoned their marks for the moment to come to the big windows and ogle my red convertible. The '54 Eldorado had already been out for a while, but the '53, the first Eldorado, still had a mystique about it that seduced all in the know. I thought I could hear the wolf whistles of one of the salesmen from behind the plate glass. My car always drew this kind of reaction whenever I stopped by on an errand on behalf of my sister, which never ceased to surprise me. The Schuman Carriage regulars were more impressed with my car than anyone, yet they were more familiar with it than anyone: they sold it to me.

I entered the showroom through the glass doors under the marquee and was hit by a wave of seductive air conditioner–chilled air and the attendant new car smell. It made me want to move in. All that was missing was a television set and a decanter of scotch, and those things were probably in the manager's office.

The haole salesmen immediately swarmed me and pelted me with compliments and questions about the Cadillac. I was rescued by Herb Cooper, the showroom manager, a tall man with a radio announcer's voice who always wore a nice suit.

"Good morning, Frankie! There's coffee and Danishes in the office. How's our Caddy treating you?"

"With kid gloves. It should, for the monthly payment."

"Here for parts for your sister? I didn't get a call."

"Sorry, Herb. I'm not here on her business today. I'm here on mine."

I brought the badge out and showed it to him. This was a mere formality. Herb Cooper knew what I did for a living. It was all over my loan paperwork. At first, he always called me "Detective" until I told him to relax and call me Frankie like all my friends. One never knew when one would need a friend at the dealership, especially when a good deal was needed for a future new car. Cooper looked at the badge and scratched his chin and nodded.

"What can Schuman Carriage do for the Honolulu Police Department?" he asked.

"I need to speak to a salesman you have here on staff. A guy named Joe Matsukawa."

"Joe? Sure. He came aboard just before Christmas. Near the top of the sales numbers already. Speaks Japanese, so he brings in a lot of older folks who have been saving up for something nice. He's in the sales office in back finishing up some agreements and layaway paperwork. You want me to get him?"

“No thanks, Herb. I’ll go back and find him.”

“Suit yourself. Help yourself to the pastries.”

I made my way to the offices behind the showroom. There were a handful of doors off a narrow hallway in what would have been the old church, now remodeled to modern workspaces to include quaint touches of contemporary design like linoleum, fluorescent lighting, and slender, stand-up aluminum ashtrays with fancy little “doors” that open and shut with the push of the button.

Herb Cooper’s door was open, so I walked in and helped myself to a paper cup of coffee. I passed on the Danishes, though they looked good. Once I had my coffee in hand and a Lucky Strike ignited, I made my way down the hallway to a door with a pebble glass window with black flake paint in large letters spelling out SALES.

I opened the door to find a single, large room filled with a half dozen desks. At one of them, a lean haole man with mousy brown hair and mousy brown eyes sat on his blotter with his feet on his chair talking to a secretary in a lemon-yellow dress and matching pumps. He was probably angling for a favor or a date or both and in his case, a date would have been a favor. They turned to look at me, nodded a greeting, and resumed their flirtation as if I hadn’t walked in at all.

The other desks were empty save for one in a corner away from the windows. A short, balding Japanese guy wearing thick glasses and shirt sleeves tapped away unevenly at a typewriter choked with carbon forms. He kept glancing at his paperwork on the blotter next to the typewriter then back to the forms he was pecking at, no doubt being extra cautious with the spelling of some customer’s name or address. He looked like the kind of guy who would make a lot of mistakes if he didn’t take the time to triple check his work. He mouthed the words and names he was typing quietly, always a sign of a limited thinker with poor concentration. You could practically see the smoke escaping from his ears, and smell it, too: the unmistakable bouquet of failure. Happy Tokuda has had some easy marks throughout his infamous career, and this guy was a Hall of Famer.

I walked up to his desk and waited patiently for him to stop his uneven two-finger typing. I sipped my coffee and took a few drags of my cigarette before he even noticed, so deep was his concentration and fear of screwing up.

He finally looked up at me from his hunched position over the typewriter, his fish-like eyes regarding me curiously through the thick lenses.

"Joe Matsukawa?" I asked.

"Yeah, that's me," he said. He looked like he was about forty years old, if I didn't miss my guess, king of his house, whose homely wife let him have the first soak in the furo while the water was still hot. I set my coffee cup down on his desk and pulled my badge out. His eyes grew wider and his slack lower lip dropped a half-inch lower.

"Yoshikawa. HPD," I said.

He said nothing. He sat and stared at my badge until I finally put it away.

"I need to ask you a few questions, Joe," I said. "This is about a friend of yours. Harry Tokuda. Folks call him Happy. Do you know who I'm talking about?"

He nodded dumbly. I looked over at Mousy Brown and Lemon Yellow whose witty banter had died down while they eavesdropped on our exchange.

"Hey, miss," I said to Lemon Yellow. I flashed the badge at her though I knew she had caught a glance of it when I showed it to Matsukawa. "Could you tell Mr. Cooper that I'll be using his office for a few minutes, please?"

"Yes, sir," she said. She scurried out of the office, leaving Mousy Brown at his desk to smile awkwardly at me. I nodded at him, then turned to Matsukawa.

"Let's go to Herb's office," I said. "I won't take up too much of your time."

He nodded and we walked out of the big room and down the hall to Herb Cooper's office. I shut the door and refreshed my coffee cup. This time, I caved in and helped myself to a sticky, sugary pineapple Danish. I devoured the thing in two bites. Having realized it was the first thing I had eaten that day, I plucked another from the white cardboard box lined with wax paper and bit and chewed a little more slowly.

"How long have you known Happy Tokuda?" I asked. My mouth was still partially full when I said it, but I was too tired to stand on ceremony. Matsukawa blinked at me and shook his head.

"Not too long," he said. "Maybe about a couple of weeks. He came into the showroom and acted like he didn't speak English that well, so Herb came and got me to help him. He told me in Japanese that he was looking at a Buick but really wanted something smaller and cheaper. I told him I heard about a Japan-made car I heard lots of things about, the Toyopet. You can see them in some Japanese movies."

"When did you find out Happy could speak English just fine?"

"He told me right then. In Japanese. He said he didn't trust the haoles in the showroom and didn't want them to hear what he was saying to me."

"And what was that?"

I had finished eating my second Danish and picked up a paper napkin from a stack next to the pastry box and used it to wipe the sugar from my mouth and fingers. Matsukawa shifted uncomfortably in his chair and blinked some more.

"He said he knew a way to make us both rich. Not just Pake rich. Haole rich. He said he could've shared his plan with any of the other guys, but he didn't trust haoles. He said he trusted me because our moms were from the same ken. He said that practically made us cousins."

"What ken is that?"

"Hiroshima."

"How'd he know that if he just met you?"

"He asked me and I told him. He seemed really excited when I did."

I had to laugh. Vintage Happy. He created ties that weren't there, fabricated relationships and false shared experiences. I didn't know for sure what ken he was really from, but he had at times been from Hiroshima, Yamaguchi, Kumamoto, and Okinawa and had even been half Chinese, Hawaiian, or Filipino when it suited his game.

"Is Happy in some kind of trouble?" Matsukawa asked. His brow was furrowed now; his curiosity was rapidly slipping into the abyss of worry.

"That's an understatement. I'm a homicide detective, Joe."

"Shit," he said.

"We can talk all you want about your 'business arrangement' with Happy later, but right now I really need to know if you have any idea where he might be."

Matsukawa screwed up his face like someone washing out a wound with salt water. I puffed on my cigarette and waited, but not very patiently.

"I never knew where he lived," he said. "But he told me about how busy he was with another business he had. Something about chicken feed."

"Chicken feed?"

“Yeah. Some kind of special food for fighting chickens to make them stronger and meaner. Better fighters.”

I laughed aloud again. Jesus, Happy. I’ll give you this: you sure have a knack for finding the world’s stupid people.

“Detective? You’ll get my money back?”

“Your money’s gone, Joe. But if I can bring Happy in, maybe you can punch him in the mouth and feel a little better.”

# 6

Because Schuman Carriage was just a few blocks from the station, I drove there and used the telephone from my own office. I had also wanted to check in with the forensics guys, but nothing definitive had come back yet; tests were still underway.

I called another sister of mine, Daisy, who lived in Wahiawa with her husband and kids and kept the books for the feed store her husband inherited from his folks. I had four sisters, all of them older, and all of them with flower names: Violet, Daisy, Iris, and Pansy. I was grateful that my folks stopped with the floral theme by the time I was born.

If anyone knew anything about special chicken feed, it would be my sister Daisy or her husband George. Of course, it hurt my pride to have to ask them something so stupid, but because I didn't have any better leads for locating Happy, I picked up the telephone receiver and dialed.

"Tanioka Feed," said my sister.

"Hey, Dais. It's your favorite brother."

"It's my only brother."

"Same thing."

"Not really. If I had another, you'd be a distant second. Aren't you supposed to be at work?"

"I am at work."

"Oh," she said. "I just thought because you never call you might be on vacation or something. How's Ellen and little Lizzie?"

"Ellen's tired and Lizzie's awake at all the wrong times. By the way, I'm tired, too. Thanks for asking."

"Oh, Frankie. If I know you, you probably just lie there and pretend to be asleep when the baby starts crying. I'll bet Ellen gets up on her own to feed her."

"Touché. Look, Dais, I know this is a stupid thing to ask, but is there such a thing as special chicken feed that makes the chicken, uh, angrier? You know, a better fighter. For chickens that do that sort of thing, anyway."

That bought me a good two minutes of listening to my sister's howling laugh.

"Stupid! There's no such thing," she said when the howling died down to a few giggles under her breath.

"Look, I thought as much, but I had to be sure," I said. "Nobody can sell anything like that. The next question is: have you ever heard of anyone claiming to sell anything like it?"

"No," said Daisy. "Anybody who said anything like that in this business would be a laughingstock. Nobody I know said that—and believe me—if someone had, we'd all know about it."

If my sister hadn't heard anything about the scam, Happy was likely to have initiated it on his own. Happy was smart enough to steer clear of anyone who'd know anything about the commodity at the heart of his ruse, which is why he spoke to Joe Matsukawa in Japanese in the Schuman Carriage showroom: he didn't want any of the sharper haole salesmen calling his bluff. He would, however, in this case, have to go to a legitimate feed merchant to purchase his magic corn and he wouldn't need much at all to perpetrate his scam. This meant I had a long day of driving around the island showing every feed store's mom and pop Happy's picture. I lit up a cigarette and steeled myself for my sister's answer to my next question.

"How many feed stores are there on this island?" I asked.

"That sell your magic fighting chicken feed?" Daisy started laughing all over again. I was beginning to regret making the call to her.

"No," I said. I sighed and took a drag off my Lucky Strike. "I mean how many feed stores like you. On this island. Selling regular chicken feed. Period."

"Well, let's see. There have to be at least a dozen that I know of. Most of us are out in the country, but there's a couple of big ones in town. Some of us get ours from them wholesale because they're right by the harbor. Why?"

"I have a suspect who's pulling some kind of scam with the magic chicken feed, as you call it. I really need to find this guy and the best lead I have is this scam. I'm thinking I have to go to every feed store on this island and show his picture and ask if anyone has seen him and if they have any information."

"Good luck with that. You'll be out all day driving around the island. I've got a list somewhere of all the shops and their addresses and owners' names. I'll give it to you if it'll help."

"Yeah, it will," I said, without really believing it. "Thanks."

"Oh, I almost forgot," said Daisy. "I was going to tell you that George said he saw one of your old friends the other day. This guy said he hadn't seen you in a while and asked George to say hello to you the next time he saw you."

"Oh? What guy was this?"

"I can't remember the name. George might. He said the guy knew you from McKinley but he was older. The guy knew all of you baseball boys."

"Is George there?"

"No. He went out to make a delivery but he'll be back in an hour or so."

"When he gets back, tell him not to go anywhere until I get there."

"Get where?"

"Out to your store. I'm leaving from town now. I mean it, Dais. This is important."

"You're visiting? Why don't you wait until you're done with work and bring Ellen and the baby over for dinner?"

"This isn't a visit, Dais. It's work. I need to talk to George about work. Make sure he stays put, okay?"

I hung up, killed my cigarette in the ashtray on my desk and put my coat on. I was so close. If Happy was the "friend" who stopped by my sister's store and talked to my brother-in-law, I just saved several hours of legwork. I had to slow down and remind myself that my sudden burst of energy was just me getting my hopes up. If it turned out the customer wasn't Happy, I would have driven all the way the hell out to Wahiawa for nothing.

Well, not for nothing, exactly. I suppose I could consider Tanioka Feed my first stop on my around-the-island chicken feed store tour. The prospect did little to brighten my mood. Still, I couldn't suppress the feeling, against better judgment, that something serendipitous had just happened, and I allowed myself a little smile.

Maybe I should call my sister more often and show her just what a thoughtful kid brother I really am.

The drive from town to Wahiawa was as it always is: long and hot. Once I got out of town and past Tripler Army Hospital high on its perch marking the edge of Honolulu, I went up then down Red Hill and hit the sea of green sugar cane that would not fall away until I reached my destination. On less urgent commutes out to the middle of the island, I'd usually pull over and take my father's old cane knife out of my trunk and chop a stalk and cut and peel a section for chewing on during the drive out. The sweet cane juice was nostalgic. It was our candy before my folks moved us into town to open their automobile repair shop. To-san's young assistant mechanic, Masataka Konishi, ended up marrying my eldest sister Violet, and they inherited the shop, moving it a few blocks away to Halekauwila Street and renaming it Konishi Automobile Repair.

Violet was the sister who used to cut and peel raw cane stalks for me when I was very small and in many ways, I preferred the pulpy, fibrous feel in the mouth to the chewing gum I had in abundant supply overseas during the war. Wally asked why I gave my entire ration of chewing gum away to the Italian kids in the streets and I told him I missed the cane. Weak and rubbery, Wrigley's was no substitute.

Wahiawa was a quaint little town filled with quaint little people and it might have been a place you would describe as sleepy if it wasn't for the fact that, in addition to the quaint little people, there was a crapload of soldiers. Wahiawa was Schofield Barracks' immediate playground, and many of the poor young G.I.s often opted to spend whatever little free time and cash they had right outside the gates in little Wahiawa Town. The buses into town were infrequent and inconsistent and cab rides were too long and too expensive.

But for a handful of bad eggs and a few isolated incidents, the boys of Schofield were generally well-mannered and polite, and Wahiawa got along with them famously, taking their government paychecks bit by bit in exchange for hot meals prepared and consumed somewhere other than the mess hall, shirts cleaned and pressed, shoes shined, and hair mowed down to regulation. And, of course, booze. An enterprising denizen of Wahiawa could live handsomely off the soldiers' disposable income.

My sister's business, Tanioka Feed Store, was one of those Wahiawa businesses that derived its sustenance from the military in a more roundabout fashion: though the Army did not raise chickens, it certainly ate them. This meant that area poultry farmers, whether they were a family with a small coop in their yard or a large-scale egg farm and hatchery, were able to unload their birds on Uncle Sam for a good price. This also meant that these folks needed feed for their birds and did not want to drive all the way into town for it.

My brother-in-law George Tanioka's folks had been small-scale poultry farmers with the brains to use their tanomoshi loan to buy a truck and build a shed. They used their truck to acquire feed from one of the big haole wholesalers near the harbor and store the bags in their shed. Other Japanese bird farmers started paying them for feed, then the Pakes, the kanakas, and the Filipinos followed and entered similar arrangements with them. When the war drove the demand for poultry and eggs up, the Taniokas stopped their own bird-raising operation and concentrated strictly on providing feed, even working out a deal for War Department gasoline for their truck to continue their feed runs into town, despite the fact that they were "enemy aliens." When the forces of freedom need to feed, they don't give a damn who holds the serving spoon.

They made money hand over fist during the war, built an actual storefront and warehouse on California Avenue, then, after the war, turned the reins over to their only son, George, and his new bride, the former Daisy Yoshikawa. My sister. She met George at UH in one of their accounting classes.

I pulled up in front of the store on the gravel-covered drive and lot and parked next to one of the Ford trucks branded with the shop name on the doors in white paint. Tanioka Feed now had three trucks, though only one was in at the moment. I guessed that my brother-in-law had not yet returned from his delivery run.

I got out of my Cadillac and walked into the shop. An old man in coveralls with a large burlap sack thrown over his left shoulder was exiting. I hurried back to the door to hold it open for him. He thanked me, though he was a tough old bird who looked like he hardly needed any help to get a single fifty-pound bag a few yards to his truck, and he shot me a look that told me so. Watching him made me think of my job as easy, though I was pretty sure that the tradeoff was that the old man would never have to beat a confession out of one of his chickens or detail one of their deaths in a report.

When the old man had left, I was alone in the store with my sister Daisy. She sat behind a counter laden with a cash register and battleship gray trays full of carbons and invoices. She peered up at me over the frames of her cat eye glasses.

"Look who's here," she said.

"Hey, Dais," I said. I looked about the shop. "Long time since I've seen the store. When did you start selling tools?" I walked over to the wall opposite the register where a number of farm tools hung from pegs. I took a hoe down from the wall and hefted it in my right hand. "This is nice and heavy. You could open someone's skull with this." I returned the hoe to its pegs.

"Very funny," my sister said. "You always think of things in terms of their use as murder weapons. To us common folks, something like that is for gardening. How have you guys been?"

"Tired," I said. "Lizzie goes off every two hours or so in the middle of the night because one end needs liquid or the other end made some. I think in a strange way, Ellen enjoys it."

"Of course, she enjoys it. She's a mother now. We all enjoy it. There is no greater pleasure in life." Daisy's eyes got dreamy as she gazed at the sunlight coming in through the shop door. Daisy's kids, my nephews Danny and Royce, were good boys, but they were probably hell as infants. Weren't they all?

"You're sick," I said. "I've never been so tired in my entire life. Not even when I had to sleep standing up in a foxhole full of rainwater."

"You're the sick one," she said. The sound of heavy tires crunching on gravel came into the store through the open door.

"You're just in time," Daisy said. "George is back."

In a few seconds, the sound of work boots on the landing announced the return of my brother-in-law. He wiped his forehead with a pocket handkerchief. His blue chambray work shirt was damp with sweat.

"That's the last one of the day, honey," he said to Daisy. He used the handkerchief to rub the smudges from his glasses. When he put them back on, he noticed me standing near the counter.

"We have a surprise visitor," said Daisy. "A long-lost relative, I think."

George's face broke into a huge grin. "Frankie! Good to see you! You have the day off?"

"Good to see you, too," I said. "I wish I had the day off, but I don't. I came out to talk to you about a case I have."

"Me?" George raised his hands in mock surrender. "I hope you're not going to arrest me."

"No," I said. "You've got plenty of grief as it is." I cocked my chin toward my sister at the register. George and I laughed. Daisy punched me in the arm. She didn't hit as hard as Violet, but almost.

"You might have talked to somebody of interest in the case," I said to George.

"Okay," said George. "Why don't we talk about it in the office? It's air conditioned now."

"Good call," I said. "Air conditioned, huh? I guess it really has been a while since I've been out to see you folks. Lead the way."

George opened the door to the office in the back of the store. I could feel the cool air immediately. I loosened my tie at the neck and removed my jacket. The great thing about interviewing family is that you never had to stand on ceremony. Especially on a hot day. We sat down, me in an old dining chair and George in a large, squeaky leather-covered office chair that had been his father's from before the war.

We chatted first about Ellen and Lizzie, then about baseball. The pennant races were about to kick into high gear and we discussed our own predictions. Daisy came in with a couple of cold bottles of Primo on a tray and set the tray down on the desk. George handed me one of the bottles and raised the other to his lips. Daisy leaned up against the wall next to the desk with her arms folded. She had made no effort to exit. It was clear that she wanted to hear what I was going to ask George. I didn't think there was any harm in letting her hang around, so I launched into my questioning.

"Daisy told me that an old friend of mine from McKinley came into the store the other day and talked to you," I said.

"The one from the other day you told me about," said Daisy. "The guy who knew all the baseball boys."

"Oh, yeah," said George. His beer was already half gone. "I think he was a coach or something. He was older, like a little older than me, even. He said he used to help out at batting practice."

"A coach?" I asked. "Coach Perreira? Coach Ross?"

"No, he wasn't actually a coach, at least not officially. He told me he helped you guys work on technique, or something like that."

"What was his name?"

George took another long swig, wiped his mouth with the back of his hand and thought hard in silence.

"You know? I don't think he said."

"How did he know we were related?"

"We were talking about baseball and I told him my wife's kid brother—you—were pretty good at McKinley and in college. I told him you might have been able to go pro if it wasn't for the war."

George was exaggerating a bit, but he was right about the war interrupting my baseball career. The last high school season I played was the spring of my junior year in 1941. In my senior year at McKinley, school was shut down for a few weeks after Pearl Harbor, and when it reopened, all sports were cancelled and stayed cancelled for a couple of years. I enlisted in the 442nd when I got the opportunity, played for our unit against the haole units at Camp Shelby during basic training just to kill time, then at Columbia on the G.I. Bill. When I came home, I played a couple of seasons for the Japanese League Kakaako team and even had a tryout for Asahi while I was a patrolman. Asahi picked me up as a backup first baseman and pinch hitter, but when I got promoted to dick, there wasn't any time for ball with all the paperwork. I never played an inning for Asahi. Thus ended my run at big league glory.

"I wasn't that good," I said. "I'm trying to think of a part-time coach who used to help with batting. Sometimes somebody from UH or Army or Navy would come down to help."

I was losing hope despite enjoying the reminiscence of my ball playing days. I tried a last-ditch attempt.

"Was it a haole guy?" I asked. "He would've been a big man. Worked at the shipyard, I think."

"No," said George. "He was Japanese."

A surge of hope ran through me quicker than the beer had. I steadied my hand and pulled Happy's mugshot from my pocket. I handed the photograph to George.

"Was that him?" I asked.

George looked at the photograph through his glasses. He nodded slowly at first, then more vigorously.

"Yep, that's him," he said. He handed the photograph back to me. "Your friend—uh, coach—is a criminal?"

"That was Happy Tokuda. He's neither a friend nor a coach, but you got criminal right. He used to come around batting practice to sell us bubble gum and chewing tobacco for cheap. Stuff he stole from Pake stores."

"I remember you talking about that guy when you were in school," said Daisy. "You were pretty upset about the whole thing. Did he do something recently?"

"Maybe," I said. "It looks like it. I need to find him and get some answers out of him."

"Wait," said George. "You're a homicide detective, right? Did this guy kill somebody?"

I said: "I don't know. Maybe."

"That's terrible," said Daisy. She glanced at the photograph I had shown George. "Too bad. He's handsome."

I rolled my eyes.

"Wow," said George. "To think, he was right here in this store, talking to me."

"What was he doing here?" I asked. "What did he want?"

"He wanted the smallest bag of feed corn," said George. "I told him we didn't sell any 'small' bags. He gave me two dollars and asked how much he could buy with that. I told him I could give him a couple of pounds and he said he had his own sack to put it in. So, I put a couple of pounds in his sack."

"Did you write out a receipt or invoice?"

"For two pounds? It was such a small amount I didn't bother."

"George!" said Daisy. "We always write a receipt! Even for small stuff! You're so lazy!"

"Sorry," I said to George. "I didn't mean to get you in trouble. I just thought you might have a record of an address."

"Usually, there is," said Daisy. She shot a cold look at her husband, who could only grin back sheepishly.

"Did he say what he was going to do with his two pounds of corn?" I asked.

"He said he had a friend who was training fighting chickens who needed some for a big cockfight in the Filipino village in Waialua. He said they ran out of feed and they needed just a little bit because they didn't expect their bird to win anyway. I guess it's something like a boxer taking a dive."

"Did he say when this big cockfight was supposed to take place?"

"He said in a couple of days. That would make it . . . tonight."

I finished up my Primo and promised George and Daisy I'd bring Ellen and the baby out to Wahiawa soon for a visit. I walked back out to my Cadillac parked on the gravel. I thought about hanging around in the country until the big cockfight when I heard my radio.

Dispatch was calling me.

It was urgent.

Meet Detective Sergeant Lau at the Medical Examiner's.

So much for hanging around in the country and saving on the gasoline.

# 7

I plowed back through the sea of sugar cane to the browns and grays of town, the drive back not as idyllic as the drive out to the country.

I pulled up in front of the Medical Examiner's and walked into the freezing home of the recently dead. The whole place had a clinical smell that immediately killed the appetite, with a faint whiff of human rot lingering just beneath the caustic surface; the antiseptic was a mere bridal veil for the septic. No amount of chemicals would completely conceal death's vile perfume.

Still, the medicinal odor was so heavy that I was afraid to light up the Lucky Strike that hung from my face. I wasn't sure an open flame wouldn't blow the roof off the edifice and make corpses of us all. I got over my fear pretty quickly, though, and lit up. The cigarette gave me something to taste beside the morgue air.

Paris sat on a steel folding chair in the hallway outside a large examination room, the kind with big, swinging double doors. His hat was in his lap like a suitor calling on his date at her parents' house. All that was missing was the roses. He looked up at me when he heard my wingtips on the linoleum approach.

"*Arys, and do thyn observaunce*," I said.

"Chaucer now, huh?" Paris stood slowly.

"Change of pace, just to keep you on your toes, professor. I got the call from dispatch, so here I am."

"Were you far?"

"Wahiawa."

"Ouch. Sorry about that."

"Don't be. The Department pays for my gasoline and I got to catch up with one of my sisters, sort of. What brings me all the way back to town?"

"What, indeed. The M.E. works fast."

"Any surprises?"

"If you mean from the autopsy and the stuff we theorized about at the scene, no. Cause of death: asphyxiation. Pillow forced down on her face while she was liquored up. Coitus prior to expiring, no signs of forced participation. Semen matches the blood type of Harry 'Happy' Tokuda, whose prints are all over everything, including the deceased's gold bangle. She was bound and blindfolded without a struggle. Some kind of sex game. Just like we said."

"Okay," I said, "I'll bite. Where's the surprise?"

"How's this—Happy Tokuda wasn't the only one in that room with a yard-long rap sheet."

"What?"

"The victim had a record, too."

I laughed aloud and almost choked on the smoke of my Lucky Strike.

"I know you're good, Paris," I said, "but to send out prints to the mainland to wherever the hell she's from and get a response that fast? You're not *that* good. Nobody is."

"I didn't say I was. Her rap sheet's not from Fill-in-the-Blanksville, Wisconsin. It's from right here in Honolulu."

"What?"

"She's got a fairly long laundry list of ordinance violations from about ten years ago, give or take."

"What kind of ordinance violations?"

"Hotel Street house rules. Aunt Meg was a prostitute and a fairly active one. Her name back then was Mary Judith Kerrigan."

"You're kidding."

"You think so?"

"No. But are you sure?"

"The prints are an exact match, Sheik. And the faces in the photos are hers," Paris said. He squatted down and picked a manila folder up from the frigid linoleum under his folding chair. He handed it to me. The paper had picked up some of the artificial icebox chill of the place.

I opened the file and looked. There was a mugshot of the woman I had seen at Wally's party, the corpse I had seen tied to the headboard of his guestroom bed. The same one that was beyond the sea foam green double doors on a steel table. The woman in the mugshots was younger and a lot more defiant looking, but no less haughty. She had been made up, brothel-style, and it went a long way to enhance the plain face I met at Wally's little get together. Her hair had been lighter back then, maybe brown, maybe red. But the eyes were the same—eyes that commanded you to take out the trash and stay out there with it where you belonged.

Had I seen this face somewhere before? *This* face. The made-up sporting girl, not the aunt at Wally's party. It couldn't have been in the course of my work. Where?

"How the hell did you know to run her prints against what we have here?" I asked.

"I didn't," said Paris. His sheepish grin came back. "It was done out of habit. Too many bodies from cane fields and Chinatown alleys. A reflex. I felt bad about wasting the technician's time after I submitted the request and had time to think about it, but by then it was too late to call off the checks."

"I was wrong," I said. "You *are* that good."

My momentary amazement with Paris's serendipitous find wore off when I thought about Wally. "Jesus," I said. "How the hell do we break this to Lydia?"

"Does she need to know?" asked Paris.

"I'll tell her," I said.

"Jesus," said Paris.

It was a hell of a thing to find out about your recently deceased aunt, and one whose passing was less than delicate. I didn't relish the task, but it felt wrong for Lydia and Wally to have to hear it from anyone else. It would have been easier to beg off and let Paris or even Gid break the dirty news to them, but it wouldn't have been right. Life was full of shitty things that had to be done, and this was among the shittiest. I'm sorry about your aunt. It must be difficult. By the way, did you know she was a prostitute here in Honolulu a decade ago?

There wasn't any good way to do it.

Aunt Meg had been a Hotel Street "sporting girl," as they liked to call themselves. It was one of those near-Victorian euphemistic labels like "adventuress" that were meant to lend an air of glamor and danger to what "respectable" society considered to be the most deplorable thing a woman could do. A roundheels for profit.

Hotel Street was crawling with sporting girls during the war. Wally and I would catch glimpses of them when we went down there to keep an eye on Clarence, his kid brother, and Clarence's shinebox when he had to take a piss.

I first had contact with the sporting girls of Hotel Street in 1942, just before graduation from McKinley. It was mid-May, and we were entering a summer of uncertainty. Wally and I had finished our coursework and were assured our diplomas from the T.H., so we appropriately threw our academic efforts into neutral and spent a lot more time on Hotel Street ostensibly looking after Clarence, but really seeking entertainment. The war brought worry to adults, but to a couple of kids denied their last year of high school ball, it brought a lot of interesting sights. Wally and I were in the habit of hanging around Chinatown, buying cheap rice cakes and tea cookies, and watching the G.I.s stand in long lines for their three minutes of heaven. Often, the lines would wind around the block, and we'd wait for a fight to break out between a soldier and a sailor or a marine and anybody.

On occasion, we'd get an empty beer bottle hurled our way and get called "dirty Japs," usually in a drunken Southern accent. But the insults and flying bottles and, alas, the fights we'd come down to watch were really few and far between thanks to an active M.P. and S.P. presence. Hotel Street was crawling with military law and the patrols were pretty efficient at beating down altercations in the whorehouse queues with the shoe-black nightsticks they swung from leather thongs like lethal yo-yos. They'd generally protect us from the hotheaded Southerners, but sometimes they'd tell us to run along or they'd call HPD to call our folks.

Sometimes we could get a friendly G.I. or a drunk to buy us a beer and Wally and I would split the bottle, passing it back and forth between us like it was Coca-Cola. Sometimes we could bum a cigarette, too, and we'd have an entire afternoon's worth of cheer. Wally, always cautious, carried Sen-Sen for the long walk home and we'd smell each other's shirts for traces of smoke. We thought those were great times. We were easily amused.

It was one of those May afternoons, when we were lucky enough to get hold of both beer—and that day we had a bottle each—and cigarettes, when we were approached by a sporting girl. We had been standing in the doorway of a Chinese tailor-and-sundries place selling cheap, tinny-sounding ukuleles, grass skirts, and hand-tinted postcards. We were taking surreptitious sips and puffs of our ill-gotten booty when a bleach blonde haole girl with Bette Davis makeup and wearing a blue dress with big padded shoulders walked right up to us. We moved aside, allowing her entrance to the tacky little shop.

"Pardon us, miss," I said. Wally nervously and hurriedly dropped and stamped out his cigarette on the sidewalk. We both hid our beer bottles behind our backs.

"No need for that," said the blonde. "Give me a sip of that, will you? I'm dying of thirst." I had not moved quickly enough; she had seen my bottle. I slowly brought it out from behind my back and held it out to her. She grabbed the bottle and the hand that held it and raised both to her scarlet, pouting mouth and took a long, lingering pull. Her manicured fingers felt hot on mine and I could smell her perfume, like hothouse orchids. It filled my head and stung my eyes.

Wally's mouth gaped and his eyes bugged, as if she had kissed me. It was the closest I had ever been to a haole woman if you didn't count my McKinley math teacher Mrs. Hastings, who weighed two hundred pounds, had sardine breath, and was the last person to call me Francis. And she only got close to me so she could hit my knuckles with a ruler.

This girl was different. Though her blonde came out of a drugstore bottle and she cracked gum to get rid of the taste of the fifty different tongues she'd chewed earlier, she might as well have stepped off the silver screen and into my personal space. She slowly released my hand and beer bottle, which was noticeably lighter, and laid her hand on my shoulder.

"Thanks," she said. "Tall, dark, and handsome." She threw a glance Wally's way and said, "You're cute, too, Shorty. I guess it's my lucky day. If you guys have a buck between you, I'll take you out back behind this store in the courtyard one at a time and help you blow off some steam."

I smirked and reached into my pocket. Wally broke out in a cold sweat and turned beet red.

"No thank you, miss," he stammered. "My mother wouldn't think it proper."

I rolled my eyes and let my fifty-cent piece in my pocket drop back down. The blonde threw back her head and laughed, snorting like a pig at the trough.

"You're cute," she said to Wally. "And funny, too."

"I'm . . . I'm not kidding," said Wally. I thought he was going to burst into tears or faint dead away.

"How about you, Big Stuff? Offer stands if you're game," the blonde said, turning back to me. "Fifty cents for the time of your short, little life."

I snickered, pulled the half dollar out of my pocket and tossed it to her. She caught it with the reflexes of a big league infielder.

"Tempting." I said, "but why don't you take care of my friend? He's got more steam than me to blow off."

"Frankie!" Wally hissed. He shot me a sideward glance of desperation and fear. "I can't! My mom would kill me and she'd kill you, too!"

The blonde snorted some more and I laughed along with her. She stepped forward and grabbed Wally's hand. He flushed a deeper red, if that were possible, and panic flashed in his puppy eyes. The blonde started tugging him toward the store entrance. Terrified, Wally yanked his hand free and held his wrist as if he gnawed it off in a trap. He broke into a full sprint mauka up Nuuanu Avenue without looking back.

The blonde snorted uncontrollably. "You're right," she shouted around the corner into an alley. "These guys are a real gas!"

From the alley, the familiar black felt beret poked itself out into view with the rugged tanned face just below it. The face grinned big.

"You boys are funny, First Base," he said.

I pushed the snorting blonde aside to get a clear shot at Happy. He pulled a tin whistle out of his pocket and held it up near his mouth while holding his free hand up in a motion to halt me.

"Come on, First Base, it's all in good fun. If you hit me, I'll blow this whistle and those two M.P.s will come and arrest you."

I looked up and caught a glimpse of two burly soldiers with M.P. armbands and nightsticks talking to a drunk sitting on a curb a few yards away.

"Shit," I muttered. I dropped my fist to my side. "You're pretty damn lucky," I said to Happy. "If I ever catch you away from Hotel Street, I'll beat your crooked ass."

"Hey, come on, First Base! We're just horsing around here! I told Goldie to proposition you boys just for kicks! She wasn't going to do nothing!"

"Yeah," said the blonde, cracking her gum. "I wasn't going to do nothing to you two babies. Me and Happy, we were just having fun. I gotta say, though, you are a cool customer."

"Yeah, you're pretty cool, First Base," said Happy. I thought I heard some genuine admiration in his voice, but I had known Happy long enough to know that genuine wasn't the first word that should come to mind when Happy was concerned. He couldn't even spell it. "Maybe you should catch Shortstop before he tells his mommy," Happy said.

He was right. I took off up Nuuanu after Wally.

"I'm not through with you," I said over my shoulder. "I'm going to get you, Happy."

I'm going to get you, Happy.

Happy knew a lot of the sporting girls back then. Aunt Meg was a sporting girl back then. Wally had told me that at his party, they seemed familiar with each other. They probably were. Just how they were acquainted eluded Wally, but it was crystal clear to me with the revelation of her wartime occupation. Happy had sampled his share of the sporting girls' wares. He and Aunt Meg probably got reacquainted by playing cowboys and Indians over a bottle of scotch in Wally Yoshida's guest room and the game got out of hand.

"Did you want to go in and see the body or ask the M.E. anything?" Paris asked. He moved his weight from foot to foot in a gesture of discomfort. He felt bad for me, as if it were my aunt lying on the steel table behind the door. He knew the truth of the matter, that I had assumed the responsibility of breaking the news to Lydia about her aunt's past and risked more than just hurting her feelings. He knew a lifelong friendship could be out to sea with the sewage, long gone and irretrievable.

"No, no need," I said. "I don't think I'm going to learn anything beyond what we've talked about. At this point, there's only what more I can learn about Aunt Meg's sordid past, and, of course, the most important thing."

"What's that?"

"Get Happy."

"What do you need me to do?" asked Paris. His collar looked a little less crisp and his eyes a little less sharp but a little wiser. Paris Lau had aged about five years in the past four hours. He really felt for me and had taken on part of the burden in his own unassuming way. It was one of the things I really appreciated about him.

"Why don't you go back to the station and update Gid, then see what more you can dig up on Mary Kerrigan? Talk to some old timers. Maybe the Army or the Navy has a file on her."

"Sure," he said.

Paris Lau shuffled out of the frigid halls of the office of the Medical Examiner and into the white sunlight beyond the glass double doors at the end of the hallway. His shoulders were slightly slumped and his gait was easy and a little bored. From behind, he looked like a homicide dick. He was in trouble when it started to show on his face. It wouldn't be long before that happened. The permanent bags under the eyes, the cigarette hanging from the lower lip like a soul about to slip into the abyss. It happened to me fast. Two years of listening to the elegiac sobs and muttering of the survivors and the mostly exaggerated statements of attention-grabbing "witnesses" looking to get their names in the papers turned me into five gallons of cynicism in an iron bucket. Every time an angel earns her wings or a devil his horns, someone here on earth cashes a check. Death is an opportunity for the living and Paris Lau was beginning to feel the weight of that revelation.

But not everybody gets a windfall or fills the newly-created vacancies left by murder. There are a handful of folks for whom death is just a pain in the ass, and I'm not talking about the loved ones who grieve and go crazy and never fully heal. I'm talking about the homicide dicks who dig up the ugly truth then prepare it as evidence for court and rub it in the wounds of the survivors. The former makes you a prisoner of your desk, the latter a prisoner of the bottle.

Chaucer would say that each new case "quites" the old one. "Quite" was a Middle English word that meant to pay back or, more accurately, to one-up. "The Miller's Tale" was told to "quite" "The Knight's Tale." Each homicide had a way of superseding the last, and it made your head spin and stomach lurch.

Eventually, it all becomes routine but never enjoyable, like a yearly visit to the dentist. Wastewater treatment is only the second most repugnant thing you can do for a City and County paycheck, and for us it's not the corpses that are the most revolting part of the job. It's dealing with the bodies that are still living and breathing.

I watched Paris push the doors open and his dark suit get swallowed by the light and heat. I killed my cigarette in the stand-up ashtray and pulled another, a burnt offering to keep at bay the God of Headaches.

I strolled down the hallway toward the doors and put a pair of dark glasses on under the snapped-down hat brim. The outside sunlight was blinding nonetheless after even just a little time under the sickly illumination of the fluorescent tubes.

The heat immediately slapped my face as I stepped out and my sunglasses fogged. I took them off, wiped the condensation with my handkerchief, and put them back on. I headed to my Cadillac and put my ass on its sunbaked upholstery.

I started the engine and rolled toward Kaimuki and Maunalani Heights. I was on my way to talk to Lydia Yoshida whether she was ready to talk or not.

But I needed to make a detour first, into Palolo Valley. I needed to have Ellen hear it from me before she heard it from anyone else.

# 8

"It's terrible," said Ellen. She said it for the fifth time since I told her everything that had transpired that morning. It was about one o'clock in the afternoon, and I was still finishing the tuna sandwich she had made for me. It was one of Ellen's special tuna sandwiches that she put her mother's kimchee in as a substitute for sweet pickle. My mother-in-law routinely made large amounts of the stuff for their store on the Kapalama Canal, but the "special" batches were just for family and we got a lifetime supply, so Ellen used it anywhere she could. She always cut the sandwich diagonally, just like they did in the okazuyas. Whenever I made a sandwich, I never bothered. Maybe that's why mine never tasted like anything special. Like many other things about me, presentation was something that I rarely thought about. My wife had proved that it can make all the difference in the world, so I let her present everything, including me.

Ellen herself had barely touched her own sandwich. She lost her appetite, or at least her interest in the sandwich, when I told her what had happened at Wally's. We had been sitting at our little Formica-topped kitchen table, eating our sandwiches and drinking coffee, mine black and hers choked with cream and sugar like a fountain treat. Lizzie was dozing in her crib; one thing she had inherited from Ellen is that they both looked positively angelic when they slept, which was a good thing for my daughter. If she had been like me when she slept, she'd seethe with her mouth open like a large hibernating mammal.

Ellen had been surprised to see me come home for lunch as it rarely happened. My work often kept me in town or in various, far-flung locales around Oahu where bodies are disposed of: cane fields, kiawe patches, desolate beaches. Nowhere near Palolo Valley. On rare occasions, though, I might have the opportunity to interview a witness closer to home and I'd take the opportunity to drop in on my little family. It was something I tried not to do very often, though, even when the geography worked out. I often found it difficult to leave once I was home, and I didn't like Ellen and Lizzie mixed up in a day that included stinking corpses or the violent individuals who made them.

That reluctance to leave home was even greater this time due to the ugly task ahead of interviewing Lydia about a murdered aunt with a sordid past. The need to bring Ellen up to speed on the day's events had brought me to my own doorstep, which was on the way back to Maunalani Heights. Nobody, not Paris, and especially not Gid, would have faulted me for not doing the interview and handing it off. I knew it wasn't an option, though, and so did Ellen.

"This is too important to have somebody else do it," she said.

"Paris is pretty good at this, too," I said.

"I know he is," said Ellen. "But what would Wally and Lydia think if you abandoned them now? They're our friends."

"Abandoned? This isn't leaving them behind on a desert island."

"Yes, it is."

"I know. I just wanted to make sure you did, too."

"Are you testing me, Frankie Yoshikawa? How dare you!"

"Calm down, darling. I'm well aware that you're the one who does all the testing in this house."

"Darn right."

"I just need you to understand that there may be a lot to lose by doing this."

"I know, but it can't be any other way. Finish this up, and when you do, you'd better talk to Gid about that desk job he has for you."

"You know about that? How?"

"Gid told me."

Thanks a lot, Captain. Gid was conspiring with my wife to take me off the streets. I took another bite of my tuna fish and kimchee on white. There's something you won't find at the Carnegie Delicatessen.

"Then you know I told him I'd think about it."

"The time for thinking is over, Frankie Yoshikawa. Now is the time for doing."

"Doing? This is the opposite of doing. It's sitting in my office proofreading reports and drinking terrible coffee. It's letting others handle the cases I should be handling."

"Didn't you just say Paris is good at this, too? And I can't imagine that there aren't other detectives who are also good, too. Are you telling me that you'd rather spend time with killers than your own daughter?"

"No, of course not."

"Then I'll call Gid this afternoon and let him know that once you're done with this case, you'll take him up on his offer."

"I think he'd like to hear it from me."

"Sure, he would, but he knows he won't. Anyone who knows you knows that you won't make up your mind about something like this and that I end up doing it for you. And Gid knows you. Why do you think he told me about this in the first place?"

"Are you saying that I can't think for myself?"

"No, I'm not. I know you're a brilliant thinker, but your problem is that you can only think about one thing at a time. The world is full of things that you need to think about, Frankie Yoshikawa, not just your current case. Maybe without one, you'll start to think about things that matter."

I shrugged and sipped my coffee. There wasn't anything more I could say in my own defense. The fact that she was right didn't make it any less irritating. At least I was learning when to shut up and quit poking the bear.

"Then you can talk to Herb Cooper at Schuman Carriage about trading in your Cadillac for a new Chevrolet Nomad."

"Don't," I said.

Ellen laughed and stood up and walked around behind me and threw her arms around my shoulders.

"Poor thing," she said. "You and your symbolic attachments. It's cute, but I know you'll outgrow them." She grabbed my wrist and turned it to look at the face of my watch. "Are you going to tell Lydia about her aunt's past?" she asked.

"I may have to," I said.

"Why?"

"Because it could have something to do with why she was killed. Wally told me that it seemed to him that Happy and Aunt Meg were already acquainted with each other, and I know that Happy knew quite a few sporting girls during the war."

"Do you think Happy could have really done this? I mean, I can see that he probably had . . . relations . . . with some of the women he knew, but do you think he'd kill one of them? Why? Is he really the type?"

"Jesus, not you, too. Of course, he doesn't seem the 'type.' That's what he does for a living—not seeming the type. If people actually thought he was capable of doing half the stuff he does, he'd never get away with it. Why would this be any different?"

Ellen laughed. "Listen to yourself. All I'm saying is that there doesn't seem to be a reason he might do this. I didn't say he didn't."

I had a cigarette at the kitchen table while Ellen bustled about and chattered about something I wasn't paying any attention to. I was thinking about Happy again. I had to agree that murder wasn't his style, but the fact of the matter was that I had no other leads. I was hoping that my talk with Lydia would be able to provide me with some direction that way, though I was not optimistic. I didn't even know how well she knew her Aunt Meg. All I knew was that Happy had a lot to answer for, and I intended to grab him by the scruff and shake him violently, if need be, until he did just that. If he didn't do it then he had the best idea of who the hell did.

Though the drive from our house in Palolo Valley to Wally's up on Maunalani Heights was only a few minutes, it seemed interminably long. Every pause at every intersection was filled with enough time to observe the flight pattern of bees or the strange, pedestrian still life images of galvanized steel trash cans with their lids jauntily tilted at rakish angles. They reminded me of Happy and his little black beret.

When I reached Wally's house, the first thing that became apparent was that the circus had packed up and moved on. The Yoshidas' stretch of Sierra Drive had quieted back down to its normal state of hushed inconsequence. You could almost feel the collective relief in the air. Boring is what these people paid top dollar for. They were the type who loved to gawk at a limp arm hanging over a Chinatown curb from under a canvas tarp but would be alarmed and sickened to see it across the street from their lanai. It wasn't just Maunalani Heights. It was in new "developed" bedroom communities all over Oahu, where life and death were increasingly separated by zoning ordinances. Not too long ago, only haoles lived in enclaves unsullied by the inconvenient reality of out-in-the-open violence. Now everybody wanted their own piece of suburban denial, content to hide their own wife beating and Benzedrine abuse and pedophilia behind a screen door and three martinis. I guess nobody wants to see one piss-soaked wino stab another over pocket change in their driveway, but it's not as if it wasn't happening only a few miles away. On an island, everything is only a few miles away.

Our sleepy little neighborhoods were full of the *harlotrye* of "The Miller's Tale" and "The Reeve's Tale," assault and rape as revenge for a slight, though there was nothing so entertaining or lyrical about what went on between the tongue-and-groove walls of the tract houses of Oahu.

Guys like Wally, esteemed candidates for public office, promised islands without that kind of shit, islands where the root causes of bad behavior would be swept out with the tide, if only you'd give them your vote. They promised everybody would get their fair share of insulation from poverty and resentment, not just the rich, the haole, and the well-connected.

I took those promises with a grain of salt and a shot of whiskey, as I took most promises that sought to deliver the impossible. It's not that I didn't think Wally and his fellow visionaries were sincere—Wally was as genuine and sincere as they come. These characters were crammed to the gills with good intentions, especially the Nisei glad-handers, ready to roll up their sleeves and prove themselves on a new battlefield. It's just that I thought that in the end, there wasn't much that they, or anybody, could do. I routinely got to see all the shit that goes on behind the curtain and I know that all anyone can really do is hang more curtains.

I took a deep breath, which I wished was a drink, and pressed the doorbell button. It rang like the belfry of Notre Dame, but tinnier and a lot less somber. The last echoes of the ersatz chimes had yet to completely fade when the door opened.

A fragrant breeze, warm and languid with the soft notes of something French and expensive, washed over my face. I looked down to see a luminous head of pale gold hair with the satiny glow of a Christmas ornament. The face below the hair had a smile to match. A Broadway smile.

"Hello, Frankie," said Lydia. She stood in the doorway in a light blue dress covered in big white flowers with stylized petals and leaves. The print said let's take a stroll, but the cut said let's have a drink. She looked fresh and vivacious and nothing like the Lydia I had seen a few hours before.

"Hello, Lydia," I said.

"I'm sorry, but Wally isn't home. I sent him to his office. He has lots of campaign finance paperwork to do before a filing deadline, and he was so sweet to hang around to make sure I was okay, but I told him I'd be fine and not to fall behind on my account."

"How are you holding up?"

"I'll live. Shall I call Wally home?"

"It's not necessary. I'm actually here to talk to you, if you're up to it."

I swallowed hard and mentally crossed my fingers in the hopes that she wouldn't break into tears and slam the door in my face, but something in her manner invited encouragement.

"Well, in that case, won't you come in?" she said.

"Thank you," I said. "I'll try to make this brief."

"Nonsense," she said. "I can use the company." She opened the door wide and stepped back to let me in. I entered the cool dimness of the entryway. This time, I removed my shoes. I thought it best to play it as a social visit. She had seen enough cops that morning to last a lifetime. The last thing she needed in her house was another heavy hand with a pencil in it.

She led me to the living room which had been tidied up to look like the reception room it had been before it was trampled by a dozen pairs of shoes and rolled over by a gurney. She asked me to have a seat. I had a seat.

"Would you like a drink, Frankie? It's no trouble. I'm making one for myself."

"In that case, scotch."

"Coming right up."

Lydia moved silently into the kitchen on her small, bare feet as only a trained dancer could. I accepted the drink to make my visit feel less like a necessary case interview and, well, let's face it, I really needed a drink. She returned in no time with a couple of old-fashioned glasses with scotch in them and sat down on the sofa next to me. She handed me one of the glasses, sat, and smoothed her dress on her lap, then raised her glass in my direction.

"Cheers," she said.

"To better times." I said. I clinked my glass against hers and took a long, greedy drink. My throat burned but my temples cooled and I could feel the dull headache I had been carrying around all morning evaporate into nothingness. The world instantly became a better place, but not so much better that I forgot why I had come in the first place. The perky little blonde wasn't there to make me drinks or keep me company. She was there to answer questions. After we exchanged niceties—her asking about Ellen and Lizzie, me asking about Wally's campaign—Lydia opened the business discussion.

"So, what can I do for you, Frankie?' she asked.

"Actually, I came to ask what I could do for you. It's been rough, I'm sure. So, if I can do anything at all for you, just ask."

Lydia smiled gratefully and nodded. She reached out and squeezed my hand and said, "Thank you, Frankie, that's really sweet."

"You may not be so grateful after I've asked some questions. I'm sorry, but it has to be done, Lydia, and I'd rather do it than have my colleagues do it. I know you've probably been answering their questions all morning, but I have some which may not have been asked yet, due to some new information which has come to light this morning."

Lydia continued to smile sweetly at me and sip her scotch. There was no flinch of fear or distaste with my request.

"Of course you do," she said. "It's your job and I'm grateful that you're doing it. You're our friend and that really helps."

"I'm relieved that you think so," I said. "I'll try to keep this short. How close were you to your Aunt Meg?"

"To be honest, Frankie, not very. Years ago, when I was very young, we were introduced by my mother, and later Aunt Meg helped me a little financially with acting, dancing, and vocal lessons. We had dinner a couple of times in New York when I started auditioning there, but beyond that and a handful of letters, we really had no contact."

"What made her decide to come clear out to Hawaii to see you, then?"

Lydia fell silent and looked absently into her scotch. She brought the glass to her lips and drank long and deep.

"Can I confide in you, Frankie?" she asked, bringing her eyes up to meet mine.

"Do you mean off the record? In a homicide investigation, it's difficult."

Lydia fell silent for a moment, then said softly, "Well, I think I understand that, but what I really mean is, can I tell you something that you won't tell Wally?"

"If it's relevant to the investigation, he may eventually find out, especially if he needs to give an additional statement to corroborate what you tell me."

"Oh," she said. She bit her lower lip and smoothed her dress in her lap again, though it really didn't need any more smoothing.

"Look, Lydia," I said, "I just have to give you the official line. But if you tell me something, I won't tell Wally. If it comes out later in a corroborative interview, it won't be from me."

She smiled wide and bright and threw her arms around my neck and hugged my head to hers. I nearly spilled my drink.

"Thank you, Frankie! Thank you! I knew I could trust you!"

She released her grip on me and scooted back to her side of the sofa. I could still smell her perfume and feel the heat of her cheek against mine. I took a sip of my scotch to chase the strange feeling of her forced nearness out of my head.

"Is this about your aunt being here?" I asked. I took a long drink and nearly drained my glass. I thought about Wally's comments to me about how uneasy Lydia had been in her aunt's company.

"Yes," she said. She paused, then asked, "You're sure you won't tell Wally? Promise?"

"Scout's honor," I said. I had never been a Boy Scout, but Wally had been. I thought about how he'd sometimes show up at church on Sundays in uniform and I'd tug the red kerchief around his neck, trying to take him to the ground. We'd get stern looks from our mothers and Reverend Takaki for horsing around in the aisle before services.

"Okay," said Lydia. "I trust you. Aunt Meg came for help."

"Help?"

"Money."

"Oh."

Lydia took a cigarette out of a large box on the coffee table and motioned for me to help myself, too. I did, and lit us up with the gargantuan table lighter.

"Your Aunt Meg certainly didn't look like the type of person who had, uh, financial issues. She had a very regal bearing, if my short observation of her was any indication."

"That's nice of you to say, Frankie," she said. She took a long drag of her cigarette and I did the same. It tasted expensive. I looked at the gold stripe running around the wrapper. Nat Sherman, New York City. Wally got his smokes from the same place he got his wife, both with the gold top. "But of course," she continued, "looks can be deceiving."

"Could you go into a little more detail? I mean, Hawaii is a far way to come for a loan, and it's not a short or cheap trip to make."

"No, it's not," said Lydia. "She came out for ten thousand dollars."

I choked on the expensive cigarette smoke in my throat and coughed. Ten grand. Did Wally have that kind of money?

"Are you okay?" Lydia asked. She patted my back gently as I hacked the last of the surprise out of my lungs.

"Yeah," I managed to rasp out. I cleared my throat and took a small sip of scotch, which was mostly thin, cold water from the diminishing ice cubes. "What did you tell her?"

"I told her I'd get it for her," she said.

"Pardon my asking, but you had ten thousand dollars to give?"

"It's savings from the shows and advertisements I'd done in New York. The show money wasn't all that much, but the ad money was really good."

"What kind of advertising pays so well?"

"The kind that gets a girl out of her clothes. Madison Avenue throws a good deal of cash at you if you're willing to model brassieres and negligees and swimwear. Then there's the kind of photo shoot that isn't arranged on Madison . . ."

Lydia's voice trailed off and she took a long drink, draining her glass.

Girlie mags. Pornography. No wonder she didn't want her brand-new candidate husband to know.

"It's okay," I said. I held a palm up with a cigarette wedged between two fingers. "Say no more. How you made your fortune is none of my business. It's just that I don't personally know many people with ten grand to give to a relative in need."

"Aunt Meg helped me when I was getting ready to hit Broadway. Voice and tap lessons, fancy cocktail dresses to bump into producers in at penthouse parties. If it wasn't for her generosity, I wouldn't have lasted a week there."

"Did you ever consider pictures? Hollywood?"

Lydia smiled. "I'm out," she said. She shook her empty glass. "I'm getting a refill. How about you?"

"Sure," I said. I handed her my glass and she got up and went to the kitchen. I watched her move across the living room with a feline grace. I imagined it was plausible for her to make a lot of money modeling for publications not seen on a lot of coffee tables or in the waiting rooms of dental offices.

"I thought very occasionally of getting out to California and I was recently thinking about it again," she said. She poured a couple of doubles after refreshing the ice. "But I met Wally. The best thing that ever happened to me. He's wonderful."

"He sure is," I said. "He has been all his life."

Lydia returned with our new drinks and sat down again beside me on the sofa. Closer, I thought, than the last time.

"Did your aunt call or wire you to let you know she'd be coming? Did she write?"

"No," said Lydia. "She dropped in out of the blue. To be honest, I don't know how she found me. I don't think she even knew I got married. I'm listed as Mrs. Yoshida here. So, seeing her was something of a surprise, to say the least."

"How do you suppose she managed to find you? It sounds like she shouldn't have even known you were here."

"Aunt Meg is—was—resourceful. Once she sets her mind to a task, she doesn't give up until it's done."

"Where was she before coming out to Hawaii?"

"She told me that she had been living in California somewhere. She had been playing the roulette tables at private houses and got into trouble with one of the owners after a run of bad luck."

"Los Angeles?"

"I think so, or somewhere close. The house she got into trouble with was owned by a friend of Mickey Cohen."

Aunt Meg was sounding more and more like the sporting girl she was on Hotel Street during the war. I thought with all this sordid information on her coming out, and her hitting up her niece for ten grand, the time was right to lower the boom.

"Did you know much about your aunt's life over the last ten years or so?"

"Not really. She was always something of a mystery."

"Did you know that she used to live here in Honolulu?"

"When?"

"During the war."

"That's news to me."

I gave her the news.

# 9

I told Lydia Aunt Meg's wartime story as recorded in her rap sheet while we drank our refreshed drinks. I told her there was no mistake, that the fingerprints and photographs matched. In short, I told her that Aunt Meg had been, without a doubt, a Honolulu sporting girl.

Lydia stared intently at the inside of her drink with a thoughtful expression as I went over each misdemeanor arrest and fine amount. I told her that the name she was booked under was Mary Judith Kerrigan, and that she worked on Hotel Street.

"She worked in a hotel here?" asked Lydia. She gave me a confused look.

"It was the kind of hotel where the guests waited in line over an hour for a three-minute stay," I said.

"Oh," said Lydia. She picked up her drink and took a good, long sip. Her blue eyes rippled with curiosity. "How is it that a place like that could not just exist, but thrive, if prostitution is against the law here?"

"Not just here," I said. "It's against the law in a lot of other places and it thrives in those places, too. But 'thrive' doesn't even begin to describe how much money these places made here during the war. Honolulu was the last stop before shipping out to anywhere Japanese guns were waiting. This island was crawling with G.I.s. I remember. Wally and I had just finished high school and we used to go downtown just to watch the fights break out. Where there are men in uniform, there are brothels."

I told Lydia about the afternoons we spent hanging around Hotel Street waiting for his younger brother Clarence to make his fortune in nickels with his shoeshine box.

"I haven't met Clarence yet," she said.

"He was a nice kid," I said. "He still is." I felt like a heel for bringing up Wally's family so thoughtlessly after he had told me that they had not yet warmed to the idea of his instant haole bride. I wondered if that included Clarence, who had gone to college at UCLA and brought a kotonk girl home. Mainland Japanese. I served with a lot of them, and they got promoted to NCO positions by the haole officers due to their "good" English. Clarence's wife, Irene, spoke with her "good" English with a nasally twang and wore sunglasses with cat eye frames everywhere, including to the Piggly Wiggly at the brand new Waialac Shopping Center where Ellen and I had run into her. She shopped there exclusively because she could find staples of kotonk cuisine like canned peaches and shelled walnuts in a bag. Wally once told me that his parents secretly complained to him about the strangeness of Irene's Waldorf salad. And she wasn't even a real haole girl.

"I'm sure he's very nice," said Lydia. "I can't wait to meet him and his wife. What did Wally's parents think about Clarence shining shoes in a red-light district? Were they upset?"

"Maybe in that quiet, brooding way that Japanese folks are when the service is slow at a restaurant. Instead of complaining, they shoot each other looks then grumble to each other behind closed doors at home. But I think the truth is that they couldn't be too upset about it if the government wasn't. The sporting girls operated with the approval—well, the support, really—of the Territory, the military, and the police. They were one of those necessary evils that kept the peace, kept the G.I.s away from 'respectable' haole girls, and brought a ton of money to Honolulu, including the nickels in Clarence's pocket."

Lydia chewed on this along with the ice cubes from her drink. I was beginning to relax a little, seeing her take the news of her late aunt's sordid past so calmly and with an almost clinical curiosity. Or maybe because the second drink was worming its way into my head and making itself at home there. The little blonde that Wally had married knew something of the mysteries of hospitality, that the not so secret secret was to keep the scotch flowing.

In my newfound relaxation, I began to ask questions I wasn't sure I could when I had first arrived.

"How exactly was your Aunt Meg related to you? Was she your father's sister or your mother's sister?"

"Oh, it was nothing so close or familiar. She was close to my mother when they were young. Aunt Meg was an orphan whose folks may have been from the same town in Ireland as my mother's. My mother looked after her, like an older sister. They lived under the same roof until my mother married my father."

"Where was this?"

"Pandora, Pennsylvania. You've probably never heard of it. It's a coal town closer to West Virginia than to Philadelphia."

"How does a girl get from Pandora to Broadway?"

"Train, mostly."

"Figuratively, I mean."

"You're not far off the mark when you say 'figuratively.' I was in the chorus line at a burlesque house downtown when I got there because I was too short to be in a chorus line on Broadway."

Lydia was flushed and glowed what haoles called a healthy pink. It looked good on her, but judging from the tone of her voice, it was more from the scotch than from any embarrassment she might have felt from divulging her professional history to me.

She must have seen the look on my face. She said, "I've never told Wally this. Can it be our little secret?"

"Sure."

Lydia had made me her co-conspirator in keeping secrets from Wally. I didn't like the feeling, but given the nature of those secrets, I felt as if I didn't have a choice. The truth would have crushed him. But so far, what he didn't know wouldn't hurt him, so I played along.

"Good," she said. She clinked her glass against mine and patted my knee. It was starting to feel disturbingly like Club Ginza in Wally's well-appointed living room, though it may have been a bias of mine after learning about Lydia's own past.

"We must have been in New York at the same time," I said. "I was at Columbia on the G.I. Bill after the war."

I thought her healthy pink got a shade healthier.

"Probably," she said. "But we were on the opposite ends of Manhattan and a world apart. I doubt that you and your Ivy League pals would have stopped in to have a drink at the place I worked."

"Don't be too sure. My teammates and I were frequently in Harlem jazz clubs and made the occasional foray into Greenwich Village and points south when we wanted a change of scenery. But I'm certain I would have remembered seeing you if we did get to your particular establishment."

"You wouldn't have remembered. I was one of ten glitter covered faces in a line where you probably saw my calves more than any other part of my body."

"You're probably right about that," I conceded. We shared a laugh. I had been to a couple of those "revues" with my teammates at the end of baseball season. We were drunk and all those haole legs going up and down onstage were just another part of the dump's decor. Lydia and I might have been three feet from each other and I would never have noticed.

"So, how does a coal town girl get from the burlesque house to the Winter Garden?" I asked. I lit up another cigarette. Lydia was still working on hers. I looked at her flushed face through the haze, like I was looking at her through the veil of time, glimpsing a younger, harder version of the pampered Maunalani Heights housewife.

"In a taxi or subway car," she said.

"Figuratively, again, or is that also not far off the mark?"

"More than you know."

"Say no more. Why don't you just tell me how Aunt Meg came into your life while you were in New York? I assume it was about at the time we're discussing."

"It was. We ran into each other at Lord & Taylor. I didn't tell her where I was really working. I told her it was off-Broadway repertory, or something like it."

"I guess that's not far from the truth," I said. "Most of those girls put on a fairly convincing act when chatting up the customers. A lot of those guys left those places really believing they were Cary Grant."

"And a lot lighter in the wallet," she said. We laughed again.

"The price of flattery is often everything you've got," I said. "Flattery is the most addictive thing in the whole world, and it doesn't have to taste much like the truth. It's what most men are really after, the real itch that needs to be scratched. The sex and boozy conversation are just gift wrapping."

Lydia regarded me with an intelligent look from behind the translucent curtain of cigarette smoke.

"You're a bit cynical, aren't you?" she said.

"Cynicism is what I have with my morning coffee. It's really the only thing that makes it taste better."

"You're so different from Wally," she said. She smiled big and broadly at me.

"Wally wants to save the world. I just live in it because I have no choice."

"Don't we all have a choice?"

"No. We just think we do when we drink," I said. I raised my glass to her and took another sip. "But, I digress again. You were telling me you ran into Aunt Meg at Lord & Taylor."

"Yes, and she told me by chance she had recently shacked up with some royal character, a deposed prince or duke from Something-ia or Something-land before the Nazis came and redrew the map of Europe. When the Nazis lost the war and the map was redrawn again, Prince or Duke What's-His-Name found that his country had disappeared. Anyway, Aunt Meg said he had inherited wealth to spare, something about escaping to London then to New York with a few gold bars from his royal treasury, and she told me if I was to get off off-Broadway, I'd need to hone my skills. So, she paid for voice and dance lessons. Classical stuff—opera and ballet. But it did the trick. I started landing small parts in big shows. I finally worked my way up to understudy, and that's where Wally found me. *Oklahoma!* The show, not the state."

"I take it at a certain point during or after her patronage of your career, she dropped out of your life again?"

"Yes. About five years ago. I hadn't seen her since until she turned up here."

"Did she ever tell you what she did during the war? Where she was?"

"No. I assumed she had been in New York, meeting all kinds of rich and interesting men, like the royal she was living with. My mother called her an 'adventuress.' I always thought the word made her sound exciting. Then I learned it was an old-fashioned word for something else."

I didn't say it, but Lydia could tell I had already filled in the blank. I simply nodded.

"You were telling me earlier that your aunt had run into some trouble in California. Could you tell me a little more about that?"

"Aunt Meg always had a taste for excitement, which included games of chance for big money. She found a place to play wherever she went. In L.A., it was easy. She was a smart player, she told me, except when she drank. When she did she was a little too bold for her own good. She told me she went on a bender one night and ran up a big marker."

"Ten thousand?" Wild guess.

"Yes. It's how much she told me she needed to get rid of her 'shadow' in L.A."

"Did the shadow have a name?"

"She told me he was a low-level Cohen enforcer named Bobby Castle. He did mostly loan-sharking and shook down strip clubs for protection money. Aunt Meg also dated him a few times. But she told me he was violent and had done some really bad things. Especially to women."

"She didn't seem like the type to scare easily."

"She wasn't, but this Bobby C really frightened her. He cut her on the inside of her left arm, as a warning. She showed me the scar. He told her the next time, it would be her face, then her throat."

I remembered seeing the scar on the corpse when I had come that morning, but didn't think much of it.

Lydia bit her lower lip and looked up toward the rafters, thinking. "Aunt Meg was frantic," she said. "She told me she took a bus up to San Francisco and got on the first flight here. She said she thought she had given Bobby C the slip."

"Have you told Wally any of this?"

"No," she said. She grabbed both of my hands and looked at me pleadingly. "Please don't tell him, Frankie. Please. Aunt Meg is gone and none of this matters any more. The scandal would kill his folks and maybe even his campaign. You can't tell him. You can't."

"I won't say anything to Wally," I said.

"Promise?"

"I promise."

Lydia threw her arms about me and started kissing my face, saying, "Thank you" over and over. I put both hands on her shoulders and gently pushed her back. I spilled a little of my scotch on the sofa. What the hell was this? Nobody had ever been this grateful for something I said I wouldn't do.

"Sorry," said Lydia, embarrassed. "I'm just so grateful."

"Sure," I said, "and maybe a little too much scotch."

"Yes, that, too," she said. She smiled sheepishly but radiantly. I pulled my handkerchief from my pocket and started to dab the spilled scotch from the sofa cushion.

"No, let me," she said. Lydia got up and went to the kitchen to retrieve a towel. I sat and thought about Bobby Castle, the Cohen goon. His appearance in the story certainly gave it a little more color.

Lydia returned with a dish towel and soaked all the excess scotch she could from the damp upholstery.

"I'm sorry about the mess," I said. "It's really uncharacteristic of me to waste good scotch."

"It's my fault," Lydia said. She smiled demurely. "I'm the one who knocked your glass."

We both laughed and she sat again. When the laughter died down, I said, "Happy Tokuda knew quite a few of these women who worked on Hotel Street during the war. Do you think it's possible that he and your aunt—given what we now know about her past here—knew each other before last night?"

Lydia bowed her head down toward her lap. All I could see was the top of her golden head.

"I don't know," she said. She said it quietly and uncomfortably. "I suppose it's possible. There was a lot of drinking last night. Even I had a few more than was probably wise. I thought that maybe if they hit it off, it was just the liquor. I was used to seeing Aunt Meg doing this kind of thing with men at parties in New York."

"Sorry," I said. "I didn't mean to bring something like that up." Lydia raised her head, shook it, and smiled. I cleared my throat and asked the question that needed to be asked in light of the new secret that had been shared with me about Aunt Meg's surprise visit.

"Did you give Aunt Meg the ten thousand she asked for?"

"Yes."

"What happened to it?"

"She kept it with her things in the guest room. I put the cash in a bag I bought in Chinatown at one of those little shops. It was a cute woven bag made of some kind of dried grass. I see a lot of Hawaiian women take those bags shopping. They hold quite a bit."

Not grass. Leaves. Fronds.

Lauhala. I didn't remember seeing anything like it in the guest room earlier that morning, and Paris would have mentioned a lauhala bag with ten grand in it.

"We didn't see it this morning," I said.

"No," said Lydia. "It's gone."

"Where was it?"

"Right next to the nightstand. She wouldn't let it out of her sight."

"What denomination were the bills?"

"Twenties. There were ten stacks, about a half-inch or so thick, maybe less. They were wrapped up in a pretty red silk scarf with Chinese flowers embroidered on it. The bundle was in the grass bag with some other scarves, different colors."

"She was going to take this back to L.A.?"

"I think that was the plan, yes."

"Did Aunt Meg see anyone during her short visit here? I mean, beside you and Wally."

"No. But she did receive a telephone call yesterday."

"Oh? Did you tell this to any of my partners earlier today?"

"No," Lydia said. Her voice grew softer and she hung her golden head. "The caller sounded rough and I didn't want it getting back to Wally, so I didn't mention it. I'm sorry, Frankie."

"It's all right. You're telling me now. Earlier today, you weren't in any shape to answer questions. Who called for her?"

"I don't know. A man. Rough voice. He asked to speak to her, I told her she had a phone call. It was very short. I did catch her asking which hotel he was staying at and saying something about meeting tomorrow—I guess that would be today—at the bar at four. I didn't think much of it. It sounded like she made a date."

"A date?"

"We were supposed to have dinner at the Japanese teahouse up on a mountain—I'm sorry, I can't remember the name."

"Shinchoro?"

"Yes, that's it. I told her the food was lovely there and that Wally and I would like her to try it, but she told me she had plans to meet a friend from out of town and could we do it the following night? Knowing Aunt Meg, this must have been a gentleman friend—she was always backing out of plans to meet me when we were in New York, when men called to take her out. She couldn't resist."

I thought of something uncharitable, but held my tongue. I glanced at my watch. Three o'clock.

"Would you excuse me for a moment? I need to check in with the station. I'll be right back," I said. Lydia nodded and I got up and put my shoes on and went out to my car, where I radioed dispatch to pass along a message to Paris to meet me at the Royal Hawaiian Hotel in a half hour. My request was acknowledged and I returned to the house to find Lydia still sitting on the sofa drinking her scotch.

"Is something wrong?" she asked.

"No, but I really need to get going. I'm sorry. I'd like to stay and talk more, but I've got to meet my partner. You've been a big help."

Lydia got up off the sofa, a little less steady than she had been earlier, but still in control. She walked up to me standing in the entryway.

"Thank you, Frankie," she said. She reached up and put a hand on my shoulder. "Please don't tell Wally what we talked about. I know you might need it for the case, but if he knew some of the things I told you, he'd worry day and night. He wouldn't be able to sleep or work. He has so much he needs to do if he wants to win this election. He can't have this, Frankie. Not a distraction like this."

Lydia was, of course, right. In the short time she had been with Wally, she got to know him almost as well as I did. Maybe better. Both Wally and I took after our mothers more than our fathers. Like my mother, I was blunt, to the point, and had a low tolerance for the long, arduous protocol of tactful human interaction. Just spit it out. Wally, like his mother, was a worrywart, and speculation paralyzed him. When that German grenade dropped into our bunker, Wally had probably overthought what it could have been until it was too late. His hesitation and over-analysis cost him a leg. Pondering an in-law with a checkered past who was able to squeeze ten grand out of his wife then ended up dead might cost him a lot more.

"Please, Frankie," Lydia said again. "Please don't tell him."

"All right," I said. "You sure know my friend. Thanks for talking to me and thanks for the drinks. We'll do it again when this has blown over with Wally and my family. And tell him I stopped by and have him call me if he needs anything."

"I will. Thank you, Frankie."

Lydia embraced me. I could feel her slight unsteadiness as I let her go. I started walking to my car. I could feel Lydia watching me as I passed the koi pond on my way to the street. I stopped and turned to see her standing in the doorway. She was smiling. The street was quiet save for the distant droning of a lawnmower a block away. It might as well have been from the other side of the world.

"Can I ask you something?" I said, without really thinking why I was doing so.

Lydia nodded.

"Why are you trusting me with all this?"

"You're a policeman," she said.

"So?"

"It means you can be trusted."

"Just how many policemen do you know?"

I waved to her and walked to my car and got in and drove down the mountain.

# 10

The drive from Maunalani Heights to Waikiki felt like it was all downhill from Sierra Drive to Waialae Avenue through Kapahulu. It all happened so fast that I only burned a single Lucky Strike by the time I pulled up in front of the iconic pink edifice that was the Royal Hawaiian Hotel.

When I radioed to dispatch to have Paris meet me there, I was making a couple of guesses, albeit educated guesses. Educated guess number one: that Aunt Meg's sudden "date" was the aforementioned Bobby Castle of Los Angeles, who had probably managed to track her down. Educated guess number two: the hotel Aunt Meg was going to meet her four o'clock "date" at was the Royal Hawaiian.

The guesses were based on Lydia's description of the caller and of Bobby Castle, and the assumption that a strongman for a gaming operator in L.A. would personally see the collection of a marker of that size through himself; it was probably cheaper for the organization to pay for a trip to Hawaii for Castle than to have local muscle do the collection and taking a twenty percent bite out of the collection. If this Castle was really tied to someone as big as Mickey Cohen, he'd book accommodations with style, even if Cohen was still doing federal time. Castle had a brand name to uphold. All those haole racketeers were the same: big men who needed the rest of the world to see how goddamned big they were.

Diamond pinky rings. Platinum blonde mistresses with chorus line legs. Custom-tailored sharkskin suits. Cars too big for a single parking stall. If this was true for the moneyed, evil-genius bosses, it was twice as true for their thuggish henchmen. Smaller dogs yap louder.

The racket strongman was about the gaudiest creature on earth after the peacock, and one might argue that the peacock at least wore his feathers in good taste. These haole goons wore more jewelry than actresses on the carpet on Oscars night, and just as much perfume. If one was coming to our fair island on a business call, there was only one place he'd stay. It's not like any visitor had a hell of a lot of options, but a clotheshorse like Bobby Castle would choose lodging on the beach over a downtown flop and though his Waikiki options were precious few, he'd grab a room at the most precious of all of them: the Royal Hawaiian, the pink palace erected by the Matson Navigation Company as a fancy warehouse to store the high-priced haole cargo they offloaded at Aloha Tower from the *Lurline* and the *Mariposa.*

Paris was already waiting for me in the lobby. He had his hands jammed in his trouser pockets and a cigarette hung from the corner of his mouth. His hat was pulled low over his eyes. He really was looking more and more like a homicide dick, with all our sloppy affectations, and he stuck out like a sore thumb among the enormous potted palms and Oriental carpets. He looked like an old beer bottle someone picked up in a downtown alley and dropped on a white linen tablecloth next to the china and silverware. There was hope for him yet.

"*Arys, and do thyn observaunce,*" Paris said, lifting his head a fraction to regard me from under his hat brim.

"*A Sergeant of the Lawe, war and wys,*" I replied. I ignited my own cigarette. "I guess we've officially switched to Chaucer."

"I thought we'd give the Bard of Avon a break. You look like you haven't slept for a week and I just saw you a few hours ago. Are you okay, Sheik?"

"Top form. And you're looking passably slovenly lately. No mistaking you for the concierge anymore."

"I'm learning from the best."

"Just don't tell your mother. I don't want to have to start doing your laundry for you when she complains."

"Not to worry. Laundry is her hobby. What's the play, Lieutenant?"

"Welcome wagon. We're going to brace some out-of-town muscle for hire. I just came from the Yoshida house and the new missus told me—confided in me—that the late Aunt Meg had a weakness for the tables and ran up a whopping tab. The joint was associated with Mickey Cohen and they turned one of their big dogs loose on her. He may be here waiting for her to meet him at the bar and settle accounts, or something."

"How do you figure, Sheik?"

"Mrs. Yoshida overheard a phone conversation yesterday about a date today she was supposed to meet in a hotel bar at four."

Paris half shrugged and nodded. He scanned the lobby from where we stood and his eyes came to rest on some haoles in their tennis whites sitting under pink umbrellas on the broad lanai stretching out toward the beach. Most of them sipped daintily and laughed raucously.

"Seems like a nice place to square things with the house," said Paris.

"Nicer than most. Keep your eyes peeled for someone who looks like a payroll thug. I'm going to check the guestbook at the desk."

I left Paris where he stood on the enormous Oriental carpet in the lobby and took a stroll to the front desk. The clerks behind the desk were handsome kanaka boys in pink uniforms with military band-style high collars and epaulettes. A pretty girl with big, luxurious hair sat partially concealed by a gold Japanese folding screen, working a switchboard. She spoke clipped, proper English and didn't chew gum. She was all class, as much as the Matson Navigation Company could buy, and they could buy quite a lot.

When I reached the desk, I removed my hat. One of the smiling faces in the pink majordomo outfits greeted me as if I were the Prince of Wales.

"Good afternoon, sir. Welcome to the Royal Hawaiian. How may I be of service?" he asked. He was all radiant dental work and pomade-slicked hair.

I pulled the shield out and showed it to him.

"Yoshikawa. Homicide. I'd like to see your guestbook if you can spare it, and even if you can't."

"Of course, sir," he said. His face was frozen in his customer service grin. He walked to the other end of the desk, retrieved a leather tome not quite as big as the Gutenberg Bible and laid it on the marble in front of me.

"Much obliged, cap'n," I said.

"Take your time, sir," he said.

I started with the page in front of me, guests who checked in that day, and worked backwards. There were five Smiths, two Joneses, two Johnsons and a Johnston, and a variety of other names you'd find on a country club mailing list.

Then I saw it among the previous morning's check-ins: R. Cassidy, Hollywood, Calif. Jesus, how tactless and pretentious. The name had been block-printed, like words in the speech balloons in the funnies, but sloppier, like the hand that wrote it had fingers as thick as bratwursts. Room 210. Second floor. A king on a budget. It probably didn't have an ocean view. All that mattered to these criminal posers was the prestige address. His hometown of "Hollywood" probably meant he could look out his walk-up apartment kitchen window over the beans on the stove and see half of the white letters on the mountain.

I caught the eye of the chipper clerk who helped me and pushed the big book back toward him and thanked him.

"How long is Mr. Cassidy booked for?" I asked. The clerk replaced the book in its proper position and stooped below the desk and pulled up a file box full of tabs and cards.

"Cassidy. Robert Cassidy . . . looks like he has Room 210 for a full week. He's all paid up, too."

"Let me guess," I said. "Cash."

"Yes, sir."

I pulled a couple of bills from my wallet and handed them to the clerk.

"Thanks for your help, kid. Go buy yourself a bad disposition. It comes in handy every now and then."

"Thank you, sir," he said. He hadn't lost his smile the whole time. "I know it does, but we're not allowed to have one here."

"Then your job is a lot harder than mine," I said. I walked back across the lobby to Paris.

"Just in time," said Paris. He looked over at the lanai bar and rested his eyes on a character making his way to one of the many tables covered by a pink umbrella. He wasn't very tall; in fact, he was probably a couple of inches shorter than I was. He was built like a fireplug and wore his jacket an inch too snug around the chest. The electric blue suit was a tad shinier than was tasteful and probably cost him a month's rent. Under the suit was a canary yellow shirt with no tie, open at the throat. He had a yellow pocket handkerchief to match the shirt stuffed into his jacket breast pocket. His cuff links were not quite as big as trash can lids and his hair was slicked back like it was varnished onto his head. His eyes were obscured by dark glasses resting on the bridge of a nose broken three times but only twice repaired.

"You've got a good eye," I said to Paris.

"For the obvious," he said.

"Give me a minute with him before you join us."

Paris nodded.

The bulldog in the sharkskin shuffled up to a pink umbrella-shaded table and lit up a cigarette. I noticed that the old-money haoles had given him a wide berth as he walked to his table and steered clear of any tables immediately adjacent to his, as if poor taste was as contagious as the plague. He pulled out his pocket handkerchief and dabbed his neck and forehead. Sharkskin. Being wrapped up in it produced the same effect that tin foil had on a baked potato. When he was seated, I approached him.

"Good afternoon, sir," I said.

"Mr. Moto," he said. He sneered derisively and looked up at me through his dark lenses. "Think fast. I'd give you my order for a double martini, but you don't look too much like a typical Jap waiter. No. In fact, if I was a betting man—and I am—I'd say you was a cop. So, how'd I do? Jackpot?"

I pulled a chair out and sat down next to him. "Winner," I said. I pulled the gold shield out and showed it to him. "Yoshikawa. Honolulu Police."

"So what? And I don't remember inviting you to have a seat at my table, Cop."

"I don't remember inviting you to visit my island, Criminal."

He glared at me from behind his dark glasses, then suddenly burst out in laughter. "Okay, what the hell," he said. "It's a free country. Won't you join me, Officer?"

"It's Detective Lieutenant. And don't mind if I do, Mr. Castle, though if I were a betting man—which I am, today, at least—I'd say that your name is really Castellano, or something else that belongs on a can of anchovies."

Bobby Castle laughed again. He called for a waiter by snapping his fingers as loud as a gunshot. A pink shirt appeared tableside.

"Double martini for me. Three olives. And something for my new friend here," said Bobby Castle.

"Scotch," I said.

"Very good," said the waiter. He bowed slightly and disappeared among the sea of pink umbrellas and the pink faces seated under them.

"I didn't know that cops here drink on the job," said Castle.

"We don't," I said. "I'm not working. I'm just here for a friendly conversation."

"No shit?"

"No shit."

"So, what do you want to talk about? The weather? It's gorgeous here."

"How about something just as nice? Something like ten thousand dollars."

Castle fell silent, but just for a short moment. A man like that probably dies of atrophy if his mouth stops moving for long.

"Ten grand is a lot of money," he said. "You think I got that kind of scratch on me?"

"You tell me."

"I'm not as well-heeled as I look."

"You're kidding."

Castle grinned. The scraping sound of a chair being pulled out interrupted our conversation. Paris sat down.

"What's this?" Castle asked. "They grow big Jap cops on trees here?"

"Sorry," said Paris, "but I'm Chinese."

"Chinese? I thought you people and the Japs hated each other."

"Sure, we do," said Paris. "But not as much as we both hate guineas posing as proper white people."

Castle laughed. "What the hell. Why don't you join us, Officer?"

"Detective Sergeant Lau."

The waiter returned with our drinks. He set them down on pink cocktail napkins.

"What're you drinking, Sarge?" Castle asked.

"Iced tea," said Paris.

"Unlike me," I said, "*he's* working."

The waiter disappeared. Paris stood up and tugged the back of Castle's chair.

"He's right," said Paris. "I am working. Get up."

"You're joking, right? What the hell are you bulls going to run me in for? I'm sitting here minding my own business and having a drink," said Castle.

"We're not running you in," said Paris. "This will only take a few seconds. Get up."

Castle shrugged and stood up.

"Hands on your head," said Paris.

Castle put his hands on his head and chuckled while Paris frisked him. The haoles at the other tables cast furtive glances our way in a manner they thought was subtle. Paris stopped at Castle's waist and pulled out a shiny, nickel-plated Colt M1911 automatic with bone grips. He placed it down on the pink tablecloth in front of me, then a switchblade found somewhere in Castle's pants leg near the ankle.

I looked at the gun. It was a strongarm's weapon. Flashy. Real assassins carried subtler, quieter tools. The switchblade handle was thin and elegant, like something out of *The Count of Monte Cristo.*

"Thank you, sir," said Paris. There was just a tinge of mockery in his voice. "You may be seated."

Paris and Castle sat back down. I dropped the Colt and the knife into my large coat pocket near my hip. I could feel the weight of the gun as I sat sipping my scotch.

Castle was now turning red around the gills.

"Hey! You can't take the Colt! I got a permit for it!"

"Not here you don't," I said.

"Give it back," said Castle.

"You can have it back when you depart our humble little island for your big city," I said. "Until then, we'll hold it for safe keeping, this giant hunk of jewelry." I patted the gun through my coat.

"It'll be safer than it would be in any hotel safe," said Paris. "You wouldn't want anything to happen to it, would you?"

Castle took a long, deep drink and placed his cocktail glass back on the table with a lack of gentleness that suggested that he was less than relaxed.

"Fucking pineapple cops! Where the hell do you think you are? Dodge City?"

"Damn straight, pardner," I said. I sipped my scotch again. "We're the westernmost corner of the Wild West and we don't take kindly to strangers bearing nickel-plated gifts. Our island home might seem a little old fashioned to the likes of you, but we try to keep it clean."

Castle picked up his glass and drank some more, then laughed. He had the laugh of a bigger man, just like he wore the clothes of a bigger man and, until a couple of minutes before, carried a bigger man's gun.

"Okay," he said. "What the hell? Keep the Colt. I'm on vacation, anyway."

"Keep it a pleasure trip," I said. "We don't want to see any trace of you doing business here."

"If I did any business," said Castle. "You'd never see any trace of it, anyway."

"Oh? You mean you don't need your big, pretty gun to get things done?" I asked. "Who needs a gun when you've got a pair of strong mitts and a pillow to push on someone's face."

I watched his reaction. He was as cool as they came. All he did was smirk and chuckle.

"It's not my style to do that to broads," he said. "No class."

"Who said anything about a broad?"

Paris reached for his handcuffs. I caught his eye and shook my head. The waiter arrived with Paris's iced tea. He took his hand off his cuffs and grabbed the tall glass. The waiter eyed my glass and Castle's, found them amply filled, and walked away.

"Hey? Who else are you going to smother with a pillow?" Castle said, and let out another one of his bigger man laughs.

"Yeah, who else? I'll bet you've had a lot of broads and pillows in your intense, short life," I said.

I thought he'd bristle at the insult but he was apparently too stupid to catch the slight, because all he did was smile and drink.

"Anyway," I said, "we were talking about ten grand, remember? If you come across that kind of cash during your stay here, be sure you let us know about it."

All Castle did was give me the same thuggish grin. I downed the rest of my scotch and nodded to Paris. We both stood up.

"Look at the time," I said. "It was lovely chatting with you, but we've got to go." I dropped a five-dollar bill on the table.

"Sure," said Bobby Castle. He picked the little skewer of olives out of his glass and started feasting on them. "It was a gas. Let's do it again real soon."

"Don't worry," said Paris. "We will."

"Great," said Castle. "Take good care of the Colt, okay? It wasn't cheap."

"Sure," I said. I patted my drooping coat pocket. "Nobody will touch it."

Paris and I started to move back toward the lobby. Though the sun was on its trajectory downward toward the sea in the west, it still baked the air around us so we steamed in our suits. We took a few steps away then I stopped and turned around.

"Behave yourself," I said. Castle chewed his olives and I shook a Lucky Strike out of the pack and lit up. "If we find you've been up to no good here, I'll personally put a bullet in your thick skull and end your worthless life. We'll feed you to the sharks off Kaena Point and the world will be a happier, sunnier place without your gaudy, parasitic ass polluting it. Nobody will give a shit that you're gone. If your employer even bothers to send someone out here to look for you as an afterthought, we'll do the same thing to him. There is no life on this island cheaper than yours."

"Just trying to keep our island clean," said Paris in a mock conciliatory tone. "We sweep out the trash that blows in."

Bobby Castle shook his head and laughed. "Tough guys, you pineapple cops," he said.

"Be good," said Paris.

"*Arrivederci*, Signor Castellano," I said. "Enjoy your stay."

We walked back into the cool shade of the lobby and watched the L.A. racket's traveling show finish his double martini.

"Next move?" asked Paris.

"Around the clock surveillance starting right now," I said. "Let's keep our eyes on this one. He may or may not have killed the wayward Aunt Meg and may or may not already have her ten grand. He played it cool. Maybe he didn't do it and maybe he still expects her to show with the cash. Maybe not. But our best bet is to sit on him and see what he does."

"Okay," said Paris. "I'll stick to him. Can I get some support, Lieutenant?"

"I'll take care of it," I said. "In fact, I'll call in the cavalry right now."

"Thanks, Sheik."

I walked to the front desk and talked to the same boy who had helped me with the guestbook. I told him that we were watching a guest, and that got him immediately excited and eager to help. While he went to fetch the manager and the house dick to talk to me, I made a call to the station. Delilah Kamanu, our secretary in Homicide, told me that she would send all available help right away.

The manager and the house dick showed a few minutes later and I briefed them about our guest of interest, though I spared them the case details. They were only too happy to help out, from providing records to access to Room 210 to keeping Paris's iced tea glass filled.

I went back to the lobby and stood next to Paris.

"What's happening?" I asked.

"He hasn't moved from the table," he said. "He's had two more drinks and looks like he's on the verge of ordering number four."

"Does it look like he's waiting for somebody?"

"Maybe, he doesn't seem to be in a hurry, though. Looks like he's in a good mood. He's been flirting with girls on their way back from the beach."

"Interesting. Maybe he's waiting for his money to show up or maybe he's already got it. In any case, he's playing it cool."

We smoked a couple of cigarettes together in the lobby and talked about Chaucer. Paris had another iced tea, went to the men's room to eliminate the ones he'd had already, and I fought the urge to order a scotch. Paris came back and lit up another cigarette.

"Did you call in for help?" he asked.

"I did," I said, "and looks like it's arrived, right on schedule."

We both turned our eyes to the lobby to see where a big man in a brown suit and brown fedora was half-limping across the big Oriental carpet toward us.

"Captain," said Paris, surprised.

"Gid, what are you doing here?" I asked. "Delilah told me she'd be sending everyone the Detail could spare."

"And you're looking at it," he said. "About an hour ago, everybody took off for Nuuanu Valley. Some old man went nuts and stabbed his wife about twenty times with a carving knife before eating his own pistol. It's a mess. I just came out of a meeting with a guy from the mayor's office, so I was the only one around to come out. Disappointed?"

"Hell no," I said. "We asked for some back up and got a legend. Why didn't you just pull a couple of bodies from central dicks?"

"Why bother them? Everyone's busy. Me, I just like stretching my legs every now and then. I don't get too many chances to do that anymore."

Captain Gideon Hanohano had sadly become another piece of furniture in his office lately. Since his promotion, he'd been loaded down with administrative responsibilities, most of them time consuming and not at all to his liking. Gid had been doing an awful lot of talking to the press lately as the Department's front man for damage control on hot investigations and spent whole days in press conferences, interviews, and meetings. I could tell that he enjoyed it as much as a head cold.

"Well, thanks for coming out, Gid," said Paris.

We filled him in on all the facts to date. I turned Castle's gun and knife over to Gid, who said he'd secure the items in the safe in his office until Castle asked for them back when and if he left town.

I waved the house dick over and made introductions to Paris and Gid, after which he retreated back to his office after saying to call him for anything, anything at all.

The three of us stood up from the plush armchairs in the lobby, Gid and Paris to take up different vantage points, me to leave.

"I'll be back in a couple of hours," I said.

"How's the little one?" Gid asked, as if he didn't hear what I just said.

"Still noisy at night," I said.

"Say hi to Ellen and relax a little," he said. "And think about what I said earlier."

"How can I not? Especially after you told Ellen."

Gid threw up his palms. "Hey," he said. "*She* called me and asked me to put you behind a desk for a while. I just told her I already offered you the opportunity to do just that."

"Why did you tell her *that?*"

"Because I did."

"I know, but couldn't you . . ."

"Lie? What for? So you can see one more case? There's always one more case, Sheik. They never stop coming. The killing won't stop just because you take a break." Gid smiled a crooked half-smile at me.

"This will be the last one before I take you up on the desk assignment. I have to do this for Wally. That means I'll be back."

"Suit yourself," said Gid. "And you can always change your mind. Paris and I will be all right."

I exited the lobby and walked to my Cadillac parked where I left it under the porte cochère. I got behind the wheel and started the engine and headed home to my two little ladies, both of whom had a lot of noise to make at me.

# 11

I watched Ellen's backside with some interest as she sautéed SPAM and watercress with shoyu in a pipe-handled wok Paris's mom had given us. It was something Ka-san had made for dinner a lot and Ellen had taken enough of a liking to it to make it for us at home. We had ours with kimchee on the side, though. Sometimes Ellen threw in some tofu, too, but I hadn't brought any from town in some time and the Waialae Piggly Wiggly didn't have tofu.

I held Lizzie while she stared up at me and made saliva bubbles with her little mouth. She made low, growling noises that felt something like a cat purring. I reached down and wiped her mouth and chin with the end of her bib. I thought she smiled at me, but she was probably just gassy.

"This Bobby Castle seems like a violent man," said Ellen. She turned the stove off and moved our dinner out of the wok into a waiting porcelain bowl, one of the big ones that they put saimin in at the chop suey places, not the smaller ones used at the saimin stands. "He seems a lot more dangerous than Happy."

"True," I said, "but Happy remains our primary suspect. Witnesses place Happy at the scene, but nobody saw Castle there."

"Don't you think that it's possible that Castle might have come in the night when everyone else left and Wally and Lydia were asleep?"

"Why are you defending him?"

"Who?"

"Happy."

"Listen to you," said Ellen. She smirked and put the wok and wooden spoon back down on the stove. "I didn't say that Happy didn't do it. I don't have any idea who did. I just think it's possible that this new, dangerous man could have."

"Sure," I said. "He could have. But where's his motive if he was going to get his money anyway? Goons like Bobby Castle don't dirty their hands unless it's the only way they could collect. They're mostly bluster and intimidation."

"What would be Happy's motive?" Ellen asked.

I paused to pull Lizzie's face up close to mine and breathe in that pristine, delicious baby smell that always made me forget the heinous reality of my professional existence just for a second. She crinkled her forehead in a frown and made more saliva bubbles.

"I don't know," I said. I had wiped Lizzie's mouth again and given myself a couple of seconds to think. "Except that Lydia said there was ten thousand dollars in cash in a lauhala bag in the guest room before the party, and when they discovered that Aunt Meg was dead, it was no longer there."

"Oh," said Ellen. "Why didn't she tell Paris earlier?"

"Because she doesn't want Wally to find out about the money."

"But she told *you* about it later, his best friend."

"I guess she felt like she needed to tell somebody. She made me promise not to tell Wally. I told her sure, I wouldn't tell him."

"I don't know," said Ellen. "I think you should tell him. Ten thousand dollars is a lot of money."

"I think so, too, but I'm okay with keeping Lydia's secret about it—at least for now—because it's not Wally's money. It's Lydia's."

"Oh," said Ellen. She brought the bowl of SPAM and watercress to the table, then went to the cupboard to fetch a couple of chawan and placed them on the table. She stood looking at me with her hands on her hips for a moment with her reporter's face. There was no doubt as to where Lizzie's frown came from. "I thought Wally's practice was doing really well. I mean, look at his new house."

"Come on, darling. Half of his clients are *pro bono*. You know people who do things for the principle of doing them? That's Wallace Yoshida, Esq. He comes to the Receiving Desk and bails out the drunk-and-disorderlies with his own money. The ten grand was Lydia's Broadway stash. So was the house. It looks to me like she's trying to shield Wally from her aunt's sordid past. There's a lot of damage an ex-hooker in-law with a taste for the tables can do to his candidacy. And I think she mentioned the money to me because she might have some hope that I can recover it for her."

Ellen's face softened. "I guess you're right," she said. "If Wally knew, he'd probably withdraw from the race."

"See? You know him, too. Wally doesn't do what he thinks is necessary. He does what he thinks is right."

Ellen walked over to the kitchen counter to the tall, frosted glass where we kept all our hashi jammed in vertically. She fished out a pointed wooden pair, a metal pair, and a blunt plastic pair.

"Do you want to be Japanese, Korean, or Chinese tonight?" she asked. She held up the three pairs for me to see. It was our little in-joke: we had collected an assortment of chopstick types since we were married, and we'd indicate which pair we wanted by their national origin.

"You choose," I said.

"Okay. You'll be Korean and I'll be Japanese for a change," she said. She laid out the metal hashi in front of me and placed the pointed wooden pair next to her own chawan. "Tomorrow night we'll both be Pake." She stuck the blunt plastic pair back in the glass. She walked around to my side of the table and stretched her arms out toward Lizzie.

"Come to Mommy," she said.

"I can hold her," I said, not really wanting to surrender my baby girl just yet.

"Please," said Ellen. She rolled her eyes. "You can't even tie your shoes and talk at the same time."

She had a point. I gave Lizzie up. I preferred doing things one at a time. Once relieved of the baby, I filled both our chawan with rice and reached for the old jelly jar full of kimchee and unscrewed the lid. I removed the wax paper under the lid. I stuck my metal hashi into the jar for some kimchee.

"Frankie Yoshikawa! Wrong end!"

"How can you tell?"

"Don't play dumb with me," said Ellen. "I know that you know where they taper. You're using the end you put in your mouth to get kimchee out of a communal jar."

Communal. Ellen used that word to describe anything I shouldn't be putting my germs all over.

"What difference does it make? I didn't even stick them in my mouth yet, so they're still clean."

"That's not the point. It's rude, Frankie Yoshikawa. You're telling the rest of the world that you don't care about keeping things sanitary."

"The rest of the world? All I see at the table are my wife and my daughter, and I've put my mouth on both of you."

"Again, you're missing the point. Yes, it's only us now, but it's not always just us. It's all about developing good habits."

"I'm a lost cause. I'm full of bad habits my mother couldn't rid me of."

Ellen narrowed her eyes. "I'm not your mother," she said. "I'm something much worse." She held her hashi points up like a dagger.

We both laughed and I stuck the wrong end of my Korean metal chopsticks into the kimchee and put some on my rice.

"You just did that to annoy me," she said.

"Yes."

Our dinners always started with an almost ritualistic scolding from Ellen followed by a reaction from me that said I didn't care. It was one of those things I had begun to associate with being home, and missed it when it wasn't there. Like on nights I was out working cases. Our little exchange made me want to get the whole matter of Aunt Meg over with. Maybe a year of pencil pushing wasn't such a bad idea.

Ellen and I talked about all kinds of things while we ate: my mother, her parents, taking Lizzie out to see my sister Daisy and her family in Wahiawa. We always talked at dinner, and lately about anything but work. But the mention of Daisy made me think about Happy again and how he must be out in Waialua at some chicken fight. The priority for the moment, though, was Bobby Castle. If I knew Paris, he would have already made a call back to the station to have somebody contact the L.A. County Superior Court for Castle's rap sheet. He was guaranteed to have one. At least two violent felonies on that record would also be a sure bet.

We were stretched thin with the Nuuanu murder-suicide, so Happy Tokuda would be placed on the back burner until we were done with the out-of-town goon. What the hell. Happy never fled the island. He never had to. Confident that it was more Happy's style to rely on his network of helpers than to skip town, I resolved to see the first night of surveillance through and follow up on Happy in the morning.

When we were done eating, Ellen turned Lizzie back over to me so she could clear the table. I once offered to do the clean up, but

Ellen found fault in my technique. I spent a few blissful moments cuddling my plump little sack of joy and inhaling that wonderful, soothing smell of baby hair. I let Lizzie's hair tickle my nose while I held her face next to mine so I could hear all the little gurgling noises she made. Since she came along, I found I rarely needed the after-dinner drink I used to pour from the decanter near the television. I stood up with her and gently bounced her around the living room in my arms until we settled down on the sofa.

Ellen came from the kitchen to join us. She was still wearing her white apron over her dress. She tickled Lizzie under her chin with the back of her fingernail.

"Hey, little lady," she said. "Is Daddy going to read you some *Canterbury Tales* while I nurse you tonight?"

"I can't," I said. It hurt to say it.

"Why not? You know she loves to hear it. It sounds funny, like German or Swedish or something."

"I've got to get back to the Royal Hawaiian. It's only Gid and Paris staking out Castle. They need my help."

"They always need your help. Them, and the rest of the world. It's fine. We can fend for ourselves." Ellen got up off the sofa and stalked back to the kitchen.

I felt wretched. I wanted so much to stay home, to breathe in the scent of baby and Ellen's perfume and to curl up with both of them and read Chaucer during Lizzie's feeding. In that moment, I became downright lustful for that administrative ball and chain for a year, for twelve blissful months of pencil pushing and going home when the day watch flatfoots punched out so I could watch my daughter grow.

But then, there was Wally. He had lost a leg and two sweethearts to circumstances he couldn't control. He might be about to lose his purpose in life, again due to circumstances beyond his control, thanks to an in-law he couldn't choose. The difference was that this time, the circumstances weren't beyond *my* control. I couldn't go back in time and save Wally's leg or change what happened with Polly Yamanaka and Marie Gouveia. But I sure as hell could do something about this. Finding killers was what I got a paycheck for, and I was supposed to be good at it.

I heard Ellen banging cupboard doors and dropping metal on the countertops. With my pronouncement of needing to return to work, I had sucked the joy out of the house. I think even Lizzie could feel it. She fussed and squirmed. I rubbed her tiny back gently and hugged her to me and dozed with her in my arms for a bit without meaning to.

"Give me the baby," said Ellen. She woke me from my short nap. I had no idea how long I was out. She leaned over and took Lizzie from me and handed me a brown paper sack. It was warm and smelled savory and salty and wonderful.

"There's three sandwiches in there," she said. "One for you, one for Paris, and one for Gid."

I got up off the sofa and rubbed the sleep from my face.

"Thanks, Darling," I said. I felt worse than I felt a few minutes before, if that was even possible. "I'm sorry. This is the last case. I told Gid as much. I'm taking up his offer to ride my desk for a year when this is done. I promise."

"It's my own fault," she said. "I should have known better than to marry a homicide dick. We could never be more important to you than all those dead people."

Before I could respond, Ellen marched to the bedroom with Lizzie and slammed the door.

"Shit," I said. I said it without volume and without gusto. I knew better than to chase after her and try to talk my way into a truce. I tried and died on that hill too many times and knew that all it would do is waste more time and make me feel worse. There was nothing else to do but get back to the Royal Hawaiian and the business of keeping tabs on Bobby Castle.

I nearly drained my hipflask on the drive out of Palolo Valley and down Kapahulu Avenue back to Waikiki. I knew I'd need a little bourbon for the long night of sitting on Bobby Castle, so I screwed the cap back on the flask and sucked on a Lucky Strike instead. Better to waste the smokes than the booze; the orange glow from the tip of a cigarette could dump the entire operation.

I thought about the icy goodbye from Ellen and my insides turned to ashes. The sweet, powdery scent of my daughter lingered in my memory but only made me feel lower.

I parked a few yards away from the porte cochère where I had a good vantage point and where I could easily maneuver out of the space and fall in behind a vehicle inconspicuously.

When I stepped into the lobby, I checked in with the boys in pink at the front desk. This was a new crew, but no less travel poster–handsome and no less chipper than the day boys had been. Neither Gid nor Paris was anywhere in sight. I showed the guys at the desk my badge and one of them flashed a hundred-watt smile and said, "This way, Lieutenant." He let me in behind the front desk and led me to the paper screen and the switchboard behind it. Gid was talking to one of the girls who sat at the switchboard. She wore a crisp, white blouse and cat eye glasses with rhinestones on the frames. A headset perched on her black hair gave her the look of an airplane pilot.

Gid was going over a notepad with the girl, who was translating her chicken scratch notations for him.

"When?" Gid asked her.

"About fifteen or twenty minutes ago," she said.

"And you're sure about the number?"

"Yes, sir."

Gid looked up at me and frowned.

"What're you doing here, Sheik? I thought maybe you'd change your mind and stay home and enjoy a night off with your family."

"I know," I said, "but overnight surveillance is a handful for just two guys. Besides, I took a night off last night to enjoy with my family and look how *that* turned out."

"Suit yourself," he said. "We're going to be moving soon, I think."

"How so?" I asked.

"This young lady just told me that Castle—I mean, Room 210—made a call about fifteen minutes ago. Number look familiar to you?"

Gid showed me the girl's notepad. It took me a couple of seconds to puzzle out her fours and her nines, but when I did, I had to read the number aloud to make sure it wasn't a mistake.

"Holy shit," I said, too oblivious to the young lady's presence to watch my language. "That's Wally's number."

Gid raised his right eyebrow then let it fall in response.

If Castle hadn't gotten his ten grand yet, he could be headed there soon to try to collect.

My pulse quickened and I felt lightheaded and short of breath. I touched the .38 in my shoulder holster to be sure it was there.

"Wally's probably not home yet," I said. "He's been at the office late with campaign people for the past couple of months. He only took last night off to introduce his friends to Lydia."

"That means she'll be by herself," said Gid.

"Captain," one of the desk boys called to Gid. "Telephone, sir."

Gid moved with an extra spring in his bum knee to a telephone at the other end of the front desk. He didn't spend three seconds on the call when he hung up and called for me.

"Sheik," he said. "Let's move."

I hurried over to the far end of the desk where Gid stood.

"What's up?" I asked.

"That was Paris. Castle just called up the elevator. He's moving."

Paris emerged beyond a pillar in the lobby. He sprinted toward us.

"Let's go! He's coming!"

"My car," I said, running along with him. "It's closest."

Gid limped as fast as he could. Impressively, he only lagged a mere five feet behind us. We piled into my Eldorado. I started the engine and left my headlamps dark.

"What the hell are you doing here, Sheik?" asked Paris. "I thought Gid said you were done for the day."

"I came to bring you guys dinner," I said. I tossed the paper sack back to him. He pulled out a sandwich and passed the sack forward to Gid. Gid pulled a sandwich out and passed the sack back to me. He unwrapped his sandwich and took a bite.

"SPAM and kimchee with extra mayonnaise," Gid said. "My favorite. Ellen knows me almost as well as she knows you."

"What a saint," said Paris. He bit into his sandwich, too. "I was starved. She can't be too happy about you out on a stake out."

"She'll get over it," I said. It came out with a lot more confidence than I felt.

Bobby Castle emerged from the lobby in a couple of minutes. He talked to one of the valets, greased him with a bill, and pulled a comb from his pocket to run through his slick hair. The valet whistled and, through a cab's windshield, we saw a newspaper being folded. The hack behind the wheel started the engine then pulled around under the porte cochère. The valet opened the door and was rewarded with another bill from the Prince of Leg-breakers. When

Castle tucked himself and his sharkskin suit into the cab, the valet shut the door and gave the cab a couple of taps on the roof with his white-gloved knuckles, then stepped away.

The cab pulled away from the porte cochère and I followed with my headlamps still off. The cab went mauka up to King Kalakaua Avenue, stopped, then made a right turn. I followed at a distance of about four car lengths. When we had traveled about three blocks on King Kalakaua, I turned on my headlamps.

We continued toward Kapiolani Park and Diamond Head when the cab hung a left turn on Kapahulu Avenue.

"Looks like we're going to Kaimuki," said Paris.

"Yeah," I said. "Looks like it. Let's see if we end up going uphill."

We took Kapahulu Avenue, past the busy lights of the new sign of Leonard's Bakery, all the way to the end, then pushed through a block of 1st Avenue before hanging a right on Waialae Avenue.

"Yep, looks like we're headed toward Maunalani Heights," said Paris. He stated the obvious just to give his mouth something to do after finishing his sandwich. He also wanted to fill the night air with something other than the non-conversation and the rush of the light breeze. I couldn't blame him. I gripped the steering wheel with white knuckles and Gid remained calm and detached, finishing the last of his sandwich then chewing slowly and thoughtfully as he watched the streetlamps above us pass. We continued steadily uphill on Waialae Avenue for a few blocks.

"I'm going to play a hunch," I said. "I think they'll be headed up to Wally's via Wilhelmina Rise. He'll have a few lights on Waialae before getting there. I'm going to take Sierra Drive up the mountain and beat him there."

"Let's go," said Paris. Gid shrugged.

Just past 10th Avenue, I took a hard left turn toward the mountain and floored it up Sierra Drive. We zigzagged back and forth, crisscrossing Maunalani Heights at breakneck speed. I almost hit a couple of trash cans and a parked Buick but luckily remained alert enough to evade them. Paris grinned and swayed with the car; Gid remained stone-faced and grabbed his hat at the turns.

We came upon the Yoshidas' block from the opposite direction that the cab would approach it from. I parked across the street behind a huge black Packard, cut the headlamps and the engine and we waited.

The seconds ticked away like fat, sluggish drops of water slowly letting go of a faucet and dying with a heavy splash at the bottom of a basin.

After a couple of minutes that seemed like a couple of hours, just when I was about to concede aloud that my gamble had not paid off, headlamps approached and came to a ponderous stop in front of Wally's redwood-framed aquarium of a house. The cab idled for an eternity before a rear door opened and Bobby Castle pulled his stocky, sharkskin-covered frame out of the vehicle.

Castle walked around to the driver's window, took a wad of bills out of his pocket held together with a gold clip that flashed under the streetlamp's yellow glow. He peeled a couple of bills off the wad and handed them to the cabbie through the window. After a short exchange of words, Castle stepped away from the cab and watched it pull away from in front of Wally's driveway. The cab first came toward us, then took a wide, sweeping U-turn in the middle of the street, and headed back past us again in the direction it came from, toward Wilhelmina Rise.

Bobby Castle strode up to the front door, illuminated by the white glow of the porch light in a modern, square-shaped fixture with a patina metal frame that reminded me of shoji, paper doors, at a teahouse. I heard the faint chime of the doorbell and kept an intent eye on Castle as he waited with his hands in his trouser pockets while he rocked back and forth on his heels. I thought I even heard him whistle tunelessly until the front door finally opened.

From my angle, I couldn't see the person who had opened the door, but it stayed open for a few seconds before Castle stepped in. He did so leisurely and without force, then the door closed behind him.

Gid, Paris, and I quietly got out of my car and moved on the balls of our feet across the asphalt to Wally's driveway. We drew our revolvers out of our holsters.

"Wally's not here," I whispered. "The garage is empty."

"I'll try to get around to a window on the lanai," said Paris.

"Quietly," I said. "Gid and I will wait just outside the front door. Come back and tell us what you see."

Paris nodded. We started moving slowly and quietly toward the house.

A scream tore the shroud of silence as we approached the front door and a shot rang out.

# 12

Without thinking, Gid and I both rushed the front door, .38s out. The door wasn't locked, so we ran into the entryway with the muzzles of our pistols leading the way.

"Police!" Gid yelled.

I looked into the living room to see Lydia standing in the center of the room, her chest heaving with hyperventilation and her eyes wide and startled, focused on the floor. Her hands were full of a gun. The gun had the tapered, slender barrel of a Luger. Wally's war trophy, taken from a dead German infantry officer.

On the floor in front of Lydia lay a man. His face was buried in the carpet near the coffee table. A large mess of a wet, dark hole graced the back of his head. The red stain under his planted face and his sharkskin suit spread like an oil slick on still water. He looked even smaller and more insignificant in death, a violent, petty life that came to a violent, petty end. Gid knelt down to touch his neck to be sure.

I holstered up my .38 and took slow, careful steps toward Lydia with my palms up in front of me.

"Give me the gun, Lydia," I said. "It's over now." I took a few more steps toward her when she didn't move. She swung the Luger around and pointed it at me. My heart nearly stopped, but I made no attempt to drop or reach for my own weapon. Then she let her arm drop and let the Luger fall to the floor. She ran to me and threw her arms around my neck and started weeping uncontrollably.

"Hey," I said. "It's all right now. Let's sit down, okay?" I directed her to the sofa and sat her down. Face vacant, she allowed me to move her, hardly blinking. Her breathing slowed down, though it was heavier.

Paris had come through the front door and I told him to grab a blanket off the bed in the master bedroom and bring it to me. When he returned, we draped the blanket over Lydia's shoulders. She had begun to shiver. Shock. I'd seen it too many times over my career as a homicide dick. Her body lost so much heat that she might as well have been in a meat locker and not in her living room on Maunalani Heights.

I sat next to Lydia on the sofa as I had earlier that day. I held her little hand, which was ice-cold and clammy. She gripped my hand for what seemed like a very long time. While I sat with Lydia, Gid went to the car to use the radio and Paris ran about the house, clearing every room to be sure Castle didn't have a hidden friend somewhere. When he returned to report all clear, Lydia finally loosened her death grip on my hand.

"Oh my God," was all she could say. She stared straight ahead at nothing. I looked down at Bobby Castle's hemorrhaging corpse. Not far from it was an open switchblade, not as ostentatious as the one we had taken from him at the Royal Hawaiian, but probably more efficient. This one had plain ebony grips and a long, nasty blade.

I gave Lydia's hand a gentle pat before releasing it. "I'm going to call Wally," I said. "Do you have his number?"

She nodded. "It's by the telephone," she said. "He's at the office."

I got up and went to the telephone on one of the kitchen counters and called Wally. I wouldn't elaborate on what happened. I just told him that I was at his house with a couple of other police detectives and that his wife, though shaken, was unhurt, and that he should come home immediately.

"On my way," was all he said. It was one of the many things I appreciated about Wally. He didn't waste any time. He didn't ask for an explanation over the telephone. He trusted me, and not because the tourniquet I put on his bleeding leg had saved his life. Wally always trusted me, though I didn't always deserve to be trusted.

I looked over at his new wife. She had the blanket pulled tight about her and had closed her eyes. She rocked back and forth on the sofa. I walked back into the living room and bent down next to Paris, who had taken a knee to examine Castle's corpse.

"Not so tough," I said.

"Not so tough at all," said Paris.

He sure acted like he was, but in the end, he went down like the frail, imperfect human being we all are. Nobody's as tough as Bobby Castle thought he was. Sure, he had a hard head, but it wasn't hard enough to stop a bullet. She didn't have to aim that high. It looked like he fell where he was shot. His head probably jerked back with the force of the round, then his knees buckled and he fell forward, face down. Lydia probably pulled the trigger from where she stood when we first came into the house. They were less than five feet apart from each other.

The carpet was in bad shape. It would have to go. It's too bad. It had a kind of Martian look to it that matched the rest of the kooky, outer space shit in the living room.

In a few minutes, the place had more cops in it than the squad room at the station. It looked eerily reminiscent of the way it had in the morning, a home turned into a circus full of olive drab and lab coat white. Gid played ringmaster and Paris gave the initial brief to the newly arrived uniforms, mercifully—or unmercifully—leaving me to the task of sitting with Lydia until Wally arrived. I had steered her into the master bedroom, away from the corpse and its examiners, and sat her down on the bed. After a long while, when the angry white flashbulbs started intermittently illuminating the hallway outside the bedroom doorway, Lydia found her voice again. It came like a flood.

"He was going to kill me. Frankie, he was going to kill me," she said. "I tell you, he was going to kill me!"

"I know," I said. "It must've been terrible, but it's over now. I'm sorry you had to go through this."

I took a couple of Lucky Strikes out of the pack in my pocket and offered her one. She took it and I lit us both up with my Zippo.

"He was coming to collect," said Lydia. "I didn't know what to expect, but I didn't know he was Bobby Castle, the man Aunt Meg was running from. When we were inside, he pulled a knife and demanded his money. I said I didn't know anything about any money. He called me a liar. He said Aunt Meg lied to him last night and now I'm lying, too. I told him I wasn't lying—but I suppose I really was because I gave Aunt Meg the money in the first place, but I knew he wouldn't believe me if I told him I didn't know where the money was. I think he could tell I was lying because he came after me with the knife. He said he'd cut it out of me."

She said all of this at the speed of a bullet from the muzzle of a Luger.

"So, you shot him," I said.

"Yes. Yes! He was going to kill me and now I know he killed Aunt Meg! He was furious that she didn't have his money. He said so. He said I deserved to die like her, that we were both liars."

"The gun," I said. "You had it when you let him in?"

"Yes," she said. "and it's a good thing I did. Wally keeps it in his nightstand drawer. When this man called and said he was on his way, I took the gun out and hid it under a shawl. Just in case. I guess

I've been a little on edge since last night." I recalled the shawl on the floor. It had been near her feet when we found her standing in front of the corpse. "He was coming at such a late hour," she said, "and with Wally out of the house . . ."

"Sure," I said. "There's no need to tell it all now. Just relax, Lydia. Or try to."

Lydia took a long drag from her cigarette and was about to start talking again when Wally walked through the bedroom doorway. She shed the blanket from around her shoulders and ran to him. She threw her arms around him and sobbed. I stepped away to give them space but looked over my shoulder at Lydia with her face buried in Wally's chest. Where the hell had she learned to handle a Luger like that? She must've known where the safety was located; did Wally teach her? Why would he, in the short time they'd been together?

Well, however she learned—and she had an interesting past—she was alive thanks to her knowledge of the pistol.

Wally held her and whispered in her ear. I moved past them, patted Wally on the shoulder and told him I'd be back. I went back to the living room.

By the time I got there, a chalk outline had already been drawn around Castle's corpse, at least where the carpet wasn't saturated with congealing blood. All the photos had been taken and the only thing left to do with Castle was put him on the gurney when it arrived.

I thought about Wally and Lydia in their bedroom, clinging to each other in the muted light of their fancy lampshades. I felt sick for them, their quiet, perfect little house in Kaimuki's blue heaven had become hell on a mountain, the first memories of their first marital home filled with a couple of corpses and an army of cops.

I walked back to the bedroom and knocked lightly on the doorframe. Wally craned his neck back at me. It looked like I'd have to throw a blanket on his shoulders, too.

"What happened here, Frankie?" he asked. Lydia sobbed and sniffed audibly.

"I'll let Lydia tell you. I'll give you guys some time together before the statements."

"Statements?" Wally blinked at me.

"Yeah, statements." I said. "I'm sorry, Wally. We'll come back for Lydia when you're ready."

"Okay, Frankie," he said.

Gid, Paris, and I sat down at the dining table and lit up cigarettes. We started writing our own report narratives in longhand on forms one of the flatfoots grabbed from his prowler, grunting at each other now and then, making sure our times were synchronized and the surveillance details consistent. I made side notes in a pad of what Lydia had told me when she started talking.

This took the better part of an hour. When we were all done, we looked over each other's narratives and lit more cigarettes.

"You think she's ready?" asked Gid.

"I'll check," I said. I got up from the table and started to move toward the bedroom. I stopped after a few steps and turned my head back toward the dining table.

"Paris," I said. "Why don't you take Mrs. Yoshida's statement?"

"Sure thing, Sheik."

I walked to the bedroom door and gave it a gentle knock. The door opened after a few seconds. Wally looked at me from the other side of a threshold with a face that looked about ten years older.

"Do you think Lydia's ready?" I asked.

"I think so."

"If she'd feel more comfortable not doing it out there in the living room, I could send Sergeant Lau in here to talk to her."

"Honey?" Wally called over his shoulder.

"It's okay," I heard Lydia say from behind him. "I'll come out."

The three of us moved out to the living room. Gid and Paris stood as Lydia approached the table, and Paris pulled out a chair for her. They took their seats and Paris started with the questions. Wally and I stood at the edge of the kitchen and watched for a little while.

"Hey," I said. "Let's have a smoke out front."

"Yeah, okay."

Wally and I walked out the front door. I pulled my crumpled pack of Lucky Strikes out and offered him one. Wally pulled one out, then I did, then I lit us both up with my chrome Zippo. I had received the lighter a mere couple of years ago, but it felt like it had been with me for my whole adult life. It was something I held longer than Lizzie, longer than Ellen. Gid's gift had gotten me through the hard cases, countless cigarettes and cigars. Cool metal in the palm of my hand. Windproof. If only I were as reliable.

Wally and I stood side by side in his driveway, looking uphill over the gables of the houses across the street at the moon. It threw a cold blue light on us and the coconut palm and the koi pond. We didn't say a damn thing for a long while.

Wally finally broke the silence.

"It's a hell of a thing," he said.

"Yeah," I said. "It is."

"I can't believe it," said Wally. "But then, again, I've been through a lot of bad shit, so I guess I should be used to this kind of stuff."

"Yeah, you've been through a lot of bad shit," I said. I thought of the German grenade that took his leg, Polly Yamanaka who took his heart, and Marie Gouveia who took his future when she got hit by a bus. Now this. Jesus. "But," I said, "you shouldn't be used to it. Nobody should be."

"Well, that's good," he said, "because I'm not."

"Did she tell you what happened?" I asked.

"Yeah, she told me."

"She's brave, Wally. And smart. And it's a damn good thing she's both, because if she wasn't, she wouldn't be alive."

Wally smiled and looked at me for the first time since we stepped outside.

"She is, isn't she?" he said.

"Yeah, she sure is. You're a lucky guy."

"Thanks, Frankie. I guess I am."

"I know you are. I think she's just great. She's held up under all the stress of the last twenty-four hours. I think she'd make a hell of a campaign manager. After everything that's happened, politics is nothing."

Wally allowed himself a smile. I smiled along with him. Then we were straight-faced again, puffing on our cigarettes and looking at the moon.

"Hey, Wally," I said. "Did Lydia tell you much about her?"

"Who?"

"Aunt Meg. Did she ever talk about the things she did?"

"Only about the support she gave her in New York. She seemed like such a classy lady. Why?"

"Did she tell you that Bobby Castle—the man on your living room floor—was a friend of Aunt Meg's?"

"She told me Aunt Meg owed him money. It wasn't easy for her to tell me, Frankie. I think she was really embarrassed about it."

"I can understand that. Did she say why Aunt Meg owed this guy money?"

"Gambling. Can you believe that?"

"She didn't look the type, but the story fits. We know who this Bobby Castle was. He was connected to some pretty bad folks in L.A. He was a strongarm in the collections racket."

"Hmm," said Wally. "I guess you can't choose your family, huh?"

"I guess you really can't."

"It really upsets me that Lydia had to get pulled into all of her aunt's shit. She was really in danger, you know?"

"So were you. By extension. And not a very far extension."

"Yeah, I guess so. But it's all over now. Lydia never told me how much Aunt Meg owed this guy, but it must've been a lot if he came all the way over here for it."

"Probably," I said. I didn't tell Wally that Lydia told me about the ten grand. No sense in bringing it up now that the parties involved were dead and gone. I had promised Lydia that I wouldn't tell him and, at that point, there wasn't any good reason to break that promise.

Bobby Castle had called Lydia to tell her that he was on his way to collect, and Lydia knew she didn't have the money. She knew his visit wouldn't go well for her and could only prepare herself for the worst: she knew where Wally kept the gun. Lydia had shot Castle in self-defense. I had no doubt that it would go that way in Paris's report. That would also be the conclusion at the inquest. Maybe the Yoshidas' nightmare was finally over.

Maybe.

There was the gnawing question: where the hell was the ten grand? Castle had come to menace whoever was in the house because he hadn't gotten it. Aunt Meg never made the handoff because she was smothered in her drunken, post-coital slumber.

There was one person who might know.

Happy Tokuda.

It might play out that Aunt Meg was killed by Bobby Castle, who had come in the night to collect and found no cash. A little bit of a stretch, but plausible. And the world was a better place with one less Bobby Castle. Everyone would be satisfied with that outcome. The things he said to Lydia before attempting to gut her in her own living room would certainly knock that conclusion home at the inquest. Even Lydia believed it, and that would let Happy off the hook once again. Another bullet dodged in his lifetime of dodging bullets. In this case, it might be more accurate to say Bobby Castle took the bullet for him.

Wally and I sucked the last of our cigarettes down to their ends and dropped the butts on the asphalt of his driveway to ground out under our shoes.

As if reading my mind, Wally said, "Didn't I tell you Happy couldn't do such a terrible thing? Even Lydia jumped to that conclusion, too, at first. I'll admit, I had my doubts, too, but after tonight, we know the truth. So, Happy will be okay, won't he, Frankie?"

"Yeah, I think so," I said. I said it in my most convincing "cheerful" voice. The problem was, I didn't have a "cheerful" voice, convincing or not. I couldn't tell poor Wally, after everything he had endured over the past day, that I was far from done with Happy Tokuda.

I took a surreptitious glance at my watch. It was nearly eleven, and there was no end in sight at wrapping up the war zone Wally's house had become. We had at least another two hours, and the meat wagon had only arrived just before ten. Happy Tokuda was probably at some post-cockfight luau, feasting on the losers' carcasses and washing it down with okolehao and Primo.

"Good thing you guys were here," said Wally.

"We had Castle under surveillance. We had eyes on him at the Royal Hawaiian, then followed him up here. Actually, if Lydia hadn't acted on her own, we might have been too late to do anything to help her, even if we were only a few feet away. She sure knows how to take care of herself."

"She takes care of me, too. I never told anyone this, but she bought this house and made a huge donation to my campaign. I found out that she had been down at Schuman Carriage to ask about surprising me with a Cadillac for Christmas."

"Coupe DeVille?"

"No. Eldorado. Like yours."

"She has good taste."

"I know. I don't deserve her."

"No, you don't."

We both laughed for the first time in several hours, but it seemed like several days. Mr. and Mrs. Yoshida had precious little to be amused about. A couple of corpses will knock the joy out of your day. Wally had seen, and made, several corpses in our time in the 442nd, way more than a couple of them, but he hadn't seen them in his guest room or his living room.

Wally was different when it came to remembering all the bloodshed we had seen overseas. He put on a cheerful face and talked about cheerful face things: handing out Hershey's bars to the children in the ruined medieval villages, playing poker using our rations as stakes, dating husky-voiced Italian girls who were about a foot taller than him. It was as if he never remembered the violence, not even the loss of his own leg. That is, except to tell folks about how I saved his life, and what a brave guy I was.

I wasn't.

I was scared shitless. Scared that Wally would bleed out and die in that bunker, halfway around the world from his mom's nishime and Polly Yamanaka. I was scared that if Wally died, it would be my fault for being too slow or too stupid to save him. I was scared that I'd have to visit his folks and tell them what happened if he died; I always got the sense that his mother never liked me, that I was a bully and a bad influence on Wally in her eyes. My bravery didn't save Wally. My fear did.

Wally was the brave one. He could live a normal life after all we'd been through and put a smile on, like some Bing Crosby tune. And he kept putting a smile on after life continued to shit on him after the war.

Not me. I turned to whiskey and I hit back when the world hit me. I was a sarcastic son-of-a-bitch who could quickly fall from wise-assed to nasty in two drinks. I chose police work not because I was brave, but because I was afraid to make my world a nicer place. I had seen hell and chose to stay there because I was already used to it. Homicide was just icing on the rotten cake. I could stay among the worst humanity had to offer, just like I had in the war. I held normal people at arm's length, but I let killers in up close because I really understood them. I detested them, but I understood them. I was incapable of embracing Wally's brighter tomorrow with a straight face.

Once upon a time, Wally and I were the same. We were a couple of kids who liked baseball and cowboy movies and pretty girls. The war changed that. Wally told me that he's a coward for not looking the violent memories in the eye, for pretending that they never happened. He's wrong. It takes courage to move on, a kind of courage I don't have.

For Wally, each new day "quites" the prior day, the Miller's bawdy colorful tale "quiting" the Knight's virtuous yarn, and the Reeve "quiting" the Miller with a story even more over-the-top. For Wally, it was all about embracing the next thing, just as the next thing in *The Canterbury Tales* was always an experience that outdid the prior by design. It was a concept I couldn't get behind. For me, each new day only outdid the prior day in the complications it brought into my life. There wasn't any wonder. There was only bracing yourself for the next shitstorm.

"Of course, you do," I said after a long while.

"Of course, I do what?" Wally asked.

"Deserve her. Of course, you deserve Lydia. She's long overdue."

"Yeah, well, she was worth the wait. And she's worth all this."

Wally looked back at his house. The front double doors opened and a covered lump that used to be a man was wheeled out on a gurney. We watched them load what was left of Bobby Castle into the meat wagon, then we watched the trail of red lights disappear downhill.

"I think they should be just about done," I said.

"Hey, Frankie," said Wally. "Do you think we could have one more cigarette before we go back inside?"

"I don't think we can," I said. "I *know* we can." I pulled the pack out of my pocket and lit us up one more time. This time, we didn't say anything. We just smoked. When we were done, we went inside.

Lydia was sitting at the dining table taking slow sips of scotch while Paris read her statement back to her word for word. All she did was sip and nod. When Paris was finished reading, he had her initial next to all the corrections he made and sign the statement. I looked at my watch. Midnight.

The M.E. had gone with the meat wagon and the forensic technicians in their white lab coats were still cleaning up their mess, putting things back into their big black leather satchels. As I suspected, it looked like we'd be there another hour.

Time dragged on and I only half heard the inane small talk made by the Yoshidas and Paris. Gid rarely engaged in any talk, small or large, while on the job. He usually deflected any attempts to engage him in conversation with polite nods, half-smiles and terse, one-syllable replies. *Yes. No. No, thank you. Yes, please. I'm fine*. It was beyond belief how such an un-loquacious man was responsible for interacting with the press on behalf of the Homicide Detail. Or maybe that was the point. Gid was damn good at it. He could shut down a line of questioning with just a look. Most reporters walked away with little more than the press release.

And Gid would shield Wally that way. "An incident" was how he'd describe it. He'd suppress key details by paying personal visits to editors and news directors, telling them that the investigation was "ongoing" and that releasing any names would only complicate—or worse, compromise—the outcome.

I was less good at avoiding the entanglements of idle chatter. My weak, vacant grunts served only to emphasize the lack of attention on my part. At that point, all I could do was apologize and look away.

This time, Happy was on my mind, and so was the missing ten grand. I could care less if the inquest pinned all this shit on Bobby Castle, and cared even less that he couldn't speak on his own behalf. Nobody really believed he didn't deserve it.

He came to do Lydia harm. She burned him down because she had no choice. If the conclusion was that a low-rent hood like Castle smothered an ex-prostitute over a gambling debt, then so be it. I didn't care and neither would the law-abiding, taxpaying world.

But the truth is a hell of a thing. It is rarely beauty queen–pretty or rich uncle–generous. Most of the time, it is a pain in the ass, and that pain gets more acute the more it is ignored. If you ignored it too long, it could make you bleed.

I knew I needed to find out just what the hell really happened. Not because I wanted to—prolonging this shitty case was the last thing I wanted to do—but because I needed to sleep at night.

As soon as I was able, I needed to make a beeline to my little Palolo Valley sanctuary and the ladies there I had slighted. I needed to patch things up with them and do it quickly because I needed to be out in Waialua first thing in the morning to get Happy.

# 13

It was close to two in the morning when I finally pulled into my Palolo Valley driveway. I was melancholy and disturbed for no reason I could put my finger on and I was tired. Not the tired of the homicide dick who had sat up all night waiting for a suspect to come home, but the tired of my parents—plantation tired—the tired that assumed that after a soak in the furo you'd drop off to sleep and stay asleep until the roosters woke you for another day of the same mind-numbing, backbreaking torture for pennies.

I dragged myself across the threshold into the living room to find Ellen sitting up on the sofa in the dark, nursing Lizzie and singing softly to her. She regarded me as she would a housefly that had slipped in through an ajar screen door, annoyed but too tired to bother to swat the damn thing. Then again, most people would look that way at that hour if they were forced into semi-consciousness to attach a twenty-pound diner to their body.

"Good morning, stranger," she said, then yawned involuntarily.

"Good morning yourself, little mommy."

I walked over to them, kissed Ellen on her tired mouth and Lizzie on her downy little head. She still smelled like a baby. At least the world had mercifully seen fit not to change that.

"What brings you to our humble abode at this hour?" Ellen cracked wearily. When all I did was smirk with my eyes closed in response, she reached out and swatted me with her free hand. My eyes opened a lot more slowly than I thought was possible for an involuntary reaction. I must've been tired as hell.

"Did you get your man?" Ellen asked. A little concern crept into her voice, knowing it wasn't normal for me not to quip back at her.

"No," I said. "Lydia did."

"Lydia did what?"

"Get our man."

"What?"

"We tailed Bobby Castle from the Royal Hawaiian to Wally's place. He rang the doorbell and Lydia let him in. We moved in closer, then we heard the shot."

"What?"

"The shot. The loud, percussive clap of thunder you hear when someone pulls the trigger of a loaded souvenir Luger."

"I know what a shot is," said Ellen. She reached out and swatted me again, this time knowing I had returned to regular form. "I meant, did Lydia actually shoot him?"

"That's what I said."

"How? Why?"

"By pointing the muzzle at his forehead and pulling the trigger, to answer your first question. It's surprisingly easy to do, though I don't recommend it to the faint of heart. And to answer your second question, because he pulled a knife on her and was presumably going to use it on her. It happens."

"Frankie Yoshikawa!"

"You asked."

"That's terrible. Poor Lydia. First her aunt, now this."

"Yes. Now this."

"Lydia had a gun?"

"Yes, but technically, it was Wally's. A Luger. More of a souvenir. He took it off a German officer we captured. But he kept it functional and loaded."

"She's brave," said Ellen. "I don't know if I'd be able to use your gun like that."

"I think you would, if you felt you or Elizabeth were in danger."

"Of course, I would. That's not what I meant. I meant I wouldn't know how to use the thing. I've never touched a gun before. Lydia's amazing. She knew how to shoot."

I hadn't told Ellen any of the things Lydia had told me in confidence about her past. She had a rough history, and maybe rougher than I first suspected, to be that prepared.

Lizzie must have sensed Ellen's tensing up. She detached herself, spit up a little, and cried. Ellen wiped Lizzie's mouth, rubbed her back gently, put her back on, and softly apologized to the baby.

"This is terrible," said Ellen.

"You were right," I said. "I should have listened."

"I was right? How long did it take you to reach this conclusion? I thought you always understood this. I thought that was the reason we got along so well. But what, specifically, was I right about this time?'

Ellen's smile returned in earnest, much to my relief. I felt lousy about having walked out earlier in the evening.

"You were right to say I should have taken Gid up on his offer to ride my desk for a year. I should've left this mess to Paris. He's good. Nobody would have blamed me if I did. I was too close. I should've backed out from this from the start. I can still, and that's exactly what I'm going to do. So, I hope the two of you can get used to having me around nights. You'll be sick of me in a week."

"No," said Ellen.

"No what? No, you won't be sick of me in a week? That's sweet."

"No, you can't quit now," she said.

"What? You were upset about me going back to work on this just a few hours ago."

"That was before Lydia was involved. Well, directly involved. You have to look out for her, Frankie. And for Wally, too."

"But it's just about over," I said. "The inquest looks like it's going to be as open-and-shut as they get."

"Do you really believe that an inquest will end all of this? With Wally running for office, I think an inquest may be just the beginning."

"Gid will take care of any press issues that might arise. It's his job these days and he's pretty good at it. They don't need me."

"Yes, they do. They need assurances."

"Assurances? Nobody is better than Gid at avoiding unwanted attention. I think relying on him to do his job is the best assurance they can ask for."

"I know he is, but that's not what I meant. They need someone they can trust, someone they can rely on, to tie up any loose ends and make sure they stay tied."

"What?" It was my turn to make the shocked one-word inquiry.

"Why did Castle visit Lydia?"

"To collect the ten thousand dollars owed to him by Aunt Meg."

"Which means he didn't have it yet."

"That's my conclusion."

"Don't you think that qualifies as a loose end?"

"What?"

"Don't play dumb, Frankie Yoshikawa. It may fool your

hapless suspects, but it doesn't fool me. Besides, dumb doesn't look good on you."

She had done it again. The reporter I married had reached into my head and pulled out what I was thinking then threw it back in my face to make me acknowledge it.

"When did you figure this out?" I asked.

"I didn't. What's there to figure out? This thug goes over to Wally's to see if he can get his ten thousand dollars, and when Lydia tells him she doesn't have it, he tries to kill her. He doesn't kill her, thank God, but his ten thousand dollars isn't there, either. So, where is it? Loose end. And if what you told me is right, that the money is Lydia's and Wally knows nothing about it, he may not be in the dark for very long. When he finds out, things could get complicated."

"So?"

"You're doing it again."

"What?"

"Playing dumb."

Ellen reached out and swatted me again. Lizzie had gone to sleep, having had her fill and the excess burped out. Ellen let her doze in her arms.

"I'm not playing dumb," I said. "I really meant it when I said, 'So?' Yes, there's the matter of the missing money, but who cares when we've got a tailor-made murderer to hang Aunt Meg's killing on?"

"You're right. You weren't *playing* dumb. You really *are* dumb. If you think that this missing money is not going to come to the surface and muddy things up for Wally and Lydia, then I'd better pray that you didn't pass the stupid gene to Lizzie."

"And you think I can do something about that?"

I was smiling at my clever little bride. She had just given her consent for me to do what I intended to do in the first place and see this thing through to the end. All I had to do was get her to think it was her idea and resist it a little. I felt that I was finally getting better at this.

Until she said: "I knew it."

"What?"

"You're going to find Happy Tokuda."

I sighed. "Guilty," I said. I threw my arms up. "He *is* the leading candidate among people still breathing who might know something about it." I sat down next to Ellen. She leaned her head against my shoulder.

"Poor thing," she said. "You really thought you had tricked me."

I threw my arm over Ellen's shoulders and stroked my sleeping daughter's soft hair with my free hand.

"I'm sorry about my little tantrum earlier," Ellen said. "You're going to find out what happened to the money and make sure everything is going to be fine for Wally and Lydia."

"Slow down," I said. "I'm going to find Happy, yes. But whether or not he still has the money is anyone's guess. And if you think I can help Wally and Lydia avoid any trouble in their lives, you give me too much credit. But I'm not going to attempt to do any of this stuff right now. I need to sleep a little first or I'm likely to end up in an irrigation ditch on the way out to Waialua."

"That's right," said Ellen. "You were on your way out there earlier. It seems like a long time ago."

"Ages. And I'm taking Gid's offer of a desk job after the loose ends are tied up. One year of a good night's sleep and being with the two of you every night. I think I've earned a break, don't you?"

Ellen leaned in closer. "You're not just teasing, are you?"

"No. I've never been more serious about not doing anything."

I could tell even in the gloom that Ellen was all smiles. She kissed me and said, "Go get some rest, Detective."

I stood with some effort and dragged myself toward the bedroom. While my heart felt lighter, my limbs felt like cast iron.

Every hour given to Happy Tokuda was another fifty-mile head start. He had built an insurmountable lead.

It didn't matter.

I'd catch him. I always did. I'd catch him because I never gave up chasing him the way every other cop did.

"Catching this guy is more than just a win or lose game with you," Gid once said to me. "It's an obsession."

"It has to be," I told him, "because he's obsessed with not being caught."

As far as I was concerned, until the Bobby Castle inquest reached what seemed to be its inevitable conclusion, Happy was still a murder suspect. He was still very much on the hook and I was going to bring him in. Again. I didn't much care if he beat the rap yet again—we had Castle to take the fall for it—but I was going to make him cough up answers, if not the money.

"No big deal, First Base," he once told me. "Nobody's keeping score."

"I am," I said to him.

And I did. So far, I've lost every inning to him. But in a game where the Territorial Criminal Code is the rules, I bat last. Everything to this point has just been one long box score.

I stumbled into the shower and let warm water cascade on my head until I could will my arm to move for the soap. I nearly fell asleep standing twice. While I was finished drying off and brushing my teeth, Ellen was already fast asleep in bed. I set the little red alarm clock on my nightstand for six thirty. If I was lucky, I'd get almost four hours of sleep. I lay down next to Ellen and closed my eyes.

I was jolted out of the blackness by the cacophonous clanging of little brass bells. Lizzie started wailing from her crib. My slumber died a violent death. It was going to be a bad day, full of yawns and headaches.

Ellen had actually beaten me to placing two feet on the floor; she actually had Lizzie in her arms before I was completely out of bed. They went out into the living room for Lizzie's breakfast while I got into the shower.

By the time I had dressed and was headed to the kitchen, Ellen had long since put Lizzie back down in the crib and was pouring us coffee.

"Are you just that fast, or am I just that slow?" I asked. I picked up my coffee and started sucking it down before my ass even hit the seat cushion of the dining chair.

"Both," said Ellen.

"How'd you sleep?" I asked.

"You know. My life is just a series of things to do for the baby between short naps. How did you sleep?"

"I didn't," I said. "Or it just felt that way."

"It just felt that way," said Ellen. "You really did sleep. Your snoring woke us before your alarm clock. Breakfast?"

"Only if I can take it on the run. I probably should have left an hour ago as it is."

"I'll put it in a sandwich."

I helped myself to a second cup of coffee while I watched my wife spread mayonnaise on a couple of slices of bread and slide a fried egg on one of them.

"Kimchee?" she asked.

"Why not? It may help me stay awake."

"Go say goodbye to the little girl. Just don't wake her or you'll be sorry." Ellen menaced me with the spatula from across the dining table.

I crept into the bedroom where Lizzie lay in her crib, eyes shut and mouth moving every now and then contentedly. I leaned down to breathe in her scent, then stroked her chubby little arm with a finger. She squirmed a little and I backed out of the room silently on the balls of my feet.

As I gave my sleeping daughter one last backward glance, I was filled with the weight of unwillingness to depart. To a certain extent, I had gone through this every morning since she was born, but that morning I was less eager than ever to leave my house and little family for a day of inevitable frustration. It was in that instant that I felt myself become more of a bureaucrat, changing from hunter to gatherer, subtly but unmistakably. Part of it made me sad, but I guess we all have to grow up sometime.

Not yet, though.

Not that morning. I'd think about it and embrace settling down as soon as I caught Happy.

I returned to the kitchen where Ellen was waiting for me with two brown paper sacks. She had marked each bag with a carpenter's pencil: BREAKFAST and LUNCH. It was a good thing that the two words didn't resemble each other. My wife's handwriting was lousy and barely legible, even when she printed in all capital letters. Maybe she became a journalist because someone would eventually typeset all her words so they could be understood.

"You didn't wake her, did you?" Ellen asked.

"Didn't even stir," I lied. The important thing, I thought, is that she went back to sleep.

"Good," she said. "I'll let you live—for now." She stood on her tiptoes in her house slippers and gave me a kiss.

By the time I stepped outside, the air had begun to warm considerably, though the lawn was still sprinkled with dew that shimmered like tiny diamonds, showing off what was left of its overnight finery before the sun burned it away.

I got into my car and headed toward Waialae Avenue and town. My plan was to check in at the Homicide Detail office then head out to Waialua.

I devoured the kimchee-and-egg sandwich Ellen made me for breakfast before I had even gotten past University Avenue. Having not brought any coffee for the road and needing it badly, I did the next best thing and stuck a cigarette in my face and set it ablaze, though it didn't do anything to make me more energetic by a long shot.

The drive to the station seemed interminable. Something I had done must have incurred the wrath of the Traffic Signal Gods, because every light I caught at every intersection was as red as my eyes.

Things opened up a little after I crossed over Ward Avenue. In a few blocks, I passed by Schuman Carriage and thought about poor Joe Matsukawa and his lost investment. While Happy robbed the unsuspecting blind, he did admittedly have a knack for picking the least sympathetic victims. While they were all gullible, I couldn't help but to harbor a secret contempt for those people, due to their greed and stupidity, while outwardly expressing outrage at their victimization. While it was my job to make sure the Joe Matsukawas of the world received protection of the law from the likes of Happy Tokuda, I somewhat reveled in the fact that they all got what they deserved.

Unlike those folks, I have never been naïve enough to believe that desire for something makes having it more possible. I wanted a great many things—domestic servants, a trust fund, peace and quiet, 21-year-old scotch—but I was never stupid enough to believe that wanting those things badly enough would bring those things to me. In fact, it's been my experience that the stronger your desire for something, the more likely life will conspire to deny it to you. We all want what we don't have. The sooner you learn that some things are never meant to be, the better off you'll be. It's not that all things aren't up to you, it's that *most* things aren't.

Don't get me wrong. It's not that I don't believe that things such as divine providence, romantic serendipity, occasional justice, and good old dumb luck don't exist. To the contrary, I've seen such things happen and such things have happened to me. It's just that when it comes to believing that other people will make good things happen for you, I just don't. Nothing screws up your plans for happiness like other people and the belief that you are somehow entitled to their grace or generosity, which is the worst kind of stupidity.

This is why I will never be victimized by the likes of Happy Tokuda. He's never even tried to put one over me. I will never be Joe Matsukawa, hope in his heart for a big payday when his trusted partner brings the soapbox-sized automobiles from Japan and showers him with cash as a return on his faith.

Parasites like Happy Tokuda rankle me not because I pity their idiot victims, but because I disdain their willingness to ingratiate themselves with the stupid in order to thrive. No amount of money is worth putting up with the insipid banter or their loathsome neediness.

The closest parking I would find to the station was about three blocks away. Walking that distance was just about the most difficult thing I had done in a long time. After about a block, I took my coat off and loosened my tie. After two blocks, my face felt heavy and shiny with oil and perspiration and my eyes itched from the lack of sleep. By the time I reached the station, I was ready to turn around and drive back home and collapse.

Nobody was in the Homicide office except for our secretary, Delilah. She was filling the stale air with the noise of her typewriter keys and the scent of her perfume and chewing gum. Gid and Paris were probably deservingly and wisely sleeping in, and the rest of the Detail dicks were probably working the Nuuanu murder-suicide of the day before or standing around at court waiting to give ten minutes of testimony. At that moment, I came to the realization that the rest of the world was smarter than me.

Delilah stopped typing when I walked in.

"Good morning, Sheik."

"Good morning, Delilah."

Delilah told me that a tip had come in from dispatch about a Japanese man out at the chicken fight. She gave me the details. Disgruntled scam victim. Magic corn.

Happy. He was there and there was a good chance he still was.

After I checked the telephone messages left on my blotter, I made a beeline for the coffee and filled four paper cups.

"What are you doing?" Delilah asked.

"Taking some coffee for the road," I said.

"Four cups?"

"Long drive."

"But nobody ever takes four cups of my coffee."

"Take a photograph. This won't happen again anytime soon."

I put the four cups in a steel letter tray and carried them three blocks back to my Cadillac, miraculously not spilling any. I started the car and headed Ewa, taking Hotel Street out of town. It made me think about Happy and his wartime friendship with the sporting girls.

## 14

Hotel Street. 1942. Wally and I had been bored. We decided to go into Chinatown for rice cakes because the manapua man had temporarily stopped bringing them around our neighborhoods. When asked for an explanation, the manapua man would simply reply, "No more," as if that explained everything from the shortage of nine-layer rice cakes to why there was so much suffering in the world. Looking back, that response really did explain everything.

Wally and I took the long walk through Kakaako and downtown to Chinatown but were first distracted by the long lines on or near Hotel Street. The vast majority of the bodies that made up the blocks-long human snakes stretching down the sidewalks and turning the corners were clad in Navy white or Army khaki, though there might be an occasional splash of color from someone's auntie's or tutu's muumuu. The poor woman thought the line was for cigarettes or liquor or other such increasingly scarce commodity. None of the G.I.s in line bothered to tell the ladies that the line was for a brothel. They were too embarrassed or too amused. Some even played along and told them that they were waiting for Kentucky bourbon or Virginia tobacco, too.

Not so deep down, Wally and I had meant to be sidetracked. The rice cakes were really something to tell our mothers we went looking for. It was a Sunday morning and I had a break. We were a few weeks out of high school, and I had made a half-hearted attempt to enroll at UH but ended up spending six days a week helping out at my parents' automobile repair business right at home in Kakaako, as a sort of penance for my missing college admissions deadlines. I was given a kind of pass from my parents because they half bought my explanation that the war had screwed up everything with my paperwork, which was entirely plausible. At the shop, I wasn't anything as glorified as a mechanic's helper—that was my eldest sister, Violet, who had quit doing it recently due to marriage to one of my folks' mechanics and opening up a radiator shop of their own. To-san tried in vain to get me to replace her, but I had neither the aptitude nor the inclination to do so. So, he hired a couple of helpers, guys whose folks were from the same Hiroshima village he had come from. I became the grunt labor; I did oil changes and moved heavy things around the place.

It was exhausting work, but I suppose it beat doing nothing. Sundays, though, were my days to goof off, and I took full advantage of them. Hotel Street was a place where we could bribe the G.I.s into buying us beer and cigarettes, usually by acting as "placeholders" in the brothel lines for them while they ran other errands and picked up our goods.

The job of placeholder was not without its occupational hazards. A couple of Japanese boys in a line of haole servicemen sometimes drew taunts and challenges from some of the drunken G.I.s, most of whom were from the South. In most cases, though, other G.I.s would come to our defense because they, too, had guys like us who acted as placeholders and were frequently in need of such services. We were always smart enough—and lucky enough—to avoid altercations. Most G.I.s understood that we weren't in line as patrons, so most weren't upset that we might be there to get our own sample of haole women for hire.

Then there were the M.P.s and the Shore Patrol and the cops. When they came around, our first strategy was to hide, and that usually worked out pretty well. Hiding was Wally's forte, being diminutive in stature. I'd usually act as a lookout to warn him—thanks to my size, I didn't hide very easily.

When hiding failed, the second strategy was fast-talking the authorities. Sometimes we'd tell them we were trying to drum up business for Wally's kid brother's shine business—though Clarence had stopped his nickel business when his folks had gotten fed up with his red light district jaunts—or our mothers' "seamstress" businesses, or our fathers' "taxi" services. The ploy seemed to work fairly well only with the haole M.P.s and S.P.s, though. When it came to local cops, there was no fooling them. They knew exactly what we were doing there.

So, when the HPD patrolman came sniffing around the queue, the third strategy had to be employed: run. This strategy meant aborting the operation and the abandonment of the prize. We usually sold this disclaimer up front to the G.I.s we acted as placeholders for, explaining that there was a limited risk that they could lose their place in line if the local cops showed. Most accepted that risk, and, truth be told, I could count all the times we had to exercise that option on one hand.

On that particular day in '42, we were just slumming, looking for our beer and cigarette fix and hoping for a little cheap entertainment of the juvenile variety: fisticuffs between soldiers and sailors, cops and M.P.s disposing of the drunk-and-disorderlies, maybe a glimpse of the hot-off-the-transport haole sporting girls in their bleached hair and padded shoulder Hollywood knockoff dresses.

It was one of our final Sundays of innocence. Wally had been taking classes at UH, like I should have been, and helping to maintain the deck of his father's sampan. In a matter of what was probably just days, his fisherman dad and my automobile repairing dad would be arrested by the Army and the FBI as dangerous Jap spies and taken to Sand Island to await a boat to the mainland and an internment camp. This would lead to our eventual enlistment with the 442nd a few months later.

But that Sunday was before all that. It was a Sunday that belonged to a couple of kids too young and immature to be bothered by the uncertainty that furrowed the brows of our elders. It was a Sunday for beer and cigarettes and cheap thrills. We probably deserved to have a hundred more Sundays like it, but the war forced us to grow up too soon. Once you had seen the red gore of the Germans you and your friends had opened up with your bayonets, booze and cigarettes ceased to be your instruments of pleasure and became your coping mechanisms.

We always walked to Chinatown. Since the war came to Honolulu, bus service was sporadic and those buses you could get were hot and uncomfortable, crammed with bodies. The military had commandeered most transport, so the number of buses for regular folks and the amount of fuel to keep them running were at a fraction of what they were a few months before. The G.I.s even hogged the taxicabs, using them to shuttle their lucky dates across town, or piling as many uniforms in a single vehicle as would fit to split the fare back to base, sometimes stiffing the hack if they thought they could get away with it.

Walking, in the end, was faster. And it was free. Wally would walk over to get me at our pink house on Kawaiahao Street from his house on Elm Street in the Sheridan Tract. For a guy with short legs, he was a fast walker, traversing the eight or so little blocks and the one big block of McKinley High School in somewhat more than ten minutes. We'd cut through the Iolani Palace grounds, where we sometimes raced each other across the open space or under the palace, weaving in and out of the supports like an obstacle course.

As soon as we hit the intersection of Bishop and Hotel, we could already see the long lines of uniforms snaking along the adjacent blocks, stretching out as far as Chinatown.

"Geez, Frankie," said Wally, "it looks busier than usual today. You think they're shipping out to somewhere tomorrow?"

"They're always shipping out to somewhere tomorrow," I said.

"Then what's so special about today?"

"Nothing. It's just that there's more of them. Every week they keep coming. But more leave than come back."

"Well, since you put it that way, I guess it makes sense."

Wally screwed up his face in what could only be confusion.

"What?" I asked.

"What?" Wally asked back.

"You don't look like it makes sense."

"Oh. I guess I understand, but it's just that, well . . ."

"What?"

"If I thought I was shipping off to the war, and thought I might not come back, I think I'd want to spend as much time as I could with my mother and father and brother instead of some strange haole girl for three bucks. Don't you think so, Frankie? I mean, it seems like a strange way to spend your last moments of peace."

I laughed aloud.

"What?" Wally asked.

"*Last moments of peace?* Where do you get that shit from? It sounds like something Reverend Takaki said at church. If it was, I didn't catch it. I was probably asleep."

"No," said Wally. His face was turning red, the way it did after he had a beer. We'd have to wait until he returned to his normal color before we walked home so his father wouldn't know he had been drinking. "No," he repeated. "At least I don't think so." He looked down at his feet, embarrassed.

"Look, Wally," I said. "For one thing, all these haoles already said goodbye to their folks on the mainland. They can't spend any 'last moments of peace' with them any more because they're thousands of miles away. For another, have you ever done it with Polly?"

"What? Done *what* with her?"

"It. Sex. Coupling. The act of sticking your genitals into hers."

"Geez, Frankie! No! Of course not! Polly's not that kind of girl!" The red on his skin got deeper. He was positively florid.

"Okay, sure," I said. "Ever do it with anyone else?"

"No! I'm not . . ."

"Not that kind of girl. You said."

"Shut up!"

"All right, already. Calm down. I'm just giving you a hard time," I said. I laughed a little more while he stood at the corner of Bishop and Hotel, fuming. "Look, Wally. Unless you've done it, you can't understand why you'd want it to be the thing you do with your 'last moments of peace.' Really."

"You'd rather do that than spend time with your mother?"

"It's not even close."

Wally looked a little less perturbed and his color was returning to normal. In a few months, he'd grow up rapidly. The same guy who wondered about this shit would spend his "last moments of peace" in Italy rutting his way through makeshift brothels in bombed out *penziones*. He'd never admit, though, that he'd choose to do it over sitting with his mother in the living room in silence, but that was Wallace Yoshida, the Boy Scout who'd grow up to be a statesman. Mere mortals like me could only marvel at the example he set for the rest of us.

I slapped him on the back. "Come on," I said. "I'll buy you a Green River from the fountain on Alakea on the way home. Let's get entertained, okay?"

"Okay, Frankie."

We headed down Hotel Street toward Chinatown. It really was our intent to get the nine-layer rice cakes. Eventually. The farther Ewa we advanced, the thicker the sidewalks became with drunken, desperate humanity. They all waited their turns with varying degrees of patience. Some were good-natured about it, passing the time by playing a few hands of poker or singing along with a radio in a nearby storefront, though seldom very well. On the other end of the spectrum, there were always a couple of blowhards spoiling for a fight, filled with cheap rum and unwittingly presenting easy targets for the M.P.s tooling around in their jeeps. Most were somewhere in between. Most just waited. And waited.

Wally and I always enjoyed this spectacle. Some of the G.I.s were no older than we were, flush with their first taste of booze and the prospect of their first taste of women. These goofy, freckle-faced farm boys were always fun to watch because they took the excursion so damned seriously, like it was a bar mitzvah or a Masonic Lodge initiation. Their uniforms were the neatest and their faces the most serious.

One line in particular seemed unusually long. It wound around the block makai down Nuuanu Avenue, but seemed to move consistently, every man in it taking a couple of steps every minute or so.

The line terminated at a doorway leading to a narrow staircase that ascended up into a black gloom. The hand-painted sign above the door was lettered in the same style as a sign for a Wild West saloon might have been, the type where there was a live piano player and the "play" had "class." The lettering was probably done by one of the dozens of tattoo artists in the area. The sign read: HOTEL METROPOLITAN.

There was a buxom, plump kanaka woman with a pleasant face and a smile framed by a generous coat of lipstick on a barstool at the foot of the staircase. She wore a bright muumuu and a big red hibiscus in her hair. She wasn't the toll collector—that was probably an older haole woman at the top of the stairs who handled all the money. This woman's job was to assess the next in line and let them pass or turn them away. St. Peter at the less than Pearly Gates of G.I. heaven.

When we saw the unusually long line for the Hotel Metropolitan, we knew we had found our entertainment for the morning.

"Show's right here today," I said.

"Yeah, it sure looks like it," said Wally.

We slowed down our pace as we walked past the queue, careful to move on the curb's edge, just out of arm's reach in case one of the more belligerent G.I.s wanted to start something with us.

We managed to walk halfway down the queue on Nuuanu without anyone so much as noticing us. A few feet before we hit King Street where the line thinned out, a voice from the queue called out to us.

"Kids! Hey, kids!"

The voice belonged to a hirsute G.I. in khaki who looked like he was in his mid-thirties. He had the kind of bushy eyebrows and hairy wrists and knuckles that suggested you'd find a bear rug under his shirt. He had a stack of chevrons running up his sleeve; some kind of ultra-sergeant.

"Hey, kids!" he shouted again at us.

We walked back toward him. He was frantically waving us over with his big, khaki-covered arm.

"Yes, sir?" Wally said.

"Hey, kids. How'd you like to make some silver? I gotta take a leak and I need to make sure I don't lose my place in line. What do you say?"

His accent was funny. East Coast. New Yorker, I'd reflect later, after I had gone to college there. It fit. He was darker and hairier than the other haoles in line with him. Mediterranean. Some kind of Italian or Greek.

"We're kind of busy," I said. "But we'll hold your place for two beers and a pack of Luckies."

The G.I. screwed up his face and hopped a little on one of his meaty legs.

"Come on, Wally," I said. "Let's get going."

"Okay! Okay!" the G.I. blurted. "It's a deal."

He put a big hand on my shoulder and pulled me into his place in line.

"These kids are holding my place," he said to the other khakis in line behind us. "Make sure you don't give them any shit."

"Yes, Sarge," one of them said.

"I'll be right back," he said, now antsy to drain his bladder. A low rumble of curses came from some white sailor suits a few feet behind.

"Shut the hell up, swabbies," said the sergeant as he hurried past them.

Wally and I flashed each other quick grins. It had only been a few minutes downtown and we already managed to secure our bounty for the morning. It looked as if we were surrounded by Sergeant Hairy's platoon so there wasn't much chance anyone would start any shit with us. We kept our chatter with each other to a minimum nonetheless; no point in drawing any unnecessary attention to ourselves. As long as we kept our mouths shut and minded our own business, the G.I.s generally left us alone.

Wally had a couple of sticks of pink baseball card bubble gum; he gave me one and we got to the business of chewing and blowing pink bubbles while moving at a molasses pace up Nuuanu Avenue with the rest of the queue. We had moved about two feet when we heard the voice.

"I guarantee you boys will see the Princess herself. She's a friend of mine. She gave me a limited amount of special tickets to see her. Just give it to the old lady at the top of the stairs, and she'll get you right into the 'Throne Room.'"

We looked up ahead to see Happy Tokuda talking up some soldiers and sailors.

"Aw, get outta here!" said a sailor in a blond crew cut. "What does this ticket look like, anyway?"

Happy produced a roll of light blue tickets from his pocket. They looked like he had swiped them from one of the taxi dance halls along Hotel Street. The sailor's eyes got big and the other uniforms around him started craning their necks and pushing forward to get a look at the tickets.

"You're shitting us," said a soldier. "You don't know the Princess."

"Sure, I do," said Happy. He deliberately fumbled around in his coat pocket until the feigned confusion disappeared from his face, replaced by a wide smile. He pulled his hand out of his pocket with a photograph in it. It looked like a glamorous shot of a haole lady in a mink stole and a message and autograph were scrawled on it.

The G.I.s pushed and shoved each other to get a look at the photograph.

"To Happy, Honolulu's best businessman," one G.I. read aloud.

"She's gorgeous," another said.

Others just wolf-whistled and jostled for a better look. Happy let them suck it up for a moment, then pulled the photograph back and stuck it in his pocket.

"Well," he said to the groaning G.I.s, "see you boys around. I see some guys I know near the end of the line who asked me yesterday about these tickets."

"How much?" asked a G.I.

"I'm going to let those boys at the end of the line have them for a half-dollar each," said Happy. He started walking toward the back of the line. He didn't get two steps when a hand attached to a white sailor's sleeve reached out and tugged him back.

"Not so fast," said the owner of the hand. "I'll give you a dollar for one of those."

"Me, too!" another voice shouted. A sea of hands waved bills and big silver coins in front of Happy. He let them rip tickets off the roll with one of his hands and collected dollars with the other. He did this with annoying speed and dexterity. The flurry didn't last longer than thirty seconds.

"That Happy!" Wally said. He couldn't conceal the admiration in his voice. He didn't even try. "You're right, Frankie! This is some entertainment in this line!"

"Entertainment, my ass," I said. I shook my head in disgust. "That crook just fleeced a bunch of G.I.s with a roll of tickets he probably stole from Dance Land."

"Geez, Frankie. You have to admit he's pretty good at it."

"At fraud? He's not good at it. He's just lucky he's never been up against somebody smart enough to catch him at it." I knew at that moment that I was smart enough to catch him at it and, though I couldn't know it at the time, I'd spend a good chunk of my future career catching him at it.

When Happy had finished lining his pockets with his ill-gotten proceeds, he started walking makai down the line toward King Street and us. He stopped as he passed us and turned around. He was smiling the smile of a dog who just shit on the rug and managed to beat a hasty retreat out to the backyard.

"Eh, First Base! Shortstop! You guys in line to see the Princess, too?"

"Nah, we're just placeholders," said Wally. "Some sergeant had to take a piss, so he asked us to wait in line for him." Wally's face was lit up with goofy admiration for the small-time grifter.

"He knows," I said. "He's just pulling your leg."

"You're always on the ball, First Base," said Happy. "I never could fool you." He smiled amiably and chuckled. Though it was meant to be disarming, it had the opposite effect on me. Happy's attempts to ingratiate himself with me always pissed me off.

"Yeah, you'd better believe you never could fool me," I said. "And you never will. Not like those idiots you just sold stolen dance hall tickets to. They'll be upstairs when they realize you put one over them and you'll be long gone."

"What did that kid just say?" said a voice a few feet ahead of us in line. I had apparently berated Happy at a bigger volume than I thought I had. More heads were now turning back our way. Wally started looking worried and anxious.

"Hey, you got it all wrong, First Base," said Happy. He threw up his hands but never lost the stupid grin. "The Princess and I really are friends, and I help her out with the ticket sales. You see this long line we're in? Well, it's all for the Princess. The other girls up at the Met are great, too, but there's only one Princess, you know. Not everybody can see her. So, she worked out a system where she takes ticket holders. I get fifty percent working the line and selling them."

"You're full of shit," I said. "How the hell did you get to know some big deal haole whore?"

"Sporting girl," said Happy. "We call them 'sporting girls,' First Base. It's not nice to use that other word."

Being chided by Happy Tokuda infuriated me, but I kept my cool. I stuck to my line of questioning. We'd go through the same kind of exchange many, many times in the years to come.

"Sporting girl," I said, correcting myself. "How the hell do you know a big deal haole sporting girl?"

"I picked her up in my friend's hack. You know Teruo Hamasaki? The cab driver who lives in the Yamada Camp near Pohukaina School? When he wants a night off, he lets me drive his cab and take fares. Well, I picked up this pretty haole girl from a party at a house by Kapiolani Park near Diamond Head. I thought she was a screen starlet. She paid me extra to drive her to town and drop her off a couple of blocks from Hotel Street. She lay down in the back so nobody could see her in the cab."

"Why?" asked Wally. "Why didn't she want anyone to see her?"

"Because she's the Princess. Sporting girls aren't supposed to leave Hotel Street. If they do, the cops arrest them. But some like to have dates and go to parties outside of town."

"Oh," said Wally. I remained skeptical.

"So, you expect me to believe that a cab ride turned into a business partnership?' I asked.

"We talked," said Happy. "I guessed that she was a sporting girl. I told her I worked the crowds downtown, too, but not for as much money as her." Happy stopped to chuckle to himself. "Anyway, she told me about how they were having problems at the Met because she got to be really popular. Some G.I.s got into a fight on the stairs and one broke his ankle falling down to Hotel

Street. The M.P.s arrested everybody and shut down the Met for the day. The guys who started the fight were both in line to see her. She said the Met madam was mad at her. I told her I could help. I came up with the ticket idea. She was going to see all those guys, anyway, so why not make some extra money and keep everybody out of trouble?"

Wally beamed at Happy. "Wow!" he said. "That's so smart!"

"Nice try." I said. "You don't know her. Even if you did meet her, you'd never split the sales with her fifty-fifty when you could keep everything yourself."

"Aw, come on, First Base." said Happy. "Business partners trust each other. That's how it works. You'll learn that when you grow up."

I was about to shout at Happy when the sergeant came back with a couple of cold brown bottles and a pack of Lucky Strikes and handed them to me.

"Thanks, kids," he said to us. He then looked at Happy, recognition lighting up his dark, beady eyes. "Is this guy your big brother or something?" he asked.

"No," I said. "He's just a crook we know."

"Frankie!" said Wally. "Be nice! Happy's a friend, sir."

"Yeah, Sarge," Happy said. "These are good boys."

"You got any tickets left today?" the sergeant asked. His voice was full of desperate hope.

"Sorry, Sarge," said Happy. "Sold out."

Happy turned his gaze upward to the fire escape landing at the backside of the Hotel Metropolitan. A platinum blonde stepped out wearing a sapphire blue dress with padded shoulders and a tiny matching hat. I couldn't see her face very well, but she wore the dress and the body inside it with class.

"Happy!" she shouted. "Sell all the tickets?"

"Yep. Got your cut, Princess Judy," he shouted back. He smiled his smarmy smile, dripping with cheap charm.

Princess.

I was too far away to see her face, so I just assumed she was as gorgeous as all those whistling uniforms thought she was. The photo from her department file that Paris had brought to the morgue. I couldn't say of the platinum blonde had the same face, but I was willing to bet she did.

Princess.

Princess *Judy*. Mary Judith Kerrigan?

Also known as Margaret Albert. Aunt Meg, to some.

A reunion in Wally's guest bedroom went south.

# 15

So, there I was. Out in Waialua, knocking on screen doors and showing Happy's photograph. I was tired and badly needed a nap. Or a drink. Neither would have been productive, but either would have evicted the headache that moved in and settled down behind my eyes.

I was having one of the most unproductive mornings I had ever had as a homicide dick. Usually, by this point, someone would break. Somebody would slip up, crack under pressure or just plain tell the truth for the hell of it. Not in Waialua. Not that morning.

I stepped down from the lanai of some obasan whose morning laundry regimen I intruded upon to show her a photograph of the con man. She put on the same act as the rest of the village. The hard squint at the photograph, the face scrunched up into a portrait of deep thought. Then the shake of the head and sometimes the dismissive wave of the hand.

No. No, sir. Never seen him before.

The whole damned world didn't know Happy Tokuda that morning. I couldn't get a break. Everything had conspired against me once I had been pulled off his trail. I began to wonder if there was really any point in my being out there at all.

The inquest the next day on the Bobby Castle matter would conclude that in addition to the attempted murder of Lydia Yoshida, his admission to her that he had done in Margaret Albert a.k.a.

Mary Judith Kerrigan would close a fast-paced, ugly chapter of Lydia and Wally's new life together and they could start to get on with the business of being a brand-new family. God knows they deserved it. They would finally be free of the ghosts of Lydia's family. All they had to worry about was the ghosts of Wally's.

Gid would make sure the press got minimal fodder out of the whole unfortunate situation and that Wally's bid for the Territorial Legislature could forge ahead without having a family scandal to handicap it. A happy ending was finally in sight for the boy I grew up admiring who lost his leg to a German grenade and his heart twice—once to infidelity, once to tragedy. Wally Yoshida had seen enough shit in his short lifetime for two or three lifetimes. It was the kind of shit that makes memoirs that people actually buy and read. If I could help him finally make all the pain go away, I would.

So, what the hell was I doing out in Waialua hunting down Happy Tokuda? Finding him wouldn't take away Wally's pain. In fact, I was pretty sure it could only bring him more. If the inquest concluded that Castle smothered Aunt Meg in an angry fit after not finding his ten grand, I should be perfectly content to let the world believe it.

But it wasn't the way I was made. I needed the ugly, ruinous truth. Ten grand was missing and Castle didn't have it. Only one person really could. Nobody cared. The world had its fall guy and everyone was satisfied, from Gid to Paris to Wally and all his future constituents. I'd be punishing all of them, including Ellen and Lizzie and, most of all, myself. Nobody was going to be ecstatic if I dragged Happy Tokuda in and booked him. I'd ruin Wally's chances for election and his marriage and probably my own, too.

I had to know.

I had to know if Happy took the ten grand. I had to know if he killed his old "business partner," the sporting girl of the Hotel

Metropolitan. I might play catch-and-release, for Wally's sake. But I had to know. And I intended to bring the full weight of the law to bear in order to catch the slippery son-of-a-bitch and reach down his throat and yank the truth out of him. At that moment, Happy was still a murder suspect until the inquest concluded otherwise, and I intended to use that as a weapon for as long as I could.

I stepped off the old lady's lanai and dragged my feet across the coral bits strewn over the red dirt toward my Cadillac. I pulled my handkerchief out of my pocket and wiped the back of my neck, then removed my hat and wiped my forehead.

As I put my hat back on my head, I was struck between the shoulder blades from behind by a small, hard object that bounced off my suit and fell to the ground. It stung momentarily, but not too badly. I looked at the object. A baseball. I bent down and picked it up, instinctively cocking my throwing arm when I stood back up.

I couldn't find a group of kids to throw the ball to. I only saw a girl in pigtails and saddle shoes. She came running up to me. She looked like she was about ten years old. She carried a man-sized piece of hickory from Louisville and wore her embarrassment on her face like a brand-new paintjob.

"I'm sorry, mister!" she said.

"Don't worry about it, kid," I said. "Where'd you hit this from?" I tossed the ball to her. She bare-handed it and stuck it in a pocket of a pair of baggy denim overalls which must have belonged to an older brother.

"Over there, by that old truck," she said. She pointed at an old Ford that was red during FDR's first term. It was a good twenty yards away.

"That's not bad," I said. "Line drive?"

"Yeah," she said. She smiled proudly and I could see that she was missing a front tooth. "It took a hop before it hit you."

"It's a good thing for me it did," I said. "Otherwise, I'd be out cold. You really knocked it."

"Aw, I didn't hit it that hard," said the girl. She flushed modestly and smiled impishly, clearly proud of the distance she put on the ball.

"What's your name, kid?" I asked.

Her face darkened to a look of concern. I smiled at her. I forget to do that a lot, according to Ellen. Smile at people.

"It's okay," I said. "You can tell me. I know your folks told you not to talk to strangers, and I'm about as strange as they come out here in my suit. But I'm a policeman." I took my badge out and showed it to her. Her grin came back.

"I'm Frances," she said.

"That's my name, too."

"Huh?" The girl frowned in confusion.

"I spell mine with an 'i.'"

"Oh. The boys' way. Mine's with an 'e.'"

"The girls' way," I said. She nodded knowingly. I smiled some more. "You're a pretty good hitter, Frances with an 'e.' Are you on a team?"

"No," Frances said. She hung her head. "No girls' teams out here. I heard they got a couple in town. I play with the camp boys here when they let me, when they don't have enough for a game. Once, they played against the boys from the Filipino camp and they needed a ninth, so they let me play right field. I had three runs, but the Filipinos complained after when we won, so they never asked me since then."

"Well, they're all just scared of you. All of them. The Filipino boys and the Japanese boys. If you're better than they are, they don't want you around to remind them how junk they are. That's the way boys are."

Frances smiled so widely that I could see that she was missing more than just one tooth. "Did you play on a team?" she asked.

"I played on five teams. I played for McKinley High, then for the 442nd against some haole units during the war, then for Columbia University. After I came home, I played for Kakaako in the Japanese League, and I even had a tryout with Asahi and got picked up for their bench."

"Wow! You played for Asahi!" Frances looked at me like I was Mickey Mantle. Then the stars in her eyes faded and she wrinkled her face. "Why'd you quit?" she asked.

"I was a patrolman during my season with Asahi. I got promoted to detective and after that, there wasn't any time. I wanted to try out again, but I just got busier and busier. Now, it's too late. I got married and had a kid."

"Oh," she said. "That sounds so sad."

I laughed. "It is, in a way. But, in a way, it's not. When you grow up, only guys in professional leagues can still play ball. But you have a long time yet, so keep swinging for the fence, okay?"

"Okay," she said.

I opened the door of my Cadillac and was about to slide in behind the wheel when the thought of the girl's mention of the Filipino camp slapped me in the face with an idea. What the hell. It was worth a shot.

"Hey, Frances with an 'e,' can you do me a quick favor?"

"Okay."

"I'm going to show you a picture of a man. Can you tell me if you saw him?"

"Okay."

I took Happy's photograph out of my pocket and showed it to her. Paydirt. Her eyes grew wide immediately.

"That's Happy," she said.

"You know him?"

"Everybody does. He comes by and sells stuff for cheap."

"Have you seen him lately?"

"He stayed at the Nakayamas' house last night. They live across the road from us. I think he slept on their sofa," she said. Then she narrowed her eyes. "Did Happy do something bad?"

"He's an old friend," I said. "He's supposed to give me something, that's all." Answers, I thought. And if I had to wring them out of him, I would.

"Well, he's not here anymore. My dad gave him a ride into town. Mrs. Nakayama asked if he was going into town. Dad said he needed to drop Mom off before going to work anyway. She had to do some shopping at Sears and Roebuck."

"Happy was going to Sears and Roebuck, too?"

"No. I heard my dad tell him the airport was on the way, so no problem."

"Did Happy say where he was going?"

"No, but he said he needed to visit relatives, or something like that."

I thought about that, but not for too long. I could think about it on the drive back to town. The drive to the airport.

"Let me see your bat," I said.

She handed me the bat. I took a few steps away from her and my car and gave it a couple of swings. Frances gasped and clapped. I handed the bat back to her.

"It's hickory," I said. "I have one just like it from college. It's too heavy for you. If you get yourself a proper bat, you could really get some distance on the ball."

"I know," she said. "It's my brother Tommy's bat. I don't have one."

"What's your last name?"

"Yoshioka."

"Frances Yoshioka. That's almost my name, too. I'm Francis Yoshikawa." I took out my badge again and showed her the credentials. She smiled again, showing me the gap in her teeth. I said, "Listen, Miss Yoshioka, get yourself a Hillerich & Bradsby Louisville Slugger in ash, not hickory. It's lighter." I took a five-dollar bill from my pocket and pressed it into her small hand.

"I can't take this," she said. She shook her head. "It's too much."

"Sure, you can," I said. "You just helped the Honolulu Police Department find a missing person. Ever heard of a reward?"

"Yeah."

"This is a kid-sized reward. Thanks for helping me out. Keep swinging. See you around, Frances with an 'e.'"

I got into my car and drove away from the aspiring slugger and Waialua. No five-dollar snitch bribe ever bought me so much as the "reward" I just gave to little Miss Frances Yoshioka. If Happy got on a plane that morning, I still had a chance of finding out where to. I was probably three hours or so behind him, and I needed to be ready to fly myself. I was chasing a slippery fish who swallowed ten thousand dollars, and if I had to gut it to get the money back for Lydia, I would.

As I drove through the pineapple fields between the North Shore and Wahiawa Town, I pulled a pint of Kentucky rye I kept in the glove box for emergencies. My headache was starting to reach throbbing, blinding levels of pain, so I felt that tapping the bottle was appropriate.

The first sip burned going down, but the second was nice and damn near cool. I could taste the spice and the dense wood and subtle sweetness on that sip, and it seemed to me that my head shrunk back down to normal size.

Happy had mentioned over the years that he had grown up on a Big Island sugar plantation, but moved in with relatives in a Kakaako camp when his mother passed away while he was a teenager. He attended McKinley about ten years before we did. My eldest sister, Violet, was a year or two behind him. Happy never talked about relatives anywhere else. Big Island and Kakaako were the only two places he referenced in my presence when it came to family. Obviously, like all of us, Happy had relatives in Japan. Hopefully, like all of us, he had never met them nor had any real clue as to who the hell they really were. I hated to think of myself on a Pan American Stratocruiser to Tokyo.

Then again, Happy could have, and likely did, lie to Frances' father about going to see relatives. The only thing I could be certain of was that he was leaving the island. In my cat and mouse history with Happy, he never left the island when trying to elude me. Truth be told, he never had to. His wits and connections kept him elusive to all but me, and when I finally brought his ass in for booking, he always managed to get released.

This time was different. This time he felt the need to get off the island. But then again, ten grand was a lot more than a couple hundred bucks and murder was a far cry from misdemeanor theft. Happy hadn't skipped town before because the consequences of his bad behavior had never been bad enough to warrant taking off.

What the hell have you done, Happy?

Everyone who knew him was willing to forgive him. His crimes were entertaining antics to his familiar observers. Even his so-called victims kissed and made up with him because he fawned and offered to make amends without really making amends. Even folks who met him for the first time, like my own wife, took an instant liking to the handsome grifter.

Not me. I neither forgave nor forgot anything Happy Tokuda ever did. I didn't find his lawbreaking endearing and was probably the only person on the whole damn island who was totally intractable to his will and his wiles. I guess I never liked guys like Happy, who parasitically preyed on those who were at a mental disadvantage, those whose desire and gullibility blinded them. Like Happy, I could pick them out of a crowd, but the difference was where he saw opportunity, I saw annoyance. Happy loved stupid people but fleeced them; I detested them but protected them.

I glanced at the pint bottle of rye in my right hand. It was half gone. I shoved the cork back in the neck and returned it to the glove box. My headache had disappeared. I ate the lunch sandwich Ellen had made for me. I had a cigarette for dessert. The drive a few miles past Wahiawa suddenly went downhill and I could see the blue of Pearl Harbor and the vast Pacific beyond and I thought about Happy Tokuda taking his leap over the water to his new hiding place. I hoped that it wasn't thousands of miles overseas, where his dark, rugged face was just one smiling puss in ten million.

I hit Kamehameha Highway and took it through Aiea. And in a few minutes, the control tower of the newly-dubbed Honolulu International Airport came into sight. In the previous year, the runway was completed and proclaimed to be the longest in the world by people who make it their business to know such things. Not just in the United States or the Pacific, but in the world. A good number of folks here were very proud of the fact, and you could hear them profess that pride in every soda fountain, bar, market, and okazuya from the airport terminal on Lagoon Drive to the Waialae Piggly Wiggly. Hooray for us. The world's longest runway. We could lay down more asphalt than anyone else in the civilized world, but we couldn't stop one person on the island from killing another. Wally campaigned on a platform of safe neighborhoods, and he lived in one of the safest on Oahu, until his house produced two corpses. Maybe he'd be better off selling projects like the World's Longest Runway. We were pouring concrete and asphalt like it was going out of style, covering up every inch of green and bad behavior.

I pulled up in front of the lei stands on Lagoon Drive and parked in front of one of them. The stand, apparently, belonged to someone named Lovey. I expected Lovey to be the large woman in a circus tent of a muumuu with a big-brimmed lauhala hat perched on her voluminous black hair. She was seated behind a small counter with a cash register, stringing plumeria with a long needle. She wasn't Lovey. Lovey was in the back, sorting orchids. I walked in the back to find a tall, slender man in horn-rimmed glasses and a tapa print aloha shirt. He was balding and looked about ten years older than he really was.

"Lovey?" I asked.

"That's me. What can I do for you?"

"I'm a police detective," I said. I showed him my badge. Lovey nodded. "That's my red Cadillac out there in front of your stand," I said. "I need to leave it there for a little while, hopefully not too long. Maybe just a few minutes."

"Sure," he said. "Take your time."

I reached into my pocket and pulled out a couple of bills. I handed them to Lovey.

"When I get back, can you have a lei ready for me to take home?"

"Sure. What kind would you like?"

"Something pretty that smells good. You choose—you're the expert."

"Sure thing, sir."

"Thanks," I said. I started to walk out the backdoor of Lovey's workshop when I stopped in the doorway and turned.

"If you don't mind my asking," I said, "How'd you get a name like Lovey?"

"From my haole grandfather. He was the original James Lovey. I'm James the Third."

"Sounds regal," I said. "I'll be back."

"Take your time."

I walked toward the terminal and stopped at the newsstand to buy a pack of Lucky Strikes and a couple of Hershey's bars. I unwrapped the candy while I walked the terminal and inhaled the chocolate. I started at the check-in counters for the airlines on the farthest end and planned to work my way down the row until someone recognized Happy's photograph.

The first counter belonged to Trans-Pacific Airlines. The girls behind the counter wore big, fat carnation leis over their military-style uniforms with fashionably cut skirts and heels. That made some of them almost as tall as me.

After identifying myself by displaying my badge, I showed the ladies of TPA Happy Tokuda's photograph, one by one. The first two looked very carefully at the photograph, then decided they hadn't seen him that morning, though they helped a few customers who "kind of" looked like him. I made them laugh by telling them that Happy looked like just about every Japanese pool hall rat, but with worse clothes.

The third girl, whose name was Alma or Alva or something like it—I couldn't make out the four-letter name on the too-shiny brass nameplate—examined the photograph for a very long time.

"I think this man checked in this morning. I'm not totally sure, but it looks like him."

"Where was he going?"

"Hold on," she said. She turned around and opened the top

drawer of a file cabinet. She pulled out a manila folder and brought it back to the counter and opened it.

"I think this is him," she said, and pulled out a carbon copy of a receipt for a one-way ticket."

"What was his name?" I asked.

"F.B. Yoshikawa."

Shit. First Base Yoshikawa. The son-of-a-bitch was taunting me.

"Where was he going?" I asked.

"Lihue," she said.

"I'd like a round trip for your last flight this evening," I said. I looked over at Lovey's Lei Stand and thought about the lei I'd be taking home.

"Make that two round trips," I said.

# 16

"It's beautiful and it smells wonderful," Ellen said. She examined the pikake lei in her hands. "Where did you get it?"

"Airport," I said. "I'll put it on you when we leave for there."

"Leave for where?"

"The airport. We're going to Kauai."

Ellen laughed aloud. "Oh, Frankie. This lei isn't going to last *that* long. Not even in the ice-box."

"Sure, it will, if you pack quickly enough. The baby's napping, so you have a little time."

"What?"

"Pack quickly. I'll listen for the baby."

"What are you saying?"

"We're going to Kauai. Let's try to leave in an hour. I don't want to catch any traffic on the way out."

Ellen sat down on the sofa. She laid the lei absently on her lap and looked up at me.

"Are you kidding?" she asked. "You want to fly to Kauai *today?*"

"Yes," I said. "I mean no. No, I'm not kidding, and yes, I want to fly to Kauai today."

"Oh," she said. She toyed with the lei in her lap absently, then the light came up in her eyes. "Wait! Are you crazy? Lizzie's still napping. These things take planning, Frankie Yoshikawa. You can't just tell me we're leaving for the airport in an hour."

"Fine, if you'd rather not go, there's no need to rush. I'll just have to go by myself."

"Oh, no. This will be our first trip as a family. You are not getting out of this. Listen for the baby. I'm going to pack."

Ellen shot up off the sofa. She handed me the lei.

"Put this on a damp towel and put it in the ice-box for me. Then get the suitcase off the closet shelf. Then look in on your daughter."

I allowed myself a smile, but not until Ellen had disappeared into the bedroom. If she had known I was amused, she would have beaten me with one of the throw pillows on the sofa. I did as she instructed with the lei. With Ellen, there were always instructions. She once told me there had to be so that mere mortals like myself didn't have any room for error when it came to carrying out her wishes. At least she didn't make me repeat them back to her. She told me that I shouldn't complain because I chose her precisely for that reason. She theorized that I needed order in my life and that I wisely selected the best there was for that purpose. If only she knew it was because I liked the way she looked in a cashmere sweater.

When I had placed the wrapped lei in the ice-box, I made my way to the bedroom to take the suitcase down for Ellen so she wouldn't have to balance precariously on a stool to fetch it. When I placed the suitcase on the bed, I saw that Ellen had picked out a few shirts for me. She caught me looking at the madras plaid she had laid out on the bed.

"What?" she asked. She crossed her arms in front of her and looked up at me from under her lashes.

"You picked out my clothes for me," I said.

"I think you look good in red. And blue. But not yellow."

"I won't be needing those."

"Why not?"

"It's kind of a working trip for me."

"Oh?"

"Happy Tokuda flew out for Lihue this morning."

"Oh."

"Look, darling. I'm sorry. I have to go to Kauai and get Happy and talk to him, with or without you. But I thought it would be so much nicer with you."

Ellen's expression softened. I knew she had been ready to pounce. I sold the explanation because it happened to be true. I had learned a while ago that there was no point in trying to misdirect her. She never fell for it.

"Okay," she said. "That's sweet. You're finally getting it, Frankie Yoshikawa. We have a family now and families stay together." She gave me a kiss and headed to the closet to pull out a couple of my suits.

"Should I put these away?" I asked. I held up the plaid shirts.

"No," said Ellen. "You'll need something to wear on the boat ride."

"What boat ride?"

"The boat ride up the Wailua River to the Fern Grotto."

"What fern grotto is this?"

"The one up the Wailua River. The boat leaves right from the Coco Palms. You *did* book at the Coco Palms, didn't you?"

"Actually, I hadn't booked anywhere yet. I was thinking we'd stay at the Kauai Inn. It's close to the airport. I heard that the Coco Palm Lodge is a dump near the sugar plantation train tracks."

"Where have you been, Frankie Yoshikawa? Don't you remember seeing that Rita Hayworth picture before Lizzie was born? It was filmed at the Coco Palms last year. They have a new manager who really cleaned the place up. It's much nicer than the Kauai Inn now. They have bungalows near the lagoon on the property. And Lizzie wants to ride the boat."

Bungalows. Near the lagoon. Shacks with fake palm frond thatching near a couple of old fishponds that probably bred more mosquitos than fish.

"How romantic," I said. I rolled my eyes after Ellen turned to put my shirts in the suitcase.

"Yes," she said. She unpacked everything to reorganize the suitcase for a third time. "You're learning, Frankie Yoshikawa. Now call the Coco Palms and check on your daughter. I still have to pack her things, too."

I called the Coco Palms and booked a two-night stay. Then I walked into the nursery we had set up next to our bedroom and looked in on my baby girl.

She was sleeping, her downy black hair standing partially up on the top of her little pink head and moving gently with the faint breeze coming in through the window. I couldn't resist. I reached down into the crib and gently stroked the hair on her warm head. Lizzie squirmed and her face wrinkled. Then she flopped more aggressively and wailed.

"Shit," I said. I picked her up out of the crib and rubbed her back gently.

"Is she up?" Ellen asked from the bedroom.

"Yeah," I said.

Ellen walked into the nursery to find me holding the baby and trying to quiet her to no avail.

"Did you wake her?" Ellen asked.

"No," I lied.

"Right," said Ellen. "Why don't you go out and put the top up on the car while I feed her?"

"There isn't a cloud in the sky."

"Frankie!"

"Okay."

I took one last, lingering sniff of Lizzie's hair then handed her to Ellen. I walked out of the nursery, then out to the driveway. When I started to put the top up on the Cadillac, the weight of my fatigue came down on me like a hammer. I managed to do it, but the short walk back into the house took some effort. I found a half pot of cold coffee in the kitchen that Ellen had left, a rare instance of neglect on her part. After a quick glance over my shoulder to make sure Ellen was still in the bedroom feeding Lizzie, I brought the pot to my lips and drained it in a desperate guzzle. I felt like my eyes could stay open for a couple more hours.

After Ellen finished feeding Lizzie, she rearranged the suitcase once more and we were off to the airport. I knew better than to help Ellen with packing; I'd be in the way at best and I'd ruin her "system" at worst. This didn't bother me. I was content to let my wife control my household and run my life. It spared me from having to put any thought into it.

We didn't talk on the way to the airport. Ellen sat in the back with the baby; the lei sat in the front seat and filled the Eldorado with its perfume.

I parked as close to the terminal as I could. When we got out of the car, I took Lizzie from Ellen and put the lei around Ellen's neck. I held the baby in my left arm and carried the suitcase in my right hand. We got to the gate with just under two hours prior to departure.

I drifted out of consciousness sitting on a chair in the terminal with Lizzie dozing contentedly on my chest. I fell into a deep, black sleep with the scent of my daughter's infant hair filling my head. It gave me thoughts or dreams—I couldn't tell which—of sitting on the sofa in my Palolo living room with nothing to do. It was glorious. I seemed to be in that place for only a few heartbeats when I was jarred back into the world of harsh sunlight and droning propellers and the reek of aircraft fuel.

"Frankie. Wake up. Our flight boards in five minutes."

Ellen's face came into focus. First, I saw only the glasses, the lipstick, and the white pikake lei. Then I felt the baby squirm in response to my sudden movement. We had both come out of our naps at the same time. I stood carefully with Lizzie still in my arms and followed Ellen to the edge of the shade of the terminal to await boarding. The march across the asphalt to the aircraft was long and unpleasant in the harsh heat and light of the afternoon sun. It was already close to five o'clock, but it was hot enough to be noon.

If the view of Oahu falling away under our ascent was breathtaking, I didn't know it. I had succumbed to a dreamless slumber as soon as we were seated. When Ellen nudged me awake, we were on the ground in Lihue.

As soon as we exited the aircraft to descend the stairs to the pavement, I was slapped in the face by the warm, moist hand of the climate. The air was thick and damp and sultry. Gray hung above the green inland, while the sky remained a bleached blue over the water.

Once I collected our suitcase in the terminal, we got a cab to the former Coco Palm Lodge, now known simply as the Coco Palms. The cab ride was surprisingly short, and not just because of the negligible distance: there was no traffic. The lack of vehicles on the road made me think of the drives To-san used to take me on out to the Leeward coast of Oahu to forage for kiawe logs for the furo. I felt uneasy. Most people love the bucolic atmosphere of a place like Kauai. Not me. I was more at home among the noise and the stink of the city, in the presence of the humanity I detested. If someone shot me in the head and took my wallet on Bethel Street, at least twenty people would see it happen, even if they didn't care. Not in a place like Kauai.

It might be months before they discovered my decomposing corpse on the side of the road. Ellen, in contrast, loved the "serenity" and chattered to Lizzie about how beautiful and empty everything looked. Beautiful and empty is how I once described my dates and I didn't like spending any more time with them than I had to.

When we pulled onto the Coco Palms property, I had to admit it did look like something out of a motion picture and probably because it had been. The Rita Hayworth picture we had seen a few months before was shot on the property, *Miss Sadie Thompson*. It was based on a W. Somerset Maugham story about a Honolulu prostitute who goes to Samoa to start a new life. A sporting girl. The irony wasn't lost on me that I was there on the same property where Rita Hayworth portrayed a Honolulu sporting girl looking to start over while I was looking for answers about the life of a Honolulu sporting girl that ended abruptly. There was no starting over for these women except in the pictures. The end came for them inevitably, whether it was at the hands of a violent pimp in a cheap hotel room or in an alley in their own piss when their livers gave out.

Everyone who worked at the Coco Palms was smiley, from the haole manager in her fat carnation lei to the Hawaiian bellboys in their pomaded hair and crisp, white shirts. We were mobbed by a host of these smiley characters and were shown to an old army surplus barracks given a fresh coat of paint and a new set of blinds in a spruce-up attempt. It was like strapping a saddle to a stray mutt and calling it a racehorse. But it was clean and more spacious on the inside than it looked on the outside, and Ellen gushed like it was the Waldorf-Astoria Presidential Suite.

Inside, the cottage had whitewashed walls, new-ish furniture, brand-new sheet covers, and modern plumbing. All the trappings of home, except for the stacks of letters from insurance companies trying to swindle you out of a regular premium in exchange for "extra" life coverage and the *Star-Bulletin* from three days ago. Ellen was positively giddy. I eyed the bed and its floral print cover longingly, but I knew there was work to do.

Ellen took Lizzie to the bed to change her diaper. I went into the bathroom to splash cold water on my face, comb my hair, and re-tie my necktie.

"I'm going," I said.

"What about dinner?" asked Ellen.

"I'll try to be back by seven," I said. "Eat without me."

"Where are you going?"

"Back to the airport. I need to hire a car, then ask around with Happy's photograph. I'm going to try to find out where he's flopped for the night."

Ellen sighed in resignation. "I guess it's dinner for one," she said. "Try to have a better dinner than a candy bar."

I gave her a kiss and kissed the freshly-changed Lizzie on her forehead. Then I left Cottage Number 10 for the front desk to get a cab back to the airport.

"Leaving so soon?" asked the grinning desk clerk. "You only just checked in, sir."

"I'm not flying out," I said. "I'm going to hire a car and get to work."

"What kind of work do you do, sir?"

"I'm a janitor of sorts for the City and County of Honolulu. I clean up messes."

"There's a mess here on Kauai?"

"A big one."

The clerk called me a cab. It arrived in ten minutes. I felt like I almost could have walked to the airport in less time. It was the same hack who picked us up at the airport.

"Hey, didn't I just drop you off?"

"Yeah, but I need to go back to hire a car and do a couple of things. Had to get the wife and kid settled first."

The hack was an older Japanese man in a crew cut and thick glasses. Though he wore a tie, he looked like a guy whose attire of choice was an undershirt and a Primo.

"You need a car?" he asked. "Why? I could take you anywhere on the island you need to go."

"That would be nice, but I might have to go places all night. I couldn't ask you to do that."

"All night? While your wife and baby sleep at the Coco Palm?" He said it singular—*Palm* not *Palms*—like its former name. Old habits die hard among locals. "You must be working then," he said. "What kind of work you do?"

"You're pretty sharp," I said. I pulled out my badge and showed it to him. "Police. From Honolulu. My name's Yoshikawa. Frankie. What's yours?"

"Fujita. Masato. But everybody calls me Fuji."

"Hey, listen, Fuji. Can you take a look at a picture for me and tell me if you've seen this guy? He would've flown in from Honolulu this morning." I took Happy's photograph out of my pocket and handed it to him. He glanced at it for half a second and handed it back to me.

"He was my first fare this morning," said Fuji.

"Where'd you take him?"

"I can take you there now, if you like."

"Okay, Fuji. How about I hire you as my personal driver for the next twenty-four hours?" I pulled a twenty out of my pocket and handed it to him. "Would that cover it?"

"Sure," he said. He licked his lips while he eyed the bill for a couple of seconds before sticking it in his pocket. "I told you that you don't need to hire a car."

"Didn't I just do that?"

"You hired a driver. That's better."

"You're right," I said. "That is better."

"Yeah. Better. Because you don't know how to get around here."

"I can read a map."

Fuji laughed aloud. Even in the fading sunlight, I could see that his teeth were stained yellow by tobacco.

"A map," he said. He laughed some more, derisively this time. "The map only shows you the main roads. I can get you around where the map doesn't show. Like the places where your guy went."

"There was more than one place?"

"You're not the first one today to hire yourself a driver."

I felt like I was always a step behind Happy Tokuda. Beaten to the punch, even with the same hired hack.

We proceeded back toward Lihue and everything around us was green on our way into town and out of town. Sometimes the blue of the ocean was visible, sometimes not. Fuji wasn't much of a conversationalist. When I was in college, New York cabbies yakked with their fares as if inane conversation were a vital part of the service they provided. Japanese hacks like Fuji knew their clientele. Most Japanese customers just wanted peace and quiet. Talking to a stranger, even at the most superficial level, was taxing and stressful, so they did their best to be invisible. I wasn't like most of his Japanese fares, though. I got a paycheck for getting answers.

"Where are we going?" I asked.

"Hanapepe."

"What was he doing in Hanapepe?"

"Paying his respects."

Enigmatic, but I didn't press him for an explanation. I felt that when we got there, an explanation would reveal itself.

A half hour or so after departing Lihue, we pulled up on a vast lawn just off the highway. Not too far off in the distance, I could see buildings resembling some Old West town in a John Wayne picture. Set back on the lawn was what looked like a brand-new church, sleek and modern with a generous gable supported by four square columns on the verandah.

"A church?" I asked

"A church," said Fuji. He pulled up to the front of the edifice. "Not a Jesus church. A Buddha church."

I looked above the doorway and saw a gold stylized wisteria crest where a cross would have been.

"A Hongwanji," I said.

"It's new," said Fuji. "They just had a dedication in May."

"It's nice," I said. "How long did our man stay?"

"Not too long. He told me to wait, that he'd be just five minutes. It was more like ten, but it was okay. He hired me for the day."

"Give me ten minutes, then."

"You're the boss."

I got out of the cab and walked into the temple. The setup was very much like a Christian church, with uniform rows of wooden pews flanking either side of a center aisle. Up front, where the altar would be in a Christian church, was the magnificent display of gold lacquer surrounding its standing centerpiece of Amida Buddha, the ornate gold housing accented with silk brocade and cords. Everything was brand new. The smell of senko rose up to greet me. It was a scent that always made me think about funerals and death. I never took a liking to it.

The priest was up front dusting one of the hanging gilt lanterns with a rag. He looked as modern and new as the temple, sporting a white Arrow shirt and businesslike blue silk necktie under his black robes, horn-rimmed glasses, and a pomade-set haircut. He looked more like an accountant than a priest. He stopped dusting when he noticed me, put the rag down on the altar, and approached me.

"Good afternoon," he said. His English was accented but had an elegant clip. "How may I help you?"

"Good afternoon," I said. I bowed and removed my badge to show him. "I am sorry to interrupt you, but I've flown in from Honolulu and would like to ask a few questions. My name is Yoshikawa. I'm a police detective."

"Of course. You are not the first visitor from Honolulu today, Detective."

"No, I didn't think so. I'm here to ask about your other visitor." I took out Happy's photo and showed it to him.

"Yes, this is the other gentleman from Honolulu," said the priest.

"Why was he here?"

"He wanted to offer prayers for a loved one and to make a donation."

"A donation?"

"Yes, a rather generous donation."

"May I ask how generous?"

"A hundred dollars."

I raised my eyebrows. I didn't know that Happy was a philanthropist, which was as preposterous to me as him being religious.

"Did he say who the prayers were for?"

"A loved one, no name was mentioned."

"Did he have a name?"

"He did not give me one."

I shrugged. No time to ruminate and linger. I thanked

the priest and asked him to contact me at the Coco Palms if the generous donor were to turn up again. I walked out and back to the cab.

"Ten minutes on the nose," I said.

"It's okay," said Fuji. "You hired me."

I got back in the car and Fuji pulled away from the Hongwanji, back onto the highway in the direction we came from.

"Where to now?" I asked.

"Back to Lihue."

Then he was quiet again.

Before we hit Lihue town, we turned off the main road down a rough dirt road surrounded by tall stalks of sugarcane. We drove for some time through the cane field until Fuji hung a turn onto a gravel-covered road which took us past a cluster of kukui trees to a handful of buildings sprawled out in a patch of open space in the surrounding cultivated and uncultivated vegetation. The sun was beginning to sink in earnest and Fuji turned on his headlamps.

"A sugar plantation?" I asked. Having been born and raised for the first few years of my life on a sugar plantation, I immediately recognized the set up.

"Yeah," said Fuji. "He said he lived on Kauai a few years ago, with his wife. She died, but he wanted to come back and visit a few folks they knew here on the plantation."

His wife? Happy Tokuda was never married as far as I knew, but who could say? It may have been one of his scams where he bilked some homely girl's folks out of a modest dowry. Was this who he offered prayers for in Hanapepe? Or maybe he was never married and just fed a line to Fuji.

"Hey, Fuji," I said. The last thought was still fresh in my mind about Happy feeding a line to the hack. "This guy didn't try to sell you anything, did he?"

"Nah, he only told me I might make more money if I got rid of this big Ford and drove a new little Japan car. He said he was going to start selling them soon. He told me they use less gasoline. He said I could be part of his company, like a . . ."

"Investor?"

"Yeah, investor. He said two grand is all it would take and I could make ten grand in the first year."

"I hope you didn't give him two grand."

"Are you kidding? I don't think I ever even saw that much money in my whole life. I told him no thanks."

"You're smart, Fuji."

"Not smart. Just broke."

He laughed again, though this time the light outside the car wasn't enough for me to see the stain on his teeth. He continued down the gravel road, past the big manor house where the haole owners lived, and some nice cottages where their honored guests flopped in style. We passed more kukui trees and an old stable that probably once housed oxen before tractors replaced the big, smelly beasts, though there were probably still horses somewhere for ranch work and surveillance, though the surveillance these days was of large machines, not indentured servants with cane knives. And show horses, of course, for haole recreation. Then we came up on a banana patch to our right and a row of camp houses across the gravel to the left. The first house was the biggest and the nicest; it had a large lanai and was whitewashed, with ti plants and red torch ginger out front. It was probably the Portuguese luna's house, though these days the luna was more and more just as likely to be Japanese. Hanging from one of the lanai rafters was a little bronze bell and a small paper banner, which confirmed the ethnicity of the luna: Japanese. Progress. We were no longer just the shit on the plantation. We were now the dung beetle, too.

After the luna's house, there was a row of typical camp cottages: rusting corrugated tin roofs, cramped little interiors, vegetable patches out front. The crops gave away the ethnicities of the occupants: shiso and turnip fronting the Japanese houses, marungay and bitter melon in the Filipino yards.

We continued down the row of camp houses until we came to the end, where Fuji rolled to a stop in front of the second to the last little tin-roofed home. I was beginning to feel glad I had made the decision to hire him and not a car on my own: there was no way I'd ever find this little shack on the edge of the known world.

"This is it," said Fuji. "This is where I dropped him off."

"This house?" I pointed at the sorry little dwelling we had come to a halt in front of.

"Yeah, this is it."

"Did he ask you to wait?"

"No, he just paid me and said thanks. I left."

I looked at the plants out front. The tender little blue-green leaves and long, thin hanging fruit of the marungay tree moved in the slight breeze. There were also bitter melon vines and eggplant. A stunted citrus tree bore some tiny round limes. Calamansi. This was a Filipino home.

"Are you sure?" I asked Fuji. "This is a Filipino house, and judging by the size of the calamansi tree, it probably has been for some time. Didn't you say he was going to see the place where he used to live with his wife?

"Yeah, he said it wasn't too far from here, but I could drop him off at this house. He said the place was too hard to get to by car, but his friend who lives here would take him."

"Oh," I said. There was a lot about Happy Tokuda I didn't know and this chapter of his life on Kauai was probably just one of many that I wasn't familiar with. If the occupant of the little house in front of me was an old friend of Happy's, then he'd be someone I definitely wanted to get to know.

"I need to talk to whoever is in this house," I said. "You'll be okay waiting for me out here?"

"Yeah," said Fuji. "It's what you hired me to do."

I nodded. Fuji somehow didn't look like a guy who would have a problem sitting behind the wheel and looking through his windshield at nothing for hours on end. I reached into my pocket and pulled out my pack of Lucky Strikes and handed it to him.

"Sorry," I said. "This is the best entertainment I've got for you."

"Thanks. It's plenty."

I looked at the little shack again. It was small and mean and probably leaked when it rained hard and, judging from the moss all over the crude little rock fence around the house's miniscule perimeter, it probably rained hard every other day. The lights were on. I caught the scent of something cooking, the tang of vinegar and salt and something more pungent on the heavy, moist air. It made my mouth water and made me think of Ellen's admonishment to have a decent dinner.

I went up the steps to the lanai and stood in the yellow light of a termite and moth magnet of a naked bulb.

I straightened my tie and my hat, pulled out my badge, and knocked on the door.

# 17

The little camp house was painted dark green like all the others along the gravel road. It was covered in what was once a deep forest green, now faded to a sickly olive drab, except for the door and window frames which were whitewashed. Though I couldn't really see it at that moment in the dying light in the sky, the corrugated roof was probably an array of rust browns with a few spots of grey where the original finish of the tin escaped the rain, thanks to the overhang of a kukui tree. The dark green paint was probably used for its ability to hide dirt better than white.

My knocks on the door were rewarded by slow, heavy steps and the turn of the tarnished brass knob.

What opened the door was a man in an undershirt and dusty work trousers. His feet were bare. He was about five feet four inches, slim, and looked about forty years old. His jet black hair was slick with grooming product. He held a bottle of beer by the neck at his side.

"Good evening, sir," I said. I showed him my badge. "My name is Yoshikawa and I'm a police detective. From Honolulu."

"I know," he said.

"You do?"

"Yeah. Our detectives here just show up in shirtsleeves or even aloha shirts and lauhala hats. You got a fancy suit and tie. Like *Dragnet*. You gotta be from Honolulu."

I had to laugh. "You saw *Dragnet*? Don't tell me it actually played on Kauai."

"It did. At the Lihue Theatre on the highway in town. The luna treated some of us guys who helped clear a dead tree off the train tracks."

"That was nice of him. How'd you like the show?"

"It was good. The wahine—the police lady—was nice looking. Except I didn't like the ending. The bad guy dies before they could send him to jail. That's not right. There wasn't any, uh . . ."

"Justice?"

"Yeah. I was going to say 'happy ending,' but 'justice' is better."

"Just like real life. Look, I was hoping I could ask you a few questions, Mister . . ."

"Fernando. Rey Fernando. Everybody just calls me Nando."

"Good to meet you, Nando. I'm sorry to bother you in the middle of cocktails," I said. I glanced at the beer bottle hanging lazily at his side. "But I need your help."

"Sure. What with?"

"Something that happened here earlier today."

"Here? Nothing happened here."

"Sure, it did. Lots of things probably did, but you don't think so because you're probably used to seeing it all the time."

Nando shrugged. "Okay," he said. "You probably better come inside, then. It sounds pretty important."

"Thanks," I said. "I promise I won't tie you up for too long."

"Just the facts," he said, doing a pretty good Jack Webb.

"Just the facts," I said. He was tickled that I repeated the trademark movie line. He opened the screen door for me as I removed my shoes.

Nando's living room was tiny. It brought back half-remembered images from my young childhood in a similar tiny house in Waipahu with my parents and four older sisters. There was even a little built-in shelf on the wall like our old plantation home on Oahu had, but instead of holding a little gilded Buddha in a box with a senko burner, a wooden crucifix and a framed color portrait of a Jesus with soft brown hair and limpid eyes sat perched surveying the room.

Nando didn't have much in the way of furniture, just a small wooden table and two mismatched chairs, orphans from some dead haoles' dining sets.

"Sit down," said Nando. "I was just about to have dinner. It's nothing fancy, but why don't you have some?"

I thought for a second about politely declining, but only for a second before I pushed that idea off the cliff.

"It smells great," I said. "Thanks."

Nando took about three steps into his tiny kitchen which had a basin and a cold water tap, no doubt the only plumbing in the little house. The toilet was in a small shed in the back. There were a couple of pots on a small kerosene stove into which he dipped a battered ladle and dumped its contents onto three tin plates. He came out and set two plates with utensils at the table and carried the third to the front door.

"For your driver," he said.

"Thanks," I said.

In a few seconds, Nando was back in the living room.

"Beer?" he asked.

"Sure," I said.

"You're not on duty anymore?"

"It's evening. And I'm pretty far away from my station."

"Coming right up."

Nando went back into the kitchen and I heard the click and hiss of an opening bottle. He came back with it and set it on the table in front of me before seating himself. Once seated, he raised his own bottle.

"Kanpai," he said. A nod to my heritage.

"Cheers," I said. I raised my bottle and clinked it against his.

We drank and we ate.

"Sorry," he said. "It's only adobo and pinakbet."

"It's great," I said. "Thank you. And my wife thanks you, too. She didn't want me having a candy bar for dinner."

"You eat candy for dinner?"

"Only when I can't get real food like this. I had a sandwich and a couple of Hershey's bars for lunch."

"That's no way to live."

"No, it isn't."

We ate and drank some more and talked about the weather. We lit up cigarettes.

"Ready for the questions?" I asked.

"I'll try my best," said Nando.

"It's easy," I said. "Just the facts."

"Just the facts," he said back to me, then laughed.

I pulled Happy's photograph out of my pocket and showed it to him. Recognition ignited his beer-clouded eyes.

"You know him?" I asked.

"He was here today," said Nando.

"What's his name?"

"I don't know. But I think Johnny called him Papa."

"Who's Johnny?"

"Johnny Tolentino. He lives here, too. This is one of the houses where the single guys live. There was four of us that lived in this house. There's me, Johnny, Ed, and Pablo. Ed and Pablo went back to the P.I. to get married. So, it's just me and Johnny right now."

"Where's Johnny?"

"He went somewhere with Papa. They were here, drinking okolehao since this morning. When I came home from Lihue, they were leaving."

"Where did they go?"

"I don't know." Nando cast his eyes down at his plate and moved a couple of stray okra stems around with his fork and spoon. He was positively engrossed with the task.

"Come on, Nando," I said. "I thought you were going to give me the facts."

"I am, sir."

"What's with this 'sir' shit? One minute we're eating and drinking together like friends, the next minute, I'm 'sir.' Look, Nando, you're not in any kind of trouble, and I'm not interested in making any trouble for your friend Johnny, but he may be in trouble if he's with this Papa."

"Are you going to arrest Johnny?"

"No. I can't. I'm a Honolulu cop, remember? I have no jurisdiction out here. I'm just interested in finding Papa. Please, Nando. It's important."

"It's important?"

"Very. You know what kind of detective I am? I'm a homicide detective."

"Homicide?"

"Yes, homicide. I'm the cop that gets called in when a dead body turns up that got dead thanks to someone else making it that way."

"Papa killed somebody?"

"I don't know. But it's my job to find out."

Nando stopped pushing the okra stems around his plate and let a sigh out with cigarette smoke.

"You promise you won't arrest Johnny?"

"I promise. Not unless he killed somebody."

Nando raised his head and looked me in the eye. He took another drag off his cigarette and blew the smoke out through his nostrils. His hair, once neatly slick, was now limp with sweat.

"They went to the Carriage House," he said.

"The Carriage House?"

"It's where Johnny knew him from. The Carriage House has more local girls and girls from China and Japan these days, but during the war time, when Papa was there, it was haole girls. From Honolulu, but from the mainland before that."

A brothel. Set up to service the plantation workers, no doubt. The unlucky dogs who didn't have wives, and some who did. Some of the more enterprising and daring Hotel Street sporting girls would set up shop on different islands to get away from the three-dollar-a-minute assembly line of the red-light district and its never-ending queues of G.I.s. The money wasn't as good but it was decent and the working conditions were much more humane, if you could call brothel conditions of any kind humane.

Happy managed a brothel on Kauai? It didn't seem his speed at first glance, but the more I thought about it, the more sense it made. He'd bring customers in—like Johnny—and get a commission from the independent contractor sporting girls who ran the place free of control of pimps, overbearing madams, corrupt vice cops, and military commanders. Their money, in the end, was theirs to keep, minus expenses like rent, hush money, and commissions to "referral services" like Happy Tokuda.

"Did you ever go to the Carriage House?" I asked.

"No," said Nando. He gave me a sheepish half-smile and looked back down at his plate. "I always liked the girls at the Flower Shop in downtown Lihue better."

"To each his own," I said. I shrugged and finished my beer. "Where is the Carriage House?"

"Well, it's further down the main road from town. It's not too far from the train tracks. It's on plantation land, but the owners let it be. They get a cut, I heard. And the cops let it be, too."

"Why is it called the Carriage House?"

"Because it was one of the plantation's carriage houses, back when they used horses for everything."

"Silly me."

Jesus. Carriage House. Flower Shop. Folks on Kauai are so literal and yet so euphemistic at the same time. They weren't being cute or ironic like haole ad men. They were being practical. Confucian filial piety, lack of a command of English, and not too much to laugh about will make you that way. I'm grateful every time I think about it that my folks fled the cramped, shit plantation life for the cramped, shit town life. At least my pau hana drinks were in a real bar and I didn't have to walk to a shed out back in the middle of the night to take a leak.

"How long does Johnny usually stay at the Carriage House?"

"Sometimes all night, but always a long time. There's a girl there he fell for, a hapa girl with light brown hair from Oahu. Stupid, him. She's only in love with his money and he doesn't have a lot of it."

"Good thing you're smart."

"Good thing."

*Not smart, just broke*, as a wise hack once told me.

I stood up and shook Nando's calloused hand.

"Thanks for dinner and drinks," I said. "It beat the shit out of a Hershey's bar and a cigarette. And thanks for the talk."

"Just the facts."

I put my hat back on my head and walked out of the little house on to the little lanai and off the little lanai into the night. The sky had turned inky blue-black and the banana leaves in the patch across the gravel road glistened like black satin in the moonlight. I walked to the Ford, gravel crunching under my shoes. Fuji had gone through at least three cigarettes, the spent butts lying like dead soldiers on the gravel under his window. He sat back up erect, snapping out of his relaxed, glassy-eyed slouch.

"Ready?" he asked.

"Yeah," I said. I made my way around the Ford to the passenger side. Fuji fired up the engine, then got out of the car to return Nando's tin plate and utensils and thank him for the meal. By the time he was back behind the wheel, I had started up a cigarette.

"Where to now?" he asked.

"The Carriage House."

"Aren't you working?"

"It's a business call, and not the way you think. Our man went there with a friend. Old stomping grounds, from the war time."

"Carriage House was fancy haole girls from Honolulu during the war time. Must've been well-heeled, your guy."

"He wasn't, but he was good at making people think he was."

Fuji adeptly maneuvered a tight U-turn on the narrow gravel road and headed back out of the camp and past the owner's compound toward the main road. Once we were at the junction of the plantation road and the main road, Fuji hung a left turn on the main road, away from Lihue Town.

The road was dark and the stalks of cane rose high on either side, waving like the chitinous legs of a thousand giant insects in the night breeze. There wasn't much else to see except the looming black outline of the mountains to the right. It was eerily silent, no sound for miles save for the hum of Fuji's Ford and the crunch of poor pavement beneath its tires.

We drove for a while, past Hanapepe and into a sea of tall, dark cane. Seemingly out of nowhere, a break in cane stalks appeared to the right, and Fuji eased the Ford into the gap, slowly and smoothly.

"How the hell did you know to turn here?" I asked. "There's no sign or marker."

Fuji laughed and rubbed the back of his neck with a gnarled, knotted hand. "I must've made this turn off in the dark a hundred times since the war," he said. "If you do it enough, you know where it is."

"Well, I'm glad as hell I didn't hire a car and try this myself."

"Yeah, me too. I needed the twenty bucks."

The road we traveled was bumpy and narrow, cane leaves brushed the sides of the Ford often. I had to roll up my window so I wouldn't have my face slashed by one of the sharp leaves. I could see in the light of the Ford's headlamps that the road was unpaved. The soil looked firm enough but uneven, and pale clouds of dust would go up when we hit a rough patch.

"What happens if it rains?" I asked.

"What do you think? We'd get stuck in the mud. It rains plenty over here. So, when it's coming down, I drop off my fare on the main road and tell him to walk in."

"How far is this place from the main road?"

"I don't know. Maybe a half-mile. Maybe less. Maybe more. About a half-mile."

"And the fares you drop off at the main road, they don't get mad? I'd be if I had to walk a half-mile through the cane with the rain coming down."

"No, they don't get mad. Most drivers drop them off at the main road even when it's not raining. Too hard for them to drive down this road. I'm the only one who does. That's why I charge extra for Carriage House. But even I'm not going to chance it when it's wet. If you get stuck in the mud, that's it for the car. Those guys know, so they don't mind the walk. They even do it in the rain to get what's at the end of the road."

"It must be something special."

"War time, it was the haole girls. Now it's cheaper than Lihue and it never gets raided."

"Crooked cops?"

"No, even though we got those. For the Carriage House, it's a crooked councilman."

"We got those," I said. "And the crooked cops."

"Good thing you're not one of those."

"I used to be," I said. I recalled my days as a part-time bagman making kickback collections in Chinatown at the brothels and the gaming rooms. "I don't have to be any more."

"Change of heart?"

"Change of paycheck. I got promoted. But my heart always hated it."

It was actually a lot more complicated—and bloody—than that. But I let that thought drift out of the crack I left in the window along with the cigarette smoke.

"It's okay," said Fuji. "Nobody's perfect."

"Almost nobody," I said. "I know a guy who is, but he's missing a leg."

"There you go. Nobody's perfect."

"I guess so. But he's closer to perfect than I'll ever be."

"A friend?"

"Yeah. My best friend. From school time."

"How'd he lose the leg?"

"German grenade."

"He was in the war?"

"Yeah."

"You?"

"Yeah. I was there when he lost his leg."

"That's rough."

"It was, but not as rough as seeing other friends lose more than a leg."

"Yeah, I guess so."

Wally Yoshida. I was really in a dark cane field on Kauai in an old Ford because of him. His life would be fixed by the inquest, but I was out in the middle of nowhere to make sure that nothing could come back to un-fix it. What Happy might have done, and what he might have taken, might be enough to put Wally's life back in the cesspool.

Ten grand was a lot of money not to be missed. Was it all Lydia's? Just how rich was she? I know that her money bought the fancy house on the mountain with the spectacular view, but ten grand in cash was a lot of money to raise for an ex-Broadway understudy. I had no idea how much money they made, but it wasn't the kind of money the leads made, not by a long shot. Did the cash come out of Wally's campaign chest? It might've, but that would be an awfully low—and illegal—thing for a loving new bride to do. Lydia looked like ten grand. She walked and talked like it, and probably sang and danced like it, too. Humble beginnings. Wayward relations. But didn't we all have them, humble beginnings and wayward relations? Burlesque and cheesecake modeling might have added to the small fortune and, if she was a smart, industrious girl—the plucky Judy Garland off the bus in the big city terminal with a heart of gold and a nose for it—then maybe it was possible to amass a small fortune.

Fuji was right. Nobody's perfect. Not even Wally Yoshida. He was almost, but not quite, and his fatal flaw wasn't his missing leg. It was that he was missing a wall. He was missing the wall we put up to keep the rest of the world out because we just didn't trust it. Wally loved everybody and everybody loved Wally. Nothing wrong with that. Wally also trusted everybody and there was something severely wrong with that. I neither loved nor trusted everybody. When it came right down to it, I loved and trusted almost nobody. That's why it was my job to be Wally's wall. And that's what I was doing right at that moment, heading out to a brothel in an old shack in the black of night in the broom closet of Kauai while my wife had a turkey sandwich on a ti leaf on a monkeypod platter with an orchid and a pineapple ring on the side for her room service dinner, and my daughter napped on a fake tapa bedspread.

After all these years, I was still the big guy hanging around to make sure my little friend didn't get pushed around. I didn't trust the world like Wally did. I could count all the people I really trusted on one hand. He was one of them. So, there I was.

The Ford bumped its way into a clearing where a long, low building shone grey in the moonlight. During the day, it was probably nice and bright, whitewashed by the girls-for-hire within and their lovestruck, by-the-hour benefactors to give the place a touch of class. Pale yellow light spilled out of the old-fashioned glass panes at the ends of the long edifice, and its six carriage doors were permanently sealed.

"This is it," said Fuji. "I'll wait out here for you. But if it starts raining, I'm going to go back out to the main road so I don't get stuck. You have to walk out to me there. So, you better hope it doesn't rain."

"No shit," I said. I peered up at the pale moon in the sky, luminous and without the long veil of clouds. "Looks clear to me."

Fuji laughed. "You think so? You're not from Kauai. Better keep your fingers crossed."

I held my hand up and crossed my fingers for him to see. I opened the passenger door and got out. I smoothed my trousers and straightened my tie and put my hat on my head. I put my right hand into my coat and felt under my left arm for my .38, and prayed silently that it would stay there. I patted my handcuffs dangling from my belt behind my left hip. I stuck my right hand into my trouser pocket and felt my hipflask. Armored at all points, I marched toward the Carriage House.

The Carriage House was exactly what the name said it was. In the days before automobiles, it housed six carriages for use by the plantation owners, some rich haoles whose forefathers came on masted ships with white sails to preach the gospel, New England–style, and set up schools for all the brown brand-new Christians. They won over the alii and kings of old, and that prestige parlayed itself into landowning wealth. The sugar cane they grew may as well have been gold—their Boston brethren couldn't get enough of it when the Civil War cut off their sugar supply from the Confederate South.

These days they drove around the island in sleek automobiles. Exhaust-belching tractors and trucks have replaced the enormous mammals that roamed the fields. The iron-framed buggies they tooled about Lihue Town in were dismantled and melted into supports for conveyor belts and water flumes. The structures that housed these conveyances and protected them from the wet weather stood empty for years until they were re-purposed to house a different type of luxury good.

The main entrance to the establishment was once a side entrance when the building actually contained horse-drawn vehicles. No doubt, there would be old stables not too far away, but such a building wouldn't be as useful as a brothel even after years of disuse due to its relatively flimsy construction. The new, perfumed livestock needed a more reliable shelter.

The once side now main entrance was a whitewashed door with a new brass knob. I could hear a phonograph behind the door playing a new Sinatra long-playing album. There was also feminine laughter and footsteps light and heavy on a plank floor laid above the original dirt surface of the carriage house.

I put my hand on the brass knob and turned it. The music and the laughter slapped me in the face with its full, undiluted volume. The first thing I saw, and smelled, was the women. There was a handful of Orientals in short silk kimono robes, loosely tied to show the lace and flesh beneath. A couple of haole girls in bleached Hollywood-style coifs lounged about in sheer coverups adorned with long strands of pearls or big, gaudy gold bangles. There was a Hawaiian girl sitting at the piano absently picking out notes in time with the record. She occasionally shook out her mane of luxurious black hair.

Then I saw her: a hapa girl with hair the color of an Irish setter, standing at a painting of an island landscape, the kind you find in the lobby of any of the handful of Waikiki hotels that wasn't the Royal Hawaiian. She wore a short red kimono robe that hung loosely on her shoulders, untied, revealing the black negligee beneath. She smoked a cigarette while she absently traced the rainbow in the painting with a red fingernail.

I took a quick look around the room. Beside the women, there were only two men, a couple of ruddy-faced haoles in aloha shirts with girls in their laps. One was probably a plantation overseer and his guest was probably a manufacturer salesman, judging by their inane conversation between sips of rye. They blathered too loudly about "margins" and "returns" as if they were magic words that impressed the whole world into sleeping with them.

I made my way to the girl at the painting. I was about halfway across the room when I felt a small, warm hand on my shoulder.

"Hi, handsome," said the voice belonging to the hand. I turned to look at a short Japanese girl with bobbed hair in a short pink kimono robe. Her slight accent and pale skin gave her away as a recent arrival, a beneficiary of the immigration floodgates opening a couple of years ago. She probably spent a lot of time with American G.I.s in occupied Tokyo and probably married one to hop across the Pacific to greener pastures.

"Hi, yourself," I said. "What's that girl's name?" I pointed at the girl studying the painting. The bob frowned at me.

"That's Annie," she said. "You don't want her. She's busy with a regular. She got three or four regulars. Me, I just got here a week ago. Fresh."

"Yeah, I can smell the freshness," I said. "I don't want to be with Annie. I just need to ask her something real fast. What's your name, Freshness?"

"Akiko."

"I'll come back and smell more of your freshness when I'm done with my business. Don't go away."

"I'll be waiting."

I broke away from Akiko and walked up to the cheap painting. I stood next to Annie.

"It's beautiful," I said. "This guy could give Cézanne a run for his money."

"I'm busy," she said without turning to look at me.

"I know. Where is he?"

"Who?"

"Your fare. Johnny."

She finally tore her eyes away from the canvas to look at me with cold hazel eyes.

"He's taking a break," she said. "And so am I."

"Where's he taking his break?"

"Where else? The outhouse."

# 18

I exited the Carriage House cathouse the way I had entered it. There were no other exits; an interior door led to the private rooms where the women regaled their paying guests. I glanced up at the sky above. So far, so good. Cloudless. Fuji's big Ford remained in the clearing, cigarette smoke rising into the night sky from the driver's window, a small campfire behind the wheel.

I walked the length of the Carriage House, hearing laughter every few feet of its length through the plank walls where the carriage doors had once been. When I reached the end of the long building, I saw the two outhouses, one for the residents and one for the guests, as noted by hand painted signs on the doors.

The tiny, moon-shaped cutout in the "guest" outhouse door was illuminated from within, probably by a naked bulb hanging from a fraying cord. I walked up to the door and grabbed the handle.

The "bar" on the door from the inside felt flimsy as I tested its strength with a quiet tug on the handle. I grasped the handle with both hands and I yanked with all my strength. I really didn't need all my strength. The little wood bar popped off the nail holding it to the inside of the door and probably hit the occupant in the head, if the yell he let out was any indication.

On the wooden bench with his trousers around his ankles was a man in his thirties. His eyes were bloodshot in the yellow light of the cheap bulb. His black hair was wet and limp with perspiration. He scowled at me and stammered inarticulately.

"Hey! What the fuck! Wait your turn!" he bellowed. He had finally found his voice.

"I'm done waiting, Johnny Tolentino," I said. I pulled my badge out and stuck it in his face. "But I'll give you twenty seconds to clean up. I'll be counting. If you're not out here when I reach thirty, I'll open this door again and I'll beat you senseless with the butt of this .38. Or maybe I'll just shoot you. I'm tired and it'll take a lot less effort to do that than to beat you." I pulled the revolver out and showed it to him. Normally, I'd have a lot more patience with someone like Johnny, but this wasn't normal. I had flown all the way from Oahu and I wasn't about to let Happy slip away when I had the opportunity to nail him down and make him talk. I might never get this close again if he took the ten grand.

"Okay! Shit! Okay!" he shouted.

I shoved the door shut and took about five steps back and counted aloud. At nineteen, Johnny came staggering out, fumbling with his zipper.

"What the hell is your problem?" he mumbled.

"My problem is that I've been getting shit answers to all my questions over the past forty-eight hours, and I'm sick of it. I'm so sick of it that I'm ready to shoot the next person who lies to me. That's my problem."

"So?" he asked. His eyes were wide and dirty with fear.

"So," I said. I brought the .38 up and pointed the muzzle up to the sky. "I'm going to ask you some questions. If you lie to me, I will not hesitate to point this gun at you and pull the trigger and cram your corpse into that hole in the bench. Is that clear?"

"Yes! Yes, goddamn it!"

"Where the hell is Papa?"

"Who?"

I brought the .38 down and pointed it at him. Johnny whimpered like a dog beaten with a rolled-up newspaper after its owner discovered shit on the rug.

"His house!" Johnny wailed. He shut his eyes tight, as if doing so would make me go away.

"What house?"

"The house he used to live in when he was here. His war time house. Up the trail. Used to be the house where the old carriage drivers used to live."

"Is he there right now?"

"Yeah, he's there. He's supposed to come back."

"Take me."

Johnny nodded vigorously. I re-holstered my .38.

"We need a light," he said. "A lantern or flashlight or something."

"I know where we can get one," I said. "Come with me."

We walked back to the front of the Carriage House to Fuji's Ford. As I suspected, he kept a flashlight in the glovebox. All good hacks did. He handed it to me through the driver's window and continued to smoke and look at the moon through his windshield. It must be grand to be so easily entertained.

"Let's go," I said. I nudged Johnny toward the back.

We returned to the outhouses, where Johnny pointed to a worn footpath leading through the gnarled kiawe and kukui trees. We started our trudge.

The ground under my feet was uneven and occasionally painful, full of twisted roots and stray stones of varying size. I had Johnny walk ahead of me, though I maintained control of the flashlight. The walk along the path was slow and tortuous and lasted a few long minutes.

By the time we saw a pale yellow light ahead of us, my feet were sore and so was my mood. The last twenty feet or so of the path appeared to be fairly straight and free of large obstructions, so I turned the flashlight off. We approached the clearing guided only by the light emanating from the little building in the clearing.

The drivers' "house" wasn't much larger than the camp house Nando and Johnny lived in, and was much less pretty. The planks that made up the walls, whitewashed ages ago, were darkened from the bottom with mildew. Light escaped from the top of the shack where the tin roof had grown holes over the years. The place had the sad smell of decay and abandonment. It was the scent of abject misery long dead, the memory of hardship and suffering tucked away in a kukui grove for the world to forget.

I brought my index finger up in front of my lips. Johnny nodded acknowledgement and froze in place with his hands hanging at his sides. I listened at the door and thought I heard a faint, irregular hissing with short, regular pauses.

I pulled the .38 out of my shoulder holster and placed my free hand on the tarnished doorknob and turned it. The knob moved with some difficulty but without much noise. It wasn't locked, but years of being drenched by passing showers and disuse had made it stubborn.

The hinges groaned loudly, so I just pushed the door in, leading with the muzzle of my revolver. The light in the place was supplied by a single sad, tarnished brass lamp with no shade on an old, scarred dining table in the middle of the room, its hand-turned legs indicative of a past era when folks made things like their own furniture and appointments with doctors who made house calls.

On the table along with the lamp was a glass jug that once held vinegar or shoyu but now held an inch of clear liquid sitting idle at its bottom. Okolehao. The little room reeked of its fumes.

Also on the table was a mop of wild, greasy hair, which was attached to the body of a man in gaudy clothes, sitting in a chair. The body puffed and deflated while the head seethed and whistled. It was the hissing I had heard though the door. Snoring. Next to the head of tangled hair was a black wool beret, dislodged from its sad perch.

Happy Tokuda had apparently drank until he passed out. Straight out of the jug. There was no glass. Why put up a front of formalities when there was no company to impress?

His snoring having confirmed he was still alive and breathing, I explored the little dwelling. A kitchen area adjoined the main room, housing a relic of a wood burning stove and oven. There was a pitcher and a basin on a wooden counter and a free-standing cabinet. There was no running water or plumbing, though the place was apparently wired for electricity. But for the bare, black wires running up the walls and along the floorboards, the cottage was a throwback to paniolo times, when sweat-soaked ranch hands flopped in shacks like the one I stood in. The basin was dry, and so was the pitcher. The cabinet was empty.

I moved to the one interior door in the place that opened to a back room. There was a single naked bulb in a small socket on the ceiling. A frayed string tied to a rusted daisy chain hung from the socket. I pulled it and was surprised that the bulb wasn't dead. It illuminated the room with a pale, weak light.

The room contained only three pieces of furniture: an ancient brass bed, an old wooden wardrobe, and a small table next to the bed. On the bed was a musty quilt, once white and probably green, stitched with a breadfruit leaf motif. The bed was neatly made and unslept in for years. On the nightstand was a tarnished silver frame. In the frame was a photograph, smaller than the frame's dimensions. It was one of those photographs with a fake beach and coconut palms background, the kind G.I.s posed in front of with fake hula girls during the war.

The subjects of the photograph weren't some haole sailor and a curvy dark girl in a grass skirt. It was Happy Tokuda as I remembered him from his Hotel Street bunco days with his arms around a plain-faced though classy haole lady with Andrews Sisters hair. That lady was Princess Judy Kerrigan, Lydia's wayward Aunt Meg.

I didn't want to read into their expressions any more than what they appeared to be: big smiles. I didn't want to speculate whether or not the smiles were genuine, whether or not they really looked content. In those days on Hotel Street, smiles sold for as little as a nickel shoeshine and as much as a three dollar, three-minute roll in the hay. Everybody smiled on Hotel Street except the cops.

I returned to the main room after putting out the light in the little bedroom. Johnny had come in out of the dark and sat on the floor near the front door, his back up against the plank wall.

"Is he okay?" he asked. He looked over at the snoring Happy with glassy eyes.

"Yeah. Just out cold after all the drinking. Did you tell me he used to live here?"

"When the Carriage House was all haole girls. War time."

"He lived in this little shack all by himself?"

"No. He lived with the madam. Everybody called her Princess."

"Did they own the Carriage House?"

"I don't know. I heard the plantation owners really owned it. Princess ran it with her girls. Papa-san—Papa—used to come to the pau hana parties at the overseer's house and drive us to the Carriage House for two bits each. We all piled in the back of his truck. He drove us back to the camp when we were all pau."

"Do you know Papa's name?"

"No. We only know him as Papa. We knew he was from Honolulu. Some big shot gambler who knew all the haole girls.

He knew Princess real good. He knew the little one with the short brown hair called Midge, and the blonde with the big okole called Molly. And the two with black hair, Jane and June. They said they were sisters, but they didn't look alike except for their black hair. Probably dyed."

"Papa was just a driver?"

"No. I think Princess gave him money for every guy he brought to the Carriage House. He was kind of picky, too. Mostly Japanese guys like him. He said the girls liked Japanese boys because they were clean and smelled good. Back then, I just came from Ilocos, so I did like the Japanese guys and took a bath in the furo and put Bay Rum on my face before I came out. Papa said the girls liked a clean guy like me, so he always picked me to come up. Lots of times, I even sat up front in the cab with him. He said I was a good customer and the girls liked me."

"When did he leave the Carriage House? It's different now."

"He wasn't around too long. Just after V-E Day they were all gone. Papa, Princess, Molly, Midge, the twins, all of them."

"Why? Sounds like they got pretty good business from you plantation boys."

"They did, but there was a problem."

"Cops?"

"No."

"What?"

"Problems. The girls. They were fighting with each other."

"What about?"

"Money."

Of course. What else?

"What was the money problem?" I asked.

"Princess ran the show," said Johnny. He rubbed his upper arms with his hands as if he were freezing in the sultry, damp

Kauai night air. "She controlled the cash. Paid all the girls, paid papa his cut, paid the councilman—but I think the councilman's payment wasn't in money. Then one day, the two black-haired sisters disappeared. Then Midge left. Then Big Molly. Princess was pretty pissed off. She thought one of them stole from her. A little bit after that, they all left. I never saw any of them again. Until today. First time I saw Papa since they left."

"What did Papa tell you?"

"He said, 'Let's drink.' We drank. Then he said, 'Let's go to the Carriage House.' For old time's sake. I said it was different. Not much haole girls like before. He said it was okay. He wanted to go. His treat."

"How did you guys get up there?"

"We caught a ride with some of the guys in the camp. We split the cab fare."

"So, you've been with Annie all this time."

"Yeah, I was going to go back with her again, but I ran into you." Johnny pulled a sour face. I wasn't moved.

"It was necessary," I said. "What about Papa? Was he with a girl?"

"No. He told me to take my time with Annie. Go as many times with her as I like. He just wanted to see the old house again. He said he would be a while."

"Apparently," I said. I looked pointedly at Happy's sleeping form.

"What's the matter?" asked Johnny. Something slowly crept up in his expression, which was probably understanding, long overdue. "Did Papa do something wrong?"

"I don't know. That's what I flew in from Honolulu to find out. Did he drink that whole jug by himself?"

"Nah. That's the one we were drinking from at home. But it was full when we started. I had a lot, too. So, he didn't really drink the whole thing by himself. But it was a lot."

"Well, I guess that's good. It means he probably didn't poison himself too badly. Is there a pump outside somewhere?"

"Yeah, on the other side of the house."

"See that pitcher over there? Go and fill it up and come back. Papa's going to need some water. The sooner we get this over with, the sooner you go back to Annie."

"Okay."

Johnny grabbed the pitcher in the kitchen area and went outside. I could hear the rusty whine of the pump and the sloppy splashes.

Happy lay still, breathing through his mouth. His head was on the table, drooling.

Johnny returned with a full pitcher.

It was time for Happy to give me what I had chased him all over two islands for: answers.

# 19

Happy squealed like a pig at a slaughterhouse and jerked his head up off the table when the water from the pitcher hit his head. I had emptied nearly half the contents when he finally woke up.

"Good morning," I said. I put the pitcher down on the table and pulled my .38 out of the shoulder holster. I pointed the muzzle at his head.

"Johnny," I said, "why don't you have a seat on this side of the room where I can keep an eye on you?"

I got no argument from him. He practically half-crawled across the room and curled his knees up to his chest and looked at the floorboards.

"Rise and shine, Happy," I said. "You're going to answer some questions, and you're going to answer them truthfully, or I will put an end to your lifetime of lying once and for all."

Happy wiped his face with his hands and rubbed his eyes. With effort, he brought them into focus, dull and bloodshot.

"First Base?" he asked. It came out as a dry croak. "What you doing here?"

"Shut up. I'll ask the questions. It all ends here and now, in this shitty little shack at the edge of the goddamn world. No more running. No more cat and mouse. I'm sick of hunting your ass down. If you try to run, I will shoot you. If you lie to me, I will shoot you.

I'm sick of your shit, and if shooting you is the only way to stop you from giving it to me, I will."

"Eh, come on, First Base. There's no need to be like that. We're old friends, you and me."

"No, we're not. Even if we were, we're not any more. Not after this shit. Not after what happened at Wally's the other night. Not after what you did there."

"Is that what this is all about?"

"Shut up," I said. I slammed the fist that wasn't full of a gun on the table. "I said no questions out of you. Only answers. Anything else out of your mouth gets you shot. Do you understand?"

"Yeah, okay. Yeah."

"Good. That's the first indication I've ever gotten that you're capable of following instructions. So, let's try another one. Why did you kill Aunt Meg?"

"I didn't!"

I raised the .38 and squeezed the trigger. The muzzle thundered. Happy wailed, and so did poor Johnny on the floor. I had aimed wide right to the side of his head. The bullet lodged itself in the wall near the bedroom door frame.

"Don't lie," I said. "Why did you kill her?"

"Please," Happy whimpered. "I didn't. I really didn't. That's the truth, First Base."

"Then why the hell did you leave her tied up like that? Why did you sneak away? Think carefully about how you answer this one. I won't miss again."

"I . . . I went out to the living room to see if Shortstop had some more scotch. I heard a noise. I saw a shadow outside on the lanai. Somebody was outside. I got scared. I hid in the kitchen on the floor. I heard the lanai door open and somebody came in. The footsteps went into the room where we were, then I heard some banging around, and somebody said 'shit' two or three times. Then it was quiet. I was too scared to move. Then, after a couple of minutes, I heard the footsteps again, but they were running this time, out of the lanai door. I waited a long time again. I was scared. Then, I went to check on her. There was a pillow on her face. I felt her. She was dead. I got scared and left."

"What did the voice sound like?"

"Low. A man's voice. Sounded haole."

"And the footsteps?"

"Heavy. But they could move fast."

Happy had his hands on his low-slung head, though whether out of fear or the onset of a headache or both, I couldn't tell. His story seemed plausible, and the intruder sounded like Bobby Castle. But I had to be sure.

"That's a hell of a story, Happy," I said. "The hiding and running away sure sounds like you. I'll give you that. But why the hell should I believe that you didn't kill her when you tied her up and gagged her like some kind of animal?"

Happy's shoulders shook uncontrollably, then his head. I felt like backhanding him for laughing until I realized that he wasn't. He was crying. The quaking of his body was soon accompanied by tortured sobs.

"I didn't kill her," he said. His voice was choked and broken. "I loved her. I couldn't kill her. She was my wife."

"Your *wife?*"

"Yeah. We got married. It was a secret. We did it just before we left for Kauai. It was so the Army and the police wouldn't hassle her about leaving the Metropolitan. They wouldn't let her out of the Hotel Street area if they knew she was going to open her own place on Kauai, but if she got married and quit being a sporting girl, they had to let her go. But me, I didn't just do it to help her. I loved her."

"You're full of shit," I said. I had to test him. I wasn't about to fall for a line like that the way his marks did unless I had proof. "Our records of Mary Judith Kerrigan didn't turn up any marriage here in the T.H. You would've had to show HPD a marriage certificate for them to approve her movement outside the red-light district."

"I got it," said Happy. He made a move for the inside of his coat and I brought the .38 up. He put his hands in the air. I reached into his inside pocket and pulled out a folded piece of paper. It was a certificate. Happy began to sob again. I put the certificate on the table where it was dry and unfolded it.

The Territory of Hawaii, Department of Health, Vital Statistics Bureau recorded the marriage of Haruo Harry Tokuda, a man of Japanese ancestry born in Kohala, Hawaii, to Margaret Kerrigan O'Donnell, a woman of Caucasian ancestry born in Chicago, Illinois.

"Margaret O'Donnell?" I asked.

"Her real name. The one she was born with. She used her mother's name as her sporting girl name. That's the one she gave to the cops when they arrested her."

"What the hell happened to your marriage? Your 'wife' took off and spent some time on the mainland. What was that all about?" I asked.

"The business here was good at first. We made lots of money. The cops never bothered us. The Princess put away a big amount. Enough to invest, buy land, buy houses. But then it disappeared when the two girls, the ones we called the Twins, disappeared. Princess was mad as hell. She started drinking. The little one, Midge, tried to calm her down when she got drunk, but Princess beat Midge up with a broomstick and called her a liar. She said she was covering for them. Midge left. The big girl, Molly, beat Princess up for beating up Midge. Then she left, too. I took care of Princess that night—Molly beat her up pretty bad—but the next morning, the Princess was gone, too. I never saw her again until the other night at Shortstop's. That's the truth."

"So, you packed up and went back to Honolulu after the girls left?"

"What else was I going to do? All the girls were gone. No sense in hanging around."

Happy sobbed again. He wiped his eyes and his nose with his coat sleeve.

"I loved her," he said. "I missed her. But I knew she had to make her money back. She couldn't go back to the Metropolitan. Besides, the war was almost over. All the G.I.s were going back home. She was smart. She went to some big city on the mainland, I guess. She looked good that night at Shortstop's. I guess she did okay for herself."

"You weren't mad at her?"

"No. I couldn't be mad. That's the way the Princess was. Free. A sporting girl. A good one, too. I knew she'd be gone someday. I was just lucky I got to be with her for a little while, and got to help her a little bit."

I suppose that was all anyone could really hope for with anyone else. A little while, and a little bit. For people like Happy Tokuda and his Princess, it was a few weeks. For others, it was fifty years. But in the end, it's all just a little while and a little bit.

I put the .38 back in my shoulder holster. I pulled out a brand-new pack of Lucky Strikes, opened it, and offered one to Happy. He took it and nodded. I shook one out for myself and lit us both up. I pulled a chair out and sat down.

"It's your lucky day," I said. I expelled smoke at the bare bulb in the lamp where it lingered in a yellow haze and dissipated. "I believe you. So far, so good for you, Happy. You may yet live to swindle another mark. Let's see how you do with this one: where's the money?"

"What money?"

I reached for the .38 again and brought it out and pointed it at his tangled, wet head.

"I told you no questions. Just answers," I snarled.

"I don't know what you're talking about! Geez, First Base! Put that thing away! I'm telling you the truth! I don't know nothing about no money!"

"There was money in that room, Happy. A lot of money. Ten grand in a lauhala bag. You're telling me you don't know anything about it?"

"No," he said. "I don't know nothing about no ten grand!"

"Okay," I said. I put the gun away again and stood up. "Why did you go to the Hongwanji in Hanapepe today?"

"To do some gassho. Pray for the Princess. She's gone."

"I didn't know you were religious."

"I felt like I had to do something. I never lost a wife before. She was the only wife I ever had."

Happy was nothing but a drunken husk. All his cheer had been bled from him and washed down the storm drain.

I thought about the answers he had given me. I thought about the story he had told me. It was all true, by the sound of it, but there was an omission. When I realized what that omission was, I smiled wider than I had for the first time since all this shit began, and I smiled unironically. Thankfully, Happy couldn't see my smile. I put my straight face back on.

"I'm not going to arrest you," I said. "At least not tonight. Stay out of trouble, Happy. I mean it."

"I know," he said. He wiped his face again. "Can I ask you a question without getting a gun in my face?"

I shrugged and nodded.

"Are we friends now, First Base?"

I smiled again, but this time I let him see it.

"Stay out of trouble," I said.

Happy smiled back. "Same old First Base," he said.

I walked behind Happy, patted his shoulder, and walked in to the bedroom. I turned on the light and looked at the framed photograph again. All smiles. Maybe one of them really was in love.

I took a quick look under the bed and saw a dark lump. I looked closer. Lauhala. Something dawned on me—actually, it dropped on my head like a ton of bricks—and I laughed a little to myself. I didn't bother reaching for the bag and looking inside. I didn't have to. I stood up, turned out the light and left the room—and the lauhala bag—as I found them.

*It snewed in his house of mete and drynke.* Well, maybe this little shack wasn't quite like the Franklin's house in Chaucer's prologue, but it was probably pretty damn close to it during the war. Happy came back to remember.

"Let's go, Johnny," I said. I shut the bedroom door behind me. "You have to finish up with Annie and I need to get some sleep."

"Okay," said Johnny. He rose to his feet. We walked to the front door. I turned around before exiting.

"Sorry about interrupting your nap," I said to Happy.

"No big deal," he said.

I shut the door and started the trudge back to my ride.

# 20

With no small effort, I made it back to our little bungalow at the Coco Palms before eleven o'clock. The stumbling stroll through the brush back to the Carriage House from Happy's little shack was faster than the walk out to the shack, but it wasn't any less painful. Lucky for me, the weather held up and Fuji was right where I left him, contentedly sucking on a cigarette and staring through the windshield at a clear, star-filled sky.

When I entered the bungalow, Ellen raised her head from her pillow. She and Lizzie had laid down on the bed hours before.

"Did you find him?" she asked.

"Yeah, I did."

"Was there any trouble?"

"No, no trouble. Happy Tokuda didn't kill Lydia's aunt. What he told me is going to make things at the inquest go even more smoothly. All roads lead to Bobby Castle and even he's gone now. So, it looks like all the police work I need to do on this is done."

"That's good," said Ellen. She let out a small, cute yawn, the Christmas Eve yawn of a child about to give up her Santa Claus vigil. Folks all over the island were starting to do the Santa Claus shit with their kids that we didn't get from our immigrant parents. I guess we were going to do it come December, too. We were all Americans now, and it only took the lives of my 442nd friends—and Wally's leg—to buy us our own piece of a Norman Rockwell vignette.

"I guess so," I said. I took off my shoulder holster and put my .38 away in the top dresser drawer and got undressed.

"You guess so? I think it's more than good. It's great. Wally and Lydia can now get on with their new life together and Wally can campaign without distractions," said Ellen. She yawned again.

"You're right," I said.

"What happened to the money? Did you ever find out?"

"Yeah. It's where it belongs. Go back to sleep, Darling."

Ellen replied with the sound of sleep. A rare nonresponse from the queen of responses.

I moved to the shower as silently as I could and let the water wash the day off me and down the drain. I brushed my teeth and climbed into bed with my sleeping wife and baby girl and sank into oblivion.

My slumber was black, dreamless, and apparently deep. Ellen told me that she and Lizzie had been up for a feeding and a diaper change and I didn't so much as stir.

I felt better rested than I had in three days. I resolved to enjoy my little family for the time we had remaining on Kauai. I had to be back in Honolulu the following day for the inquest, and I booked the first flight out for the next morning. I made a couple of expensive telephone calls from our bungalow while Ellen took Lizzie for a stroll on the Coco Palms grounds after we had some papaya and a ham omelet for breakfast. First, I called one of my contacts in the L.A. Sheriff's Office and had a conversation about Bobby Castle and learned that his criminal roots went all the way back to New York City. No surprise there; I caught as much from the dropped and added *r*'s in his speech. Then I chatted at length with my old Columbia roommate and teammate Hank Charles, who had become one of the first Negro investigators for the Manhattan District

Attorney. When I was satisfied my itch was scratched on the matter of the late Bobby Castle, Hank and I talked a little about old times until he had to run off to court. Ellen and Lizzie returned just as I got off the telephone with Hank. I allowed myself the satisfaction of knowing I now had all the missing pieces and could finally put the whole ugly case to rest in my own way.

We took the little boat tour up the Wailua River to the Fern Grotto. The *Lady Jane* departed from a moist, squishy bank a few steps away from our bungalow door. I remember grunting in agreement with Ellen's incessant remarks about the beauty of the cave we floated through. I could take or leave the experience, but the important thing was that Ellen was as happy as a clam. After the boat ride we went into Lihue Town, had lunch there, and walked around for the rest of the afternoon. Ellen shopped for foods we couldn't get on Oahu while I sat on benches outside various bakeries and general stores in the shade of their awnings. We went back to the Coco Palms and watched their nightly torch-lighting ceremony with conch shell-blowing, drum-beating boys in loincloths and bare feet, then ate the luau food which turned out to be better than expected, especially the haupia. Ellen smiled and Lizzie gurgled the whole time. A couple of happy girls. I smiled along with Ellen and put all thoughts of the case blissfully out of my head until the alarm went off on my rattan nightstand next to my head in the cool dark of our bungalow. The air was heavy with the sharp aquatic scent of rain.

Ellen barked orders at me to dress and pack and we were at the airport just before light started tinting the sky.

I fell asleep on the flight back to Honolulu. We landed, deplaned, and I groggily carried Lizzie and our suitcase back to the Eldorado, which had grown a healthy coat of coral dust. We got in and I drove us home to Palolo Valley.

I kept the motor running in our driveway and stayed only long enough to get Ellen and Lizzie settled back into the house, then headed downtown.

I made the inquest with just a half hour to spare. Gid and Paris had been waiting for me, smoking cigarettes and sipping coffee with the same expression cows have when they stand in the middle of the pasture chewing cud.

"You're looking better, Sheik," said Paris. "The day off helped."

"Yeah, I took my family on a short trip."

"Oh?" said Gid. "Where'd you go?"

"Kauai," I said. "It was long overdue."

"Well, if you need a longer break, just say the word. You've earned it," said Gid.

"Yeah, we'll hold down the fort, Lieutenant," said Paris.

"Okay," I said. "I'll let you know after the inquest. It might be nice to review reports for a little while."

"It might be," said Gid. He nodded and his mouth formed up in what was his idea of a smile.

The doors to the hearing room opened and we went in.

The inquest was a quick affair. It didn't last more than two hours. As expected, the findings were that Bobby Castle had entered the Yoshidas' Maunalani Heights home in the early morning hours after Wally's party had broken up, made his way to the guest room, and smothered an inebriated an unconscious Margaret "Meg" Albert, a.k.a. Mary Judith Kerrigan, and, as I now knew, Margaret Kerrigan O'Donnell. She had been restrained willingly as a part of some sexual game with Haruo Harry "Happy" Tokuda, who had left her before Castle entered the Yoshida residence.

The inquest further concluded that Castle, who had been under surveillance by detectives of the Honolulu Police Department's Homicide Detail, departed the Royal Hawaiian Hotel by taxi on the following evening for the Yoshida residence, and was let into the house by Mrs. Lydia French Yoshida. While inside, Castle attacked Mrs. Yoshida with a knife, and was shot by her in self-defense. He had come to demand money which he told Mrs. Yoshida was owed to him by her aunt, Margaret Albert. The inquest concluded that Castle had likely entered the Yoshida residence on the prior night in an attempt to collect directly from Albert, and smothered her in a rage when he could not get her to respond or find any money.

Because the inquest was a sealed affair, the press wasn't present or even knew about it. Gid had done his job admirably. Wally and Lydia could begin to pick up the pieces and get on with their lives without the specter of bad press to nag them into misery.

After the inquest, I declined an invitation to have lunch with Gid and Paris in Chinatown so I could join Wally and Lydia. We had sandwiches at the Kress counter as it was near Wally's downtown law office.

We ate in silence with occasional small talk about baseball, Broadway, the weather, and my little family vacation. I omitted my true purpose for flying to Kauai. Toward the end of lunch, I asked them if I might get a short statement from Lydia to close out my paperwork on the case, and they consented. Wally told me he had more campaign finance paperwork to prepare for filing by a deadline, but we were welcome to use his office as long as we didn't mind the small, private space that passed for a conference room.

"You know what?" I said. "I'll just take her home after we're done at the station. All I really had on my schedule today was the inquest. You've got enough work to do without working around my interview."

"Are you sure? It seems like so much trouble for you," said Wally.

"No problem. I can surprise Ellen and Lizzie with an early appearance when we're done."

"Thanks, Frankie. And thanks for everything."

"Are you going to be okay?"

"Sure. I'll manage. I always do."

That was an understatement. All Wally had ever known in his adult life was loss, and yet he managed to smile ten times more often than I ever did. My own life wasn't all that tragic, it was just a series of things that wore me down.

We parted ways outside the Kress. Wally walked back to his office and I walked with Lydia toward the station.

"Am I finally going to get to see where you work at the station?" Lydia asked.

"It's not all that interesting, unless you like old military surplus office furniture and stale cigarette smoke. I thought I'd just take you home and talk to you there. That way, you'd already be home, I'd be close to home, we'd avoid afternoon traffic out of downtown, and we'd keep the conversation confidential. I think you'd probably be more comfortable in your own living room, anyway."

"Sounds like you have all the bases covered," she said. "You're so thoughtful."

"I'm not as thoughtful as Wally. Who is? But I try."

We walked to my Cadillac and got in and I drove us out of downtown, down King Street to Waialae Avenue and up Wilhelmina Rise to their house overlooking Diamond Head and Maunalua Bay. On the drive, we chatted about my little vacation with Ellen and Lizzie and our little boat ride. Lydia told me she had found a good cleaning service and how they had done a really great job on the living room. She told me that they were already getting quotes on a replacement carpet.

When we pulled into the Yoshida driveway, I thought momentarily about taking the top back down on the Eldorado. The top had been up the whole time it was parked at the airport while we were on Kauai, and though the day was glorious and the ocean was a deep azure beyond Diamond Head, I thought for a moment about Fuji's admonishment about Kauai and its sudden rains and decided to leave the top up. There was plenty of time to take the top down later. I was becoming the disciplined creature that Ellen was training me to be, and I felt strangely fine about it.

Lydia unlocked the front door and I entered after her, removing my shoes as she had before me. There was no reason to treat this as a professional call. The inquest had concluded the official matter once and for all. I was just there to tie up some loose ends and make sure that Wally could get on with his life with a minimum of complications from the events of the past few days. And to settle some of my own professional—and admittedly, personal—curiosity.

"I think the hardwood looks nice," said Lydia, looking at the floor where the bloodstained carpet had once been. "Maybe I'll just keep it this way. I'll just get a Tabriz or Chinese rug under the coffee table. What do you think, Frankie?"

"Sure," I said. "That would be nice."

Lydia moved to the kitchen to fetch two tumblers from a cupboard and filled them with scotch.

"Sorry," she said. "We're out of ice."

"Ice is overrated," I said. "All it really does for scotch is water it down and make some noise in an otherwise quiet drink."

She brought the drinks over, handed me one of them, and sat down next to me on the sofa. She raised her glass. I raised mine. She brought her glass forward and clinked it against mine.

"Cheers," she said.

I nodded and we drank in silence for a little bit.

"So," she said. "What can I do for you and the Honolulu Police Department?"

"Mostly for me. The Department is satisfied with your answers at the inquest. I just need a few answers to put this whole mess to rest once and for all."

"Amen to that. Poor Wally. He won't say so, but he's been through so much since this all began. I feel terrible about it. It's my fault this has happened to him. He didn't ask for any of this. I want to make this up to him, to make everything right."

"I'm glad to hear that," I said. "I think Wally's been through a lot, too. Did he ever talk to you about the war?"

"He told me how he lost his leg and how you saved his life. He said you made a tourniquet, that he's lucky that you were there to do it, because if you weren't, he would have bled to death."

"I'd always like to be around to save him," I said. "I was there that day in the bunker. But there were times after that I hadn't been around to save him."

"From what? I don't think his life was in danger after that."

"From losing his heart," I said. I took a good long drink and set my tumbler down on the coffee table. "Did Wally ever tell you about Polly Yamanaka from McKinley?"

"No," said Lydia. She shook her blonde head.

"How about Marie Gouveia from Radcliffe?"

Lydia shook her head again.

"I wasn't there when he lost Polly to infidelity. I wasn't there when he lost Marie to tragedy. Both times, he lost his heart, and I couldn't do a goddamn thing to help him. I could fight his battles for him in the schoolyard and I could prevent him from bleeding out of his leg on the other side of the world. But I couldn't protect him from heartbreak."

"Wally never talked to me about those girls," said Lydia. "Were they his sweethearts?"

"They were."

"Well, you must not blame yourself for not being able to help him. Nobody could have. Nobody can save a friend from heartbreak."

"I didn't," I said. "I couldn't. But you're wrong. Friends can save friends from heartbreak, just like they can from bleeding to death. It's really the same thing if you think about it. I couldn't help him with Polly or Marie. I didn't have the knowledge. But I can help him now. That's why I'm here, Lydia. That's why we're here."

"I don't understand," she said.

"I don't want to see Wally lose his heart again, or worse. Do you?"

"No, of course not."

"Will you help me, then?"

"Of course, I will, Frankie. How do you need me to help?"

"By telling me the truth," I said. "I need your story. Your real story, from the beginning."

"What are you talking about?"

"I need your *real* story, Midge."

## 21

"I'm sorry," said Lydia. "What did you call me?"

"Midge. It's what they called you at the Carriage House on Kauai, during the war. They probably called you that at the Metropolitan on Hotel Street, too. Or whichever establishment you were associated with before you joined up with the Princess on her Kauai venture," I said.

"I don't know what the hell you're talking about," she said. It came out rough and shopworn, the voice of a veteran who had gone to war with the temptation of money and lost.

"Don't you? Don't be coy, Lydia. We don't have the time for it and you're insulting my intelligence by trying. Though I get it every day from a wide array of people, I don't have to take it from you. Not now. If you persist in playing dumb and treating me like I am, too, we'll leave for the station right now and have them pull your record." I reached for her glass on the coffee table. "I'll just have them lift your prints from this glass and have them run them. Maybe they won't find anything if you've never been pinched, but are you willing to take the chance that there's nothing on Midge?"

Lydia made a half-hearted attempt to snatch the tumbler from my grasp. I moved it out of her reach without much effort. She collapsed against the back of the sofa and started weeping. I pulled the handkerchief from my pocket and pressed it into her hand. She cried into it more, then recovered and looked at me with eyes as blue as the ocean outside her window, but shot through with the red that had stained her carpet.

“Tell me how,” she said.

“How I knew? I could say something arrogant and glib like it’s my job to know, but the truth is, it took a while. It started with your phony family relationship with the late Princess Judy. The unease of your behavior whenever you interacted with her. I got that from Wally. That was strange, even for a wayward relation. Wally didn’t know it, but he wasn’t describing your unease, he was describing your fear.”

“Fear?” she asked. “What would I be afraid of?”

“Exposure. Your brand-new husband had no idea about your past. Furthermore, any leak about it could be disastrous to his political ambitions. The Princess knew this. That’s why she came to visit. Yes, it was for money, but it wasn’t to cover a gambling debt. She was here to blackmail you.”

Lydia played with the hem of her skirt, looking for a loose thread to pull that wasn’t there. Her eyes weren’t really focused on the pseudo task. They looked like they were sinking. Drowning. I took a sip of my scotch. It had come out of the same bottle as the last time I had it, but this time it had a bitter edge, a sour, lemon-like bite. It didn’t bother me. I wasn’t imbibing a libation. I was taking medication.

“Next,” I continued, “there was your concocted story of a generous aunt who became a financial benefactor. Knowing what we knew about Princess Judy’s activities here did not fit the timetable comfortably. True, she could have crammed all that fast living into a handful of months after leaving Hawaii, but it seemed unlikely. It’s also true that she could have lied to you, and that was my initial assessment because I gave you the benefit of the doubt. My mistake.”

“You don’t trust me,” she said. She actually looked hurt.

"I'm not Wally. You must know that by now. Don't take it personally, though. I trust almost nobody."

"I guess that makes you a good cop."

"But a lousy human being. The nice cops work with school children and give little old ladies warnings instead of tickets. Guys like me end up in Homicide talking to people like you."

"Please don't be hard with me, Frankie." Lydia started to cry again.

"I'm not. I'm being straight with you. There's a difference. If I was being hard, you'd be in cuffs. But I'll get to that in a moment. First, I need to hear your story. The real story. And I suggest you tell it without embellishment. It may make a difference in my disposition."

I had to give Lydia credit. She told it without any sugarcoating. The sweet, perky Broadway understudy dropped away to reveal the as hard as nails Midge. In the telling, she transformed. Her cigarette hung slack from her lips and her eyes grew a cast-iron edge. The sporting girl had come out to talk at last.

She told me of a girl named Ludmila Wojskowicz from Pandora, Pennsylvania, whose Polish immigrant father worked in the coal mines. The man drank too much, and beat the girl and her mother when he did, which was almost nightly.

Ludmila couldn't take it anymore. She stole her father's stash of silver dollars and bought herself a train ticket to New York City. When she arrived at Grand Central Station with only three days worth of food and lodging in silver in her pocket, she was "discovered" by a man in the terminal who told her that he was a talent scout and agent. He even had the engraved business cards to prove it. Robert Castle was the name on the cards. He told her that if she signed a contract that day, he'd put her up in a Manhattan apartment with some other girls and get her started on some modeling and entertainment work. Ludmila told Castle that her name was Lily Jones and she agreed and signed his contract.

She wasn't stupid. She knew Castle was a pimp. She went along because she didn't have much choice. She was young and alone with no skills or education beyond a coal town sixth grade. She was determined, though, to transform herself, and was smart enough to understand that the road to her destination of prosperity would be a hard and ugly one.

And so began a rough year of working conventioneers from places like Ohio and stag parties where she was the paid guest of honor. Her "agent" Castle kept a full fifty per cent of everything she made. But she ate and had a roof over her head and a few nice things to wear. And though Castle occasionally beat her for her smart mouth, he didn't do it nearly as much as her father had. By her math, she was way ahead of where she would have been if she had stayed in Pandora, and she was alive to boot.

"I met her during that time," said Lydia. Her eyes were distant and her voice was as thick as the cigarette smoke it came out with. "We were in the same 'house.' It was more like a dorm room, really. Judy was Irish, like most of the girls in the house. Bobby liked Irish girls because their English was good and he could pass them off as something classier, something rich men really wanted. She was nice to me. She gave me lessons on how to talk and she gave me books to read. She called me Midge because she thought I was like one of those biting bugs that kept coming out to pester her during the summer. That, and because I was small. The name stuck."

I was out of scotch. She nodded toward my glass. I shrugged and gave it to her, along with her own glass. I had no need of her fingerprints anymore now that the cat was out of the bag. Lydia rose and went to the kitchen and filled them up. I lit another cigarette. She came back with our drinks and sat down again. She still looked hard, but somehow a little lighter than she had earlier. I knew the look. Confession took years and pounds off some people in an instant.

"How did the two of you end up in Honolulu?" I asked.

"Bobby decided after a year or so of being with us in New York that it was time to take his show out West. Pictures were attracting money to L.A. He had an opportunity to work with a brother or cousin or something like that who was working for Mickey Cohen. He thought it was a good opportunity and, if he could bring his stable of New York girls, he could boost his influence with Cohen, who was just getting set up in L.A. at the time."

"You worked in L.A.?"

"For a while. Mostly motion picture types. Studio execs, producers, directors, and the occasional actor. At least the ones whose tastes didn't run to boys."

"Better conditions than New York?"

"Different conditions. Nicer house, nicer clothes, more money. But the tricks out West had strange tastes and some got really violent. The richer they were, the weirder they were, and the harder they hit. Not that I wasn't used to it, but guys back East from the Masonic Lodge or the brush sales conventions only wanted a girlfriend for an hour. The silver screen types were really sick."

If the memory of it all tormented her, she did a damn good job of hiding it. Her words came out as easily and indifferently as a court reporter reading a transcript back. Lydia was a lot tougher than I ever gave her credit for, and I thought she was pretty damn tough.

"So, what happened next?" I asked.

"Pearl Harbor," she said. "The war. Honolulu was going to be a gold mine for the sporting girl, and Judy was smart enough to be one of the first to see it that way. She talked Bobby into fronting us our passage from Frisco to Honolulu and she said we'd pay him back double."

"He actually bit?"

"Of course. Besides, he was getting too busy in the muscle racket as an enforcer and collector for Cohen's underground casinos to be worried about running girls. And Judy made him a really big offer—ten grand to buy us both out. She told me that we could make it in no time, and that she had no intention of actually giving it to him. She said he'd forget, anyway."

"He didn't, obviously."

"No, I guess not. He probably fell on some hard times during and after the war. Bobby had a weakness for the tables himself. Not a good habit for a collector. With us, he kept his hands off because he said it was bad practice to mix business and pleasure. But I guess that rule didn't apply to the casinos."

I gave her a smile as hard as the one she was giving me. I took another sip of scotch and put the tumbler down on the table.

"Nice try," I said. "It's my turn."

"I'm all ears," she said.

"I'll buy your life story up until the point of your arrival in Honolulu. I'll even buy that Princess Judy was, in a twisted way, a benefactor aunt of sorts to you. But to say that Bobby Castle was out here to collect on an old low-life promissory note is a stretch."

"Is it? Why don't you explain? This should be good."

"Not really. It's actually pretty obvious. Bobby came out here to put the bite on you, too."

Lydia threw her head back and laughed like a sailor. In that moment, all remaining veneer of the pretty, plucky new bride was stripped away and out with the trash.

"That's pretty good," she said. "I can't wait to hear what you have for an encore. That's a pretty tough act to follow."

"Oh, believe me, I can," I said. "You'll want to refill your drink for this. Go ahead, I'll wait."

Lydia grinned and went to the kitchen to fetch the scotch. She sat back down with the bottle and filled us both up. We both stuck one of her fancy cigarettes in our faces and I lit us both up.

"Please," she said. "Continue."

"You and Princess Judy arrived at Hotel Street and worked the Metropolitan in the three-dollar love assembly line. You managed to squirrel away quite a bit doing that while supplementing that income with bigger money from private parties and house calls outside the red-light district, violating police rules. That's when the Princess concocted a plan to make even more money. She entered into a joint venture, if you will."

"That's interesting," said Lydia. She took a long drink and looked amused. "With who?"

"Her husband. Happy Tokuda."

The smile on her face didn't disappear, but it strained. Her eyes glazed over momentarily before recovering.

"Interesting," she said.

"Yes," I said. "I think so. You thought so back then, too. Kauai. Lonely plantation workers. Not as many as there were G.I.s, but with a little more to spend as repeat customers and, best of all, no need to pay such a high percentage as you would to a big house like the Metropolitan. Sure, you had a built-in madam you needed to give a cut to, but the low overhead meant more money for all of you. Not to mention the more humane—if you want to call it that—working conditions. But the amount you had to fork over to the Princess didn't bother you because you planned to take it back all along, and then some."

Lydia's smile stretched and finally broke. She hugged herself as the temperature of her blood dropped a degree.

"You all had a nice, lucrative, protected operation on Kauai," I said. "The Carriage House. You knew that the Princess couldn't just walk into a bank in Lihue Town and deposit all her brothel earnings. You knew where she stashed it. You made your move when the time was right. You paid the two black-haired girls to leave to make it appear as if they made off with the cash. Then you told the Princess you'd leave, too, because there was no way the house would make it with the shortage of labor. Princess lost it and beat you, but it wasn't anything you didn't expect and it wasn't anything you weren't used to. You took your licks to help deflect any suspicion that you filched the house cash. Molly came to your rescue and you used the altercation to cement your reason for leaving."

Lydia was now quiet and stone-faced. First, she had ceased to be attractive, then she ceased to be clever. Now, there was only the truth, and it wasn't flattering at all on her.

"How much was it, Lydia?" I asked.

She looked down at her lap. Her silence told me the answer.

"Ten grand," I said. "The Princess eventually figured it out. You went back to New York as a blonde and parlayed that stash into a lot more. Gambling?"

"Investments."

"Better. It suits the new you."

She bitterly raised her tumbler in a mock salute acknowledging my crack and took another long drink.

"You said you could follow your tough act," she said. "So far, I haven't heard anything worth the price of admission."

"Sorry," I said. I took a long drink myself. "I was just getting to that. You made your fortune. You finally arrived. Now, you just had to get far enough away from the monsters of your past whom you ripped off to enjoy your new life. The new life you earned through your resourcefulness and sacrifice. I'll give you that: I think you earned it. You went to a cocktail party full of new high-class friends. You met a one-legged lawyer from Honolulu. That was your ticket, as ironic as it was. Why the hell not? It was far away and the least likely place the Princess would look for you, and the least likely place she'd go back to. So, you latched on to poor Wally, and here you are."

I drained my glass and Lydia refilled us both. We sipped in silence for a short time before she motioned for me to proceed.

"It was like heaven, but it wasn't meant to last," I said. "Nothing that perfect ever does. The Princess got wind of your presence in Honolulu. She was in L.A., working for Bobby Castle again because she had no choice. Her wartime windfall turned to dust thanks to you. She figured out it was you, not the black-haired twins. She's not stupid. She and Castle came out to blackmail you. The ten grand you took from her was what it would take to shut them up about your sporting girl past. I called New York and L.A. and asked about Midge. They have all your names. And your booking photographs. It wasn't hard for me to figure this out even without seeing the pictures in their files. Princess and Bobby came out, one at a time, each thinking they'd eventually double-cross the other and keep all the money. After all, as you said, Castle felt he was owed ten grand in the first place."

Lydia nodded and drank. There wasn't much more she could do. She stared blankly at the coffee table. I took a small sip of scotch.

"Ten grand is a nice chunk, even for you," I said. "But you were willing to pay it to get free and clear. Then, something happened that threw a wrench into everything. Happy Tokuda, the Carriage House Papa-san, turned up on your doorstep along with me and the rest of Wally's old friends. This wasn't something you accounted for. Now, instead of two people who could expose you to Wally, there were three." Happy kept his mouth shut to spare Wally. Sometimes, he's considerate that way.

I took a drag off my cigarette and looked at her. She was a

shell. Every last impulse to do anything at all had been drained from her. All she could do was sit there and breathe.

“But things have a funny way of working out sometimes,” I said. “Happy and the Princess had their marital reunion in your guest room, and she was passed out and tied up. Happy came out to look for more scotch. You stole in and smothered her. It didn’t take much time. She was out cold, and you’re light on your feet. One down, two to go. Happy came back, and you made a deal with him. He could have the ten grand if he kept his mouth shut about your past and disappeared. Happy was upset. He had found the wife he knew and missed, only to lose her again. But he took your payoff and made himself scarce, something he’s good at doing. He was so upset and got the hell out of your house in such a hurry that he didn’t even bother to untie her. So much the better for you. Two down, one to go. You set up Castle, told him to come to the house where you’d give him the money. You knew he’d have a weapon and you badgered him into drawing it. You already had Wally’s Luger in hand. Bang. Three down. Self-defense. You even had police witnesses. Well played. The big bad criminal gets the blame for the body in the guest room and Happy’s silence has been paid for. He ran away again, but this time, it was out of grief and a refusal to hurt his old friend, Shortstop. He’ll never say a word about it. Very well played, indeed.”

Lydia drained her tumbler again and refilled it again. I had lost count of her drinks. I almost lost count of my own. She looked over at me, raising the bottle and preparing to pour. I shook my head in declination. I was done drinking because I was done talking.

“You’re right,” she said. “That was a showstopper. Will you be arresting me now?”

“No,” I said. “All that I’ve said is nothing I can prove unless you confess and I’d say that doing so is clearly not in your best interest. I could try to beat the confession out of you, like we sometimes do with our other suspects we know to be guilty, but I won't, because beating women is not my style and trying to beat anything out of you probably wouldn't work anyway. You've been cleared by an inquest and I don't have enough to overturn its findings. Besides, though it isn't my place to judge, I don't think the world will miss Princess Judy or Bobby Castle. I don't care about them, to be honest. Although if I thought I could do my job properly, with proper evidence, I wouldn't hesitate to drag you in and book you. But I do care about Wally."

"So, are you going to tell him everything you've just told me?"

"No, not if I don't have to."

"What do you mean?"

"I mean I don't have to tell him if *you* do. All of it. The truth, Lydia. If you don't, then I will."

"And do you think that telling Wally the truth isn't going to hurt him?"

"It will. But you owe it to him. You owe it to me. I'm not going to have you tell it to a grand jury, but you will tell it to my best friend."

I stood up and grabbed my hat off the coffee table and put it on my head.

"Tonight," I said. "You'll tell him tonight or I'll tell him tomorrow. You can think about it for the next couple of hours while he's still at the office. But I suggest you do it. It may not get you happily ever after with him, but at this point, it's your only shot at it. I suggest you aim in and take it."

I headed to the front door. I stopped at the entryway to put my shoes on. Lydia remained on the sofa until my shoes were tied and I was standing upright once again with my hand on the doorknob.

"Frankie," she said. She walked over to the entryway with her scotch still in her hand. "Bravo. You got it all right except for one thing."

"Oh?" I said. "What's that?"

"I didn't latch on to Wally because he could bring me back here. I latched on to him because I fell in love with him. I love him, Frankie. You may not think that a girl like me is capable of that, but it's true. He's the purest, kindest man I've ever met. I love him."

"Then prove it," I said. "Tell him the truth."

I turned the doorknob and opened the door. I stepped out onto the light and heat of outside. I took a few steps until I was next to the koi pond and looked down at the fish. They'd come to the surface with sucking lips. They had mistaken me for someone who was going to feed them. Everyone wanted something from me, even Wally's goddamned koi.

I looked back to see Lydia standing in the doorway, holding her scotch and starting to look once again, slowly, like the Lydia I had first met.

"Look," I said. "I caught up with Happy the other night on Kauai and gave him the third degree. He told me about the Carriage House during the war, and he told me his story about hearing the footsteps of a man the night he was here. He said nothing about you. He kept his word to you, so I let him keep the money. I saw it, and I let him keep it. For what it's worth, it's not the money that will keep his mouth shut. It's because he won't hurt his friend, Shortstop. He might be a grifter and occasional felon, but even I must admit his loyalty is admirable. So, it's just you and me, Lydia. The only two people left in the world who can tell Wally the truth. For your sake and for his, it better be you."

I left Lydia standing in the doorway with her drink and the koi sucking air in the pond. I walked back to my car without looking back at any of them.

I got in and drove away.

## 22

"She's gone."

It was a two-word telephone call. It was all Wally said through the line after I had picked the receiver up out of its cradle on my desk. I stared for a second at my ink-stained green blotter, then told him I'd be right over.

Gid simply grunted and nodded when I stuck my head into his office and told him I was going out to talk to Wally, who must've had a few more questions about the case. In truth, Wally probably really only had one.

The drive up to Maunalani Heights was a fast one; traffic had already died down for the morning and I was lucky enough not to have caught a single red light. I had been dreading my next conversation with Wally since leaving his house and his wife standing in the doorway the day before, hoping in vain that she'd come clean with him and tell him everything. Wally's two-word telephone call was enough to tell me that she passed on taking my good advice.

When I got to the front door, Wally opened it and handed me a piece of paper. It was a handwritten note on a girly piece of stationery, white with pink roses, embossed with "From the Desk of Mrs. Wallace Yoshida." Lydia didn't waste any time diving into her new life with Wally, and she didn't waste any time climbing out of it, either.

The note was short, and, some would say, sweet. I certainly thought it was sweet, knowing the whole story as I did:

*Dearest Wally,*

*I had to leave. I'm so sorry for the pain and trouble I've brought into your life, but know that you've brought nothing but happiness into mine, for however short a time we could be together.*

*The house is yours. I have also left a small amount in our bank account, and I'd like you to have this, too. I wish it could be more.*

*I didn't want to go, but I had to. Find success and happiness as I know you will, and remember me as I was during our time together.*

*I will love you always.*

*Lydia*

"Come in," Wally said.

I removed my shoes and followed him into the living room and sat on the sofa where I had the day before.

"Drink?" Wally asked. It wasn't even ten o'clock in the morning.

"Yeah, thanks."

Wally came back with the same two tumblers from the day before, filled with the same scotch. He handed one to me and fell heavily onto the sofa next to me, where his wife had sat.

"I don't know what to do," he said.

"Can't help you there," I said. "I'm sorry. I don't know what to say."

It was true. Lydia's response to the ultimatum I gave her was one I didn't anticipate.

"Why?" Wally asked, and not to me in particular. "Why did she have to go?"

"I don't know," I said. That was the biggest lie I had ever told, and would ever tell, to my best friend. "Did she tell you anything else?" I asked.

"No," said Wally. "She was asleep when I finally got home, and when I woke up, she was gone. All her dresses are still in the closet, all her shoes, everything. She didn't take a thing. But she left the note. Hey, Frankie! The harbor, the airport . . . do you think . . ."

I shook my head. Wally looked up at me with tears in his eyes.

"I'm never going to see her again," he said.

I nodded.

"Frankie," he said, "you might have been the last person I know who talked to her. Did she say anything—give you any hint—about what she was going to do, or why?"

I decided that I was going to play along with Lydia and the plan she had executed. When I read Lydia's letter, I realized that her disappearance removed the need to tell him the truth. She was right; he could only be hurt by it, and with her out of his life, the only thing the truth could bring him was pain. She came up with a viable solution for herself and protected Wally at the same time. Her plan was brilliant, in a way, and it really was a supreme sacrifice on her part. Whether she told him the truth or I did, Wally would be ruined emotionally. Lydia spared him by disappearing. In that moment, I decided that I would spare him, too, by keeping my mouth shut.

"She only told me that she had a lot of regret about the trouble she caused you," I said. "The rest were just stray details. Times that needed to be corroborated. Shit like that. Shit I needed to close the matter on my end." And that was the truth, if downplayed a little.

"Oh," said Wally.

"Look, for what it's worth, I really liked her. I don't know for sure, but I've dealt with a lot of folks with shit in their past that changes them for good. Shit they can't get away from, no matter how far away they run. They keep running until they can't run any more. This was the case with Aunt Meg. I'm not saying this was Lydia, too—I didn't know her well enough—but sometimes there are reasons people leave, and it's not their fault. I certainly don't think this is *your* fault, Wally. I'm just saying that there are reasons people do shit like this and they rarely explain why to the ones they leave behind."

"I know," said Wally. "But I don't like it."

"You don't have to."

"I guess two horrible deaths in two days is a lot for anyone to take. Maybe she just broke inside."

"Maybe."

"I just can't believe she's gone, Frankie."

"Neither can I."

We sat and drank in silence for a little while. The scotch tasted different again. Sweet and ancient, heavy with regret. It was a good taste, though.

"Well, she left you the house and a little bit in the bank. That's something," I said.

"Yeah, that's something," said Wally. "But you know what? I called the bank this morning. Do you know how much a little bit really is?"

I smiled. I knew somehow. But I asked anyway.

"Ten thousand dollars," said Wally.

"That's something," I said.

We drank some more and talked about our time at McKinley and our time in the war. We talked until the talk ran out. Then I got up, put my hat and shoes on and opened the door.

"Are you going to be all right?" I asked.

"I lost a leg and three different girls three different ways," said Wally. "I don't think I have any other choice but to be all right."

I laughed and Wally laughed back. I slapped his shoulder and got into my car and drove down the mountain and back to the station.

For the rest of the day, I sleepwalked through investigative reports and signed off on most of them. It was tedious, mind-numbing work. But it made my heart light knowing that at the end of the time clock day, I'd be on my way back to my house in Palolo Valley and the two ladies who lived in it.

I asked Gid for the year of desk work and he gave it to me. With some community relations stuff on occasion, just so I don't grow roots in my office.

I stopped by The Liberty House and bought a brand-new pink dress for Lizzie, then a dozen roses for Ellen at a florist near my parking spot on Bethel, and drove home, without making a stop at the morgue, some favorite bar of an informant, or some witness's musty old living room.

It was going to be a nice, boring year.

# 23

The next few weeks flew by like the reports on my desk, reports written by other dicks in Homicide who were actually working cases. I never had to return any of Paris Lau's reports for revisions or corrections. His English—modern and Middle—was admittedly better than my own.

I accompanied Gid Hanohano to more ribbon cuttings, groundbreakings, and press conferences than I could count. Being a parade grand marshal's errand boy was a pain in the ass, but not as much as being his stand-in when he couldn't make it. I had to keep reminding myself that it was all for the opportunity to watch my daughter grow.

Wallace Yoshida, Esquire won his bid for the Territorial Legislature and became the Honorable Representative Yoshida of Kaimuki. He had a personalized name plate on the long table in the big room at Iolani Palace. Newspaper analysts credited his victory over the haole incumbent to his war hero status and a war chest of thousands. Humble as always, Wally credited his hardworking campaign staff and the good folks of Kaimuki with his victory.

At my encouraging—though she hardly needed it—Ellen took on some freelance assignments from her old employer, the *Honolulu Record*. She wrote from home, sitting at her typewriter at the kitchen table when Lizzie napped during the day, and in the evenings when I spent time with the baby. It was better than spending my evenings with the television and the scotch in the decanter. Ellen took Lizzie with her to the *Record* on Wednesdays when she went in to drop off her articles for the weekly.

Happy Tokuda was brought in and booked only once during that time. I was the one who made the arrest at a Territorial fair where I happened to be one of the "celebrity" judges of a pie eating contest. It was one of those irritating community relations appearances I had to make in uniform. Happy was a contestant. Of course, the complainant and rival pie eating contestant, Joe Matsukawa of Schuman Carriage, ended up recanting his accusation and renewing faith in his investment partner. Happy was released when the charges were dropped. I never did see a Toyopet on the streets of Honolulu.

Once again, Chaucer's Miller upstages his Knight. "Quites" him in typical fashion, to the amusement of all except for the Knight.

The cable came in on a November day after Wally had been elected. I was in my office reviewing reports when Delilah, the Homicide Detail secretary, brought it to me.

"Looks important, Sheik," she said. "It's from overseas."

"Everything is from overseas if it's beyond Kaena Point," I said.

"Well, this one is from really far away."

Delilah left my office and I picked the cable up off my blotter. It was from the United States Embassy in Kuala Lumpur. The cable was the result of inquiries I made with the State Department through an FBI agent I had worked with in the past.

The cable stated that Ludmila Wojskowicz, a United States citizen who had become the third wife of a prince who was one of the sons of the Sultan of Selangor, had died at sea along with the prince's other wives when the prince's private vessel was attacked and destroyed by pirates in the Strait of Malacca. There were no survivors and no trace of the vessel.

I crumpled up the cable and threw it in the wastebasket.

Selangor. Malaya. Strait of Malacca. Lydia had run far away indeed until she couldn't run any more. She buried Princess Judy and Bobby Castle, and now she had buried herself.

A part of Lydia, though—a part she left behind—sat in a chair at a long table in Iolani Palace and wrote laws to keep our neighborhoods safe and our streets clean. Laws to curtail behavior not approved of by decent folks. Laws which she may have flouted in a different time.

She would have appreciated the irony.

## Acknowledgements

A detective book from a venerated literary press seemed highly improbable and four detective books unbelievably so.

And yet, here we are.

The following people have my ardent gratitude. Without them, this fourth anomaly wouldn't be.

Cathy Song is our poet laureate here, and I had the unbelievably good fortune to have her as my editor. If the book you just read made any sense and sounded good, it was because of Cathy.

Normie Salvador is a real detective when it comes to verifying historical claims made in my manuscript; his copy edits enable me to get this novel out with the confidence that few challenges will be made to the facts I portray and that I will face a minimum of ridicule for the language.

Joy Kobayashi-Cintrón, our Managing Editor, always manages to make my books happen. An ardent supporter of me and my work, she has inspired me to keep doing this.

Wing Tek Lum, our Business Manager and my mentor, has shared his wisdom and has steadily drawn me into the space under the hood of Bamboo Ridge Press. This operation and consequently my books do not exist without him.

Ken Tokuno and Darlene Javar spent hours writing grants and chased down the money. Books don't print themselves.

Tommy Hite, whose cover artwork has become synonymous with my work between the covers, and Jui-Lien Sanderson, who makes my books look like something worth the price of admission, give me unrivaled packaging.

The Bamboo Ridge Study Group is the most literary talent in a single room in Honolulu. They were extremely patient to have endured the chapters I had submitted for their consideration and improved my work with their skill and insight.

Gail Kuroda, who was the Archives Manager at the Japanese Cultural Center of Hawai'i, had the materials I felt needed ready for my perusal, as well as materials I didn't know I needed until she brought them to my attention.

Susan Kakuda was my guide on Kaua'i. She took me everywhere, trod the streets of historic Līhu'e with me, waited patiently while I conferred with archivists and priests and drove me out to cane fields in the west and resort grounds in the east. I would have been lost without her.

Moises Madayag, curator of the Grove Farm Museum, shared period photographs and enlightened me with his knowledge of a plantation in transition to a modern, automated operation ironically when agriculture would start its decline as the driver of Hawai'i's economy.

Reverend Tomo Hojo of the West Kauai Hongwanji Mission opened the structures and the grounds of the Hanapepe Hongwanji to me and was generous with his time and resources, including photographs from the dedication of the Hanapepe Hongwanji in 1954.

My family lets me do this. They support my writing endeavors and generally leave me alone while I research, ruminate and compose. Solitude is the greatest gift.

## About the Author

Photo by Brandon Miyagi

Scott Kikkawa is the author of a series of noir detective novels set in postwar Honolulu. He has been honored with an Elliot Cades Award for Literature and a crime fiction short story of his was selected as one of the "Other Distinguished Stories of 2021" in the 2022 *Best American Mysteries and Suspense Anthology*. He is a columnist and Associate Editor for *The Hawai'i Review of Books*. He lives in Honolulu. *Sporting Girl* is his fourth full-length novel featuring Francis "Sheik" Yoshikawa.